A Night To Remember

"Do you not think, my darling, that tonight would be an excellent time to begin our real marriage?"

Anthony was sitting on the edge of the bed now, his hands holding Belinda's arms lightly. The real pressure was being exerted by his eyes which she would swear were drawing her heart right out of her body. "Yes, please," she whispered.

His mouth came down on hers, warm and persuasive, producing a jolt of pure pleasure deep inside her. She was barely aware that her husband had expeditiously removed her tentlike bedgown until he said in a hoarse whisper, "My word, but you are even more beautiful than I dreamed. Did you not know that I have been starving for you, you stubborn little mule?"

Belinda's arms went around his neck, and her lips began their own exploration of his jawline until he shuddered and pulled her tightly against him, flesh against burning flesh, as they fell back onto the bed. Anthony's delicious depredations reduced Belinda to a state of quivering response. She was transported by the subsequent ripples of delight that rose to a crescendo of sensation, and afterward could only cling weakly to the man who wielded such sweet power over her being. . . .

SIGNET REGENCY ROMANCE
Coming in June 1995

Sandra Heath
Magic at Midnight

Emily Hendrickson
The Abandoned Rake

Mary Balogh
Lord Carew's Bride

A Temporary Betrothal

by

Dorothy Mack

A SIGNET BOOK

SIGNET
Published by the Penguin Group
Penguin Books USA Inc., 375 Hudson Street,
New York, New York 10014, U.S.A.
Penguin Books Ltd, 27 Wrights Lane,
London W8 5TZ, England
Penguin Books Australia Ltd, Ringwood,
Victoria, Australia
Penguin Books Canada Ltd, 10 Alcorn Avenue,
Toronto, Ontario, Canada M4V 3B2
Penguin Books (N.Z.) Ltd, 182–190 Wairau Road,
Auckland 10, New Zealand

Penguin Books Ltd, Registered Offices:
Harmondsworth, Middlesex, England

First published by Signet, an imprint of Dutton Signet,
a division of Penguin Books USA Inc.

First Printing, May, 1995
10 9 8 7 6 5 4 3 2 1

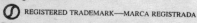

Prologue

April, 1810 Gloucestershire

A well-aimed kick from a sturdy half boot propelled the pebble forward in an arc. Seconds later another and better kick improved on the distance and brought a fleeting expression of satisfaction to the kicker's face. A benevolent Nature had intended well by this face, but its owner, a girl in her mid-teens, seemed determined to negate its natural appeal. Her lips were tightly bunched together and a ferocious scowl distorted her fair brow as she stomped along the lane, insensible of the crisp clean air around her, the swept blue sky above her, and the tender green of new spring growth at her feet. Nor did she hear the occasional cheerful snatches of bird calls that rang out in the afternoon stillness; her ears were full of her own grumbling.

"This has been positively the worst birthday of my entire life, Princess," she said, addressing a small brown-and-white dog whose ancestry was regrettably more plebian than the name proclaimed. "First there was Dreadful Deirdre's letter boasting of the japanned pianoforte her adoring father gifted her with on her birthday in February. She must think me simple beyond belief to be taken in by all that 'dearest cousin' piffle when everyone knows we cannot be in the same room for an hour without quarreling. She has always considered that her measly two months' seniority entitles her to command my obedience to her will in everything. You may take my word on it, Princess, her only purpose in writing that letter was to gloat over me, despite her sanctimonious wishes for Papa's return in time for my birthday. Miss Fenton says I must exhibit a moral superiority by ignoring her taunts and acting as if I swallowed her pious protestations. She promised to help me compose a

reply that will annihilate my cousin with magnanimous gentil-
ity. I shall enjoy that," the girl said with relish.

The intelligent animal cocked an ear and signified her approval with a short, sharp bark before trotting on ahead to in-
vestigate some mysterious scent at the side of the lane. The
girl resumed her trek, her brow darkening again.

"Of course it isn't really Deirdre who is important, it's
Papa," she confided in a voice that had lost the snap of aggressiveness. "It was bad enough that he packed up and left Millgrove within a sennight of Mama's funeral, but at least I could
fully enter into his feelings of sadness even if I did not quite
understand why he should wish to go off by himself. And I did
have Grandmother and Miss Fenton to look after me. But I
must say that I consider three brief letters in eleven months a
niggardly allotment. And not the tiniest hint in any of them
that he had formed the intention of remarrying. To simply appear on the doorstep with a new wife without any advance
warning was the outside of enough—and on my birthday too!
Not that Papa even recollected so trivial a circumstance," she
added bitterly, pulling back her foot and drawing a bead on another pebble.

Just as her boot made contact with the stone a masculine
voice called out behind her, "I say, miss, can you help me?"

The startled girl spun around off balance and landed awk-
wardly, giving her ankle a severe wrenching that brought her
gasping to her knees in the dirt. She collapsed onto her seat,
grasping the injured ankle tightly in both hands in an instinctive attempt to hold the pain at bay. She bent over the ankle,
biting her lips to keep from crying out, and firmly rode the
wave of pain, ignoring her pet's frantic barking and the concerned utterings of the rider, whose poorly timed shout had
caused the accident, as he came up to her and dismounted. She
was still fully engaged in preserving her stoicism when a pair
of dusty boots, one of them adorned with a wicked-looking
spur, invaded the edges of her vision. The owner of this footgear squatted down and said in kindly tones, "Come, you cannot remain sitting here in the dirt."

Her eyes stubbornly fixed on the white-knuckled fingers
gripping her own footgear, the girl snapped through gritted
teeth, "What do you suggest I do, get up and hop all the way
home on one foot?"

A rich chuckle sounded above her ear. "What an ungracious little crosspatch it is, to be sure."

This unfeeling remark brought the girl's head up smartly. Through a pain-induced fog her eyes beheld a modern reincarnation of Apollo, complete with sun bright curls, sky blue eyes, and distinctive features chisled in bronze. She shook her head to clear her vision, but before her benumbed senses could reevaluate this apparition, the godlike being swooped closer and plucked her from the bosom of the earth, rising easily to his feet as though the girl in his arms weighed no more than a feather.

Alarmed, she beat on his chest with her fists. "Stop this! What do you think you are doing? Put me down this instant!"

Like the heroes of old the sun god ignored her protests. Unlike the archetypal hero, however, he did not ignore the blows she was raining upon him. "Stop hitting me unless you wish to be dumped on the ground again," he commanded with unheroic impatience before softening his tone as he felt her stiffen in apprehension. "I am merely going to put you up on Titan while we assess the damage."

He was lifting her onto the back of a big bay stallion as he spoke, his hands spanning her waist. He flashed her a swift smile, removed one hand to gentle the neck of his sidling horse, and addressed soothing words to the little dog barking furiously at his ankles. The bay's nervous movements halted, Princess ceased barking, and the accident victim, drawing reassurance from both events, ventured a shy smile at the stranger whom she had been studying while he quietened the dog.

"There, that's better," he said. "You are getting your color back." Seeing that she was in no danger of sliding off the saddle, he removed his steadying hand from her waist and casually brushed the long black hair that had escaped from the ribbon at her nape back behind her shoulder, a gesture that added more color to her cheeks. "Obviously my call was very ill-timed," he said with a puzzled look in his eyes, "but whatever were you doing that you should lose your balance so completely?"

The girl hung her head. "I was kicking stones," she muttered with a touch of bravado.

The young man, who could not have been much above twenty himself, threw back his head and laughed. "A very ladylike occupation indeed," he observed teasingly.

The girl tilted her chin upward and gave him a haughty stare down her short, straight nose. "There was a good reason. Why did you call out to me?" she added, going on the offensive.

"All in good time, my child. It was your left ankle you turned, was it not?"

She nodded, adding quickly as he took her shod foot in gentle hands, "It was painful for a moment, but it is much better now. I am persuaded I can walk on it with no trouble."

He moved her foot slowly to the left, then to the right, watching her face for signs of discomfort. "Does that hurt?"

"Barely at all. If you will help me down, sir, I'll be on my way once you have told me what I may do for you."

He did not immediately fulfill her request, saying with another charming smile, "I merely wanted to know if I am heading in the direction of Lynton Abbas. I have yet to see a signpost."

"You should have gone left at the fork where you entered the lane. That was the most direct route, but if you continue to the end of the lane and turn left you will not have lost much time. You are not familiar with this locality?"

"No, it is the first time I have been in the area. I am going to visit an old schoolmate before leaving for Portugal next week to join Lord Wellington's Army."

"You look singularly pleased to be going off to war," the girl exclaimed in some dismay.

"The army is an excellent place for a man to make his way in the world, but enough about me. Tell me, fair maiden, why you felt called upon to stroll along a dusty lane engaging in the inelegant pastime of kicking stones." Perfect white teeth gleamed in a playful smile.

The girl was not to be so easily beguiled into confession, however. She declined to provide him with another reason to laugh at her, repeating her request for assistance in dismounting from his beautifully mannered horse.

"It hardly seems fair that I should have divulged my most intimate secrets to you and yet you refuse to satisfy the innocent curiosity of a man going off to risk his neck for king and country," the gentleman complained, assuming a wounded air.

Suddenly the girl capitulated to his infectious charm. After all, what did it matter if a man she would never meet again laughed at her? She did not begrudge him an amusing memory to take away with him to a foreign battlefield. "Today is my birthday," she said in a rush as he extended his hands to her waist again. "My father has been away since my mother's death eleven months ago, but he returned today without warning, bringing a new wife with him."

The gentleman emitted a silent whistle, his hands tightening around her waist. "Small wonder you felt like kicking something. I cannot suppose a stepmother was one of your desired presents."

Her lips twisted briefly before framing a weak smile. "He has no recollection that today is my birthday. Most likely it will not be too bad; his wife seems a pleasant woman. Thank you," she added as he set her on her feet, keeping his hands at her waist for a moment while she put her weight gingerly on the left foot. She took a couple of halting steps, then moved more confidently. "It's all right," she said in relief, turning to smile at the stranger, who no longer seemed like a stranger. She came back and offered her hand. "Good-bye and God be with you in Portugal, Mr.—?"

He clasped her hand warmly but declined the clear invitation. "If I told you my name you would feel compelled to reciprocate, which would present a quandary, since a well brought-up young lady should never divulge her name to a chance-met stranger." He raised her fingers to his mouth and pressed a kiss on the knuckles. "Happy birthday, flower face," he said, a smile in eyes and voice. As she gaped at him in astonishment, he released her fingers, only to take her chin between his while his bright blue gaze ran over her face as if trying to commit it to memory. Suddenly he bent forward and gently kissed her parted lips, taking his time about it while she stood frozen with shock. Just as swiftly he pulled back, spun on his heel, and vaulted into the saddle.

The bemused girl staring after him, her fingers fluttering about her lips, barely heard his farewell salute. It was several minutes before her muddled brain could formulate a message to send to her heavy limbs. As she moved off slowly she took a deep breath and smiled at the dog frisking at her heels.

"Princess, this is absolutely the best birthday of my life!"

Chapter One

Winter, 1815 Gloucestershire

Paper-dry eyelids fluttered and the frail form beneath the faded quilt quivered soundlessly. A few feet away from the massive carved bed a young woman knitting by the light of an oil lamp paused and raised her head, alerted by some sense beyond hearing. She folded her work, laid it aside, and rose from the velvet wing chair she had occupied. She went to the fireplace, added another log to the small blaze within, and poked the embers, her movements smooth and purposeful. The sudden flare-up of the fire lent a golden glow to her pale complexion and set red lights in the inky hair that had fallen over her shoulder as she bent to her task.

Despite her caution, the occupant of the bed had wakened; the girl could detect a faint gleam below the nearest eyelid in the flickering light. "Are you cold, Gran? Or in pain?" she asked in a soft, low-pitched voice.

"No, but my throat is a little dry."

The young woman made short work of easing her arm beneath her grandmother's shoulders and slipping extra pillows behind her back to raise her to a more comfortable position. She poured water from a pitcher resting on a good-sized table placed near the bed and held the glass while her grandmother sipped briefly.

"Thank you, dearest; that was most refreshing." The old lady settled back against the pillows and glanced around the shadowy room. A small frown altered the pattern of wrinkles on a face that still bore remnants of former beauty in the clean oval of its design and the delicate modeling of the nose. "What time is it?"

"Nearly five."

"Should you not be changing for dinner, Belinda?"

"I have already asked Polly to make my excuses to my step-mama and tell Cook I will be sharing your dinner here."

"It isn't right for you to be cooped up in this room around the clock, my love," said Mrs. Gordon, a troubled expression in her faded blue eyes.

"And who took care of me all hours of the day and night through every childhood illness?" Belinda posed the question but went on without waiting for a reply. "Polly will be here shortly with a tray. Shall I wash your hands and face before she comes? You will feel fresher, and it will perk up your appetite."

"Thank you, dear, that sounds very nice."

Mrs. Gordon submitted to her granddaughter's gentle ministrations and listened with an appearance of interest to a light-hearted recounting of four-year-old Albert's latest peccadilloes and the continuing discussion going on between Sir Walter Melville and his wife as to the proposed extent and style of some long overdue refurbishing of the principal rooms in the house.

When the maid arrived with their dinner, Mrs. Gordon praised the attractive appointments of the large tray and sent her compliments to the cook for the appetizing selection she had sent up. She smiled benevolently at the young maidservant, and dismissed her for her own dinner.

The invalid maintained a smooth flow of family reminiscences, interspersed with appreciative comments on the food during the next half hour that had a thankful Belinda believing her appetite had miraculously returned. When she retrieved her grandmother's plate, however, she was quickly undeceived. There was no way to disguise the nearly full plate, though an attempt had certainly been made by redistributing the contents more compactly in the center. At Belinda's distressed murmur, Mrs. Gordon looked up with pleading eyes.

"Everything was delicious, dearest, but one doesn't require large quantities of food when one is confined to bed."

Belinda bit her lip but forbore to continue the familiar argument, offering instead to read to her grandmother, whose relief to have done with the touchy subject of eating was patent.

For the next hour or two the comfortable room resounded with the merry antics of Miss Austen's Bennet sisters and their friends until Belinda became aware of her grandmother's increasing restlessness. "Can I make you more comfortable, Gran?"

Mrs. Gordon heaved a sigh of resignation. "One becomes rubbed raw all over after months confined to one's bed. Even the smoothest of sheets become abrasive."

"Before she died, Nellie taught me how to make her special lotion and showed me how to smooth it into the back and shoulder muscles. It is very relaxing. Will you allow me to do this for you, Gran?"

"Poor Nellie, I do miss her sorely. Ladies should never outlive their maids." Seeing her granddaughter's anxious face, Mrs. Gordon relented. "Thank you, dearest, that sounds most comforting."

Twenty minutes later, clad in a fresh bedgown and tucked back among the pillows, she sighed wearily and muttered, "I didn't realize dying would take so long."

"*Gran,* don't say that!" Belinda protested in a shaken voice. "You aren't going to die!"

"Of course I'm going to die, Belinda, and not before time either. To my sorrow I have outlived my husband and both my daughters. I have made my peace with the Lord and am quite ready to depart this earth. Indeed, I should do so gladly were it not for my concern for your future, my love."

"Gran, you should not be worrying about me. There is no need. You know I never hankered for a social life the way my cousin did. There is always much to keep me occupied at home."

"That is precisely what troubles me, child, watching you squandering your youth taking care of other people's children. It isn't right that you are chained to this house just when you should be trying your wings in a wider society, flirting with attentive young men, and seeing something of the world beyond this small corner of England. Why, you couldn't even attend your cousin's wedding last November because Nellie had just died and it would have meant leaving me to the care of unfamiliar servants."

"You know perfectly well that Deirdre and I have never been bosom friends despite Mama's and Aunt Laura's attempts to reproduce their own closeness in us. Pray, believe it was no sacrifice to forgo her wedding."

"It would have been an opportunity for you to visit London had I only been strong enough to undertake the journey. This wretched heart of mine! You will be twenty in less than three months' time."

"Not such an advanced age that I must consider myself at my last prayers," Belinda said cheerfully, trying to jolly her grandmother out of her depressed humor.

"Your father told me Will Belknap approached him last month for permission to pay his addresses to you, and you refused him outright. Last year George Smythe made overtures that you turned down summarily—not that I quarreled with that decision, for he is the veriest nodcock without two words to say for himself."

"Will Belknap has plenty to say, all of it on three topics: hunting, fishing, or farming. We do not share a thought in common and would run out of conversation before the ink had dried on the marriage lines. Be truthful, Gran. Would you like to see me married to George Smythe or Will Belknap?"

"Rather than see you dwindle into an old maid at your stepmother's beck and call, yes. She is fond enough of you, but she is one of those ineffectual creatures who are all too willing to shift their burdens and responsibilities onto the shoulders of more capable persons. At least a husband, any husband, would make you mistress of your own establishment with a position of respect in the community. That isn't to be despised, my love."

"I know, Gran, and I solemnly promise you I have no intention of allowing a sense of martyrdom to make me whistle a promising suitor down the wind."

After trying to combat her grandmother's anxieties on her behalf, Belinda found it difficult to get to sleep herself. She was not so sanguine about her future as she would have her grandmother believe, but she was prepared to lie her head off if it would ease that dear lady's difficult departure from the world.

The melancholy truth was that she was armored against advances from the men she knew because she had long ago given her heart into the keeping of a chance-met stranger who had doubtless forgotten her existence within a month of their meeting. How could she expect anyone to comprehend that a five-minute encounter with a total stranger on her fifteenth birthday had sealed her fate? From what lexicon might she extract language that could somehow communicate the magical and lasting effect the audacious but kind young man had had on her?

She had told no one save Miss Fenton, who had been her governess at the time, of the meeting with the would-be soldier, whom she had christened "Apollo," and not even to this sympathetic listener had she divulged the entire incident. The stolen kiss remained a cherished secret locked in her heart.

Pure desolation sank an anchor into her heart. It would be an exercise in cruelty to confide the events of her fifteenth birthday to Gran, who would surely find confirmation of her nebulous fears for her beloved granddaughter's future in this pathetic and senseless clinging to a dream. She had no choice but to continue to make light of those concerns while she battled the chill sense of impending loss she was powerless to prevent or delay.

Chapter Two

A trill of birdsong floated into the book-lined room on a breeze that stirred the heavy brocade draperies at the edges of the open window. It reached the ears of Sir Walter Melville who laid the letter he was reading down on his desk and walked over to the window. He leaned out, breathing in the nascent odors of early spring, relishing the damp yeastiness of newly turned earth beneath him awaiting planting. This past winter had been excessively long and dreary, culminating in the recent death of his former mother-in-law. After seemingly endless weeks of dull gray skies and copious rainfall, there was a softness in the air today that presaged better times ahead.

Sir Walter's lips twitched as he pictured the probable joy of the two scamps in the nursery at the improvement in the weather, not to mention the concomitant relief of their nurse, who had recently likened her small charges to caged wild animals in his hearing. Still smiling, he took another breath of the scented air before returning to his desk, where his eye went immediately to the epistle that had arrived the previous day. It was not his sons' but his daughter's welfare and happiness that occupied his thoughts this fine morning, and not before time, he acknowledged with a belated pang of conscience on Belinda's behalf.

After several years of the gut-wrenching agony of striving unavailingly to keep his first wife from slipping out of life, her death nearly six years ago had released him to a state of numbed misery. In an effort to combat the lethal lethargy that was tightening its grip on him, he had turned the running of Millgrove over to his bailiff, left his daughter in the care of her grandmother and governess, and fled—almost literally—for his life. He recalled little from those first few months of aimless wandering. He had traveled as far north as the Scottish lowlands, dallied in the lake region much of the summer, and visited with two old friends in Leicestershire during the hunting season. By the time winter settled in he was feeling alive again physically, thanks to weeks of hunting, but it was not until he arrived in Bath in December that he had allowed himself to be persuaded back into something approaching mixed society. It was in Bath that he had met the shy spinster daughter of his old Cambridge don and had begun to wonder if it might be possible to begin life anew at one-and-forty. It was not that he had ceased to mourn the loss of his lovely Maria— some part of his soul would always ache for her presence, but his land called to him as winter dwindled, and the timid sweetness of the don's daughter awoke a dormant feeling of protectivenss in his breast.

Sir Walter's eyes were fixed unseeingly on the sheet of paper in his hand while he considered the painful question of whether or not he had neglected his daughter's well-being these past few years. His own personal life had suddenly become so all-engrossing with his second marriage, the subsequent births of Albert and Robin, and the constant demands of the estate on his time and energy. He had noted with relief and approval the rapid achievement of a cordial relationship between Belinda and her stepmother, and he had had reason over the years to be grateful for his daughter's generous assistance and support of Louisa in her somewhat tentative efforts to take over the reins of a large household and cope with two lively little boys. Louisa was not robust, and she had been raised a cosseted only child of scholarly parents in modest circumstances, living always in cities, none of which fitted her to step confidently into the unfamiliar role of a rural landowner's wife. He had been aware of his wife's dependence on her stepdaughter, but he had never questioned a situation that seemed agreeable to everyone. Belinda had appeared perfectly content with her existence and had displayed no sign of resentment when tentative plans for a London stay had had to be canceled on several occasions during the past two years.

The death of Belinda's grandmother, though expected, had jolted his eyes open with respect to his daughter's future. Her pale, grieving face had wrenched at his heart and conscience. Belinda had endured more of loss and sacrifice than most girls her age, and throughout her trials she had remained uncomplainingly sweet-natured. It was time to move his daughter's interests to the forefront. The proposal contained in the letter in his hand might represent a suitable beginning in this direction.

A tap on the door was followed by the entrance of the subject of his conscience-prompted musing.

"You sent for me, Papa?" asked Belinda, slightly out of breath. "I am sorry to have kept you waiting, but Beddoes had to search all over the house before tracking me down in the stillroom."

An unexpected stab of pain shot through Sir Walter at the sight of his daughter. She was very like her mother, but at Belinda's age Maria had possessed a lighthearted gaiety that was infectious and drew people to her. As a child Belinda had shared this trait. Why had he not noticed that the sparkle had dimmed somewhere along the way? When had this occurred? As he poised the questions, he realized he should have asked them years ago.

"Papa?"

Belinda's questioning expression brought Sir Walter's distasteful self-examination to a halt. "Come over here, my dear," he invited, summoning up a smile as he indicated the chair in front of his desk. He reseated himself, noting that Belinda had inherited all Maria's grace and economy of movement even if she lacked the vivacity that had distinguished her mother. "I have received a communication from your cousin which I wish to discuss with you."

"A letter of condolence, Papa? I received one too, last week, in answer to mine telling her of Gran's death."

"Actually it was more than that. It seems that before her death your grandmother wrote to Deirdre requesting that she invite you to make her a visit in the near future."

A sad little smile flitted across Belinda's lips. "Gran was rather obsessed with the idea of my going to London parties to meet eligible gentlemen in the hope that one of them would sweep me off my feet and into marriage. I hoped that I had convinced her that I did not long to do anything of the sort."

"In the light of your recent bereavement, it would not be quite the thing to be going to parties this spring, but Deirdre won't be in London anyway. She writes that she is increasing and feeling too poorly to accompany her husband to town for the parliamentary session this year."

"Deirdre is going to become a mother? How lovely. She did not mention it in my letter. Somehow I cannot picture her with a baby in her arms."

"From my knowledge of your cousin, I'd guess that the baby will not be in her arms but the nurse's," Sir Walter said dryly. "However, that is a question for the future. For the present, Deirdre says her husband's mind would not be at rest about leaving her at Archer Hall, his country seat, without the companionship of a family member. Reading between the lines, I gather that the viscount has proposed his elder sister for the role of companion but Deirdre would greatly prefer to have you with her instead. Though she cannot offer you London entertainments, she says the genteel families in the area have been most cordial and welcoming to her, so you will not be entirely without society." Sir Walter had been watching his daughter's face closely and now he added, "You do not appear as thrilled as I expected at the prospect of a visit to what is reputed to be a magnificent estate with a correspondingly lavish style of living."

"Well, I don't think I am," Belinda replied frankly. "I have never found Deirdre exactly congenial and I fear I would be out of place in a luxurious atmosphere. Besides, Louisa needs my help with the boys."

Sir Walter continued to study his daughter's face, his expression thoughtful. "Nevertheless, I am coming around to the opinion that a change of scene at this time would be beneficial to you. You were devoted to your grandmother, and your loving care of her during her final illness is greatly to be commended." Sir Walter looked away from the tears glistening in Belinda's eyes and his voice hoarsened a bit as he continued with difficulty. "Now you have to let go of her for a while. Grief can be like a . . . a yawning black hole that you must not fall into if you are to go on with your life, as we all must. A new environment will demand more of you, and that is all to the good at present."

"Is . . . is that what *you* did, Papa, when . . . when Mama died?"

Sir Walter's lips tightened, and Belinda regretted her presumption, but after a fraught moment he said gruffly, "I fell into the hole. I know I was of no use to you and your grandmother, but at the time I could not see beyond my own suffering." He fixed his gaze on his daughter's sympathetic countenance. "Did you resent it when I remarried within a year of your mother's death, Belinda?"

"At first," she replied, meeting his difficult honesty with her own, "but Gran explained to me that it didn't mean you hadn't loved Mama dearly, and that Mama would want you—all of us—to be happy again. I think I knew that already, but I needed to be reminded of it. Besides, I liked Louisa right from the start."

"Thank you, Belinda. You have a generous heart just like your mother and your grandmother had." Sir Walter smiled at his daughter and then quirked a quizzical eyebrow. "Do you need reminding that your grandmother wished very much for this visit for you? I am aware there is little real affection between you and your cousin, but you are both beyond the stage of childish squabbling now. It may just be that in her delicate situation Deirdre would feel comforted to have someone of her own blood with her."

"Very well, Papa, I'll go." Belinda smiled warmly back at him.

"That's my good girl." Sir Walter nodded his head, crowned with thick waves of steel gray hair that in combination with lean cheeks and a well-shaped nose and brow gave him a look of mature distinction. "Now to get down to practical matters. Lord Archer is naturally eager to see his wife comfortably established with a companion so that he need not miss too much of the parliamentary session. This means there will be no time to assemble a fashionable wardrobe for you, so I propose—"

"But, Papa, I am in mourning for Gran—as is Deirdre, for that matter—so there will be no need for fashionable clothes."

"As to that, my child, your grandmother was strongly opposed to the custom of draping young people in unalleviated black for months on end. Naturally you would not wish to go about in public wearing crimson or suchlike colors, but it is my firm opinion that you will be showing proper respect for your grandmother's memory if you wear ordinary garb with black ribbons for the next few months."

"If you say so, Papa."

Belinda still looked doubtful, but Sir Walter proceeded at once to explain that he proposed to give her a sum of money with which to acquire a suitable wardrobe with her cousin's advice and assistance. "For Deirdre is a married woman now and has been to London recently. She will know what is appropriate for you," he added, with the rather touching male confidence in the married woman's ability to safely navigate the tricky seas of fashion. Belinda's jaw dropped when he mentioned the amount of money he had in mind.

"Two hundred pounds! I don't see how I could spend the half of that, Papa."

Her father's gray eyes gleamed with amusement as he came out from behind his desk. "If you cannot, I am persuaded your cousin can teach you."

"But can you really spare such a large sum at present, Papa, what with all the costs of redecorating the main saloon and the dining room?"

Gazing down into the sweet young face that, with the exception of silver gray eyes instead of blue, was almost a perfect copy of her mother's, Sir Walter felt a mist coming over his own eyes. He put his arm around his daughter's shoulders and raised her from the chair. "Should my only daughter be any less worthy of adornment than the dining room walls?" he asked with an assumption of jollity, though his voice was husky as he guided Belinda over to the door.

The girl smiled delightedly at her father's nonsense and reached up to kiss his cheek as she left the room, her head in a daze at the unanticipated changes hovering on her horizon and approaching with the speed of a summer storm.

Two days later there was no sign of a smile as Belinda prepared to embark on the journey that would wrest her from her cozy cocoon and cast her down into an alien environment.

It seemed as if the entire household had assembled in the vicinity of the carriage drive to wish her Godspeed. From his perch on the box of the solid carriage that had served the Melvilles for nearly twenty years, John Coachman directed the footman, who was cording Belinda's trunk on top, along with the tapestry valise and misshapen bundle that contained the worldly goods of an excited Polly Watson, the parlormaid who had been promoted by Sir Walter to the elevated position of abigail to his daughter during her stay in Somersetshire. Beddoes and Cook, who considered that they had had a hand in raising Miss Belinda from infancy, stood silently to one side, having said their private farewells earlier, while two of the maids and the kitchen boy could be seen through the open front door, eager to miss nothing of the momentous event. Belinda's old nurse, still serving her small brothers in the same capacity, was keeping the adventurous Albert tethered to her side with one hand while her eyes never left a tearful Robin, who, from his sister's arms, was giving unbridled reign to his vociferous displeasure at her impending departure.

"There, there, sweetheart, I'll be back before you know it, and I'll bring you a lovely surprise," Belinda promised, hugging the round little figure in his knitted blue coat once again before allowing Lady Melville to detach him.

"Have a wonderful time, my dear, and remember to write often. We shall miss you," Lady Melville said distractedly, while trying with a conspicuous lack of success to soothe her sobbing infant.

Nurse took Robin over at this point but in so doing released her hold on Albert, who promptly took advantage of this freedom to make a dash for the team of horses, his precipitate action, accompanied as it was by a joyous shout, causing a nervous wheeler to bolt. Order was restored by the coachman, who got his team under control in a few seconds, as Albert's irate father seized the culprit in a grip from which there was no escape.

"You'd best get inside the coach, my dear, before the situation deteriorates any further," Sir Walter advised his daughter. He kissed her hurriedly as Beddoes assisted Polly to climb aboard and then performed the same service for a dry-eyed but solemn Belinda. As he prepared to close the carriage door while still clutching a chastened Albert, Sir Walter said his own farewell, adding softly, "I hope you enjoy the experience greatly, Belinda, but do not permit your cousin to change you." He stepped back and signaled the coachman to start.

His daughter's face as he had last seen it, reflecting an uneasy mixture of anticipation and trepidation, recurred to Sir Walter's imagination at odd moments during that day as the household settled back into its normal routine. An hour after Belinda's departure he sat in his bookroom staring at nothing, a prey to mixed feelings himself. It was time, more than time, that the country-bred girl tried her wings in a society beyond this backwater. Any attempt to launch her in London so soon after her grandmother's death would have been frowned upon by high sticklers, and in any case, neither he nor Louisa was much at home in that sort of society. Belinda's mother's family had been well connected, but her branch had died off in the last few years, leaving no one he could call upon to invite Belinda for a brief visit to give her a little town polish. It was Deirdre or no one, but Sir Walter had not been without some reservations about accepting this invitation. With no desire to be hard on the girl, he could not gloss over the fact that he had found Deirdre St. John shallow and selfish in the past, and he did not welcome the thought that she might pass on her own taste for frivolity to his daughter. Deirdre's last visit to Millgrove had taken place before her mother died, over two years ago. She might well have matured and improved since then. It did not seem entirely fair to judge the girl on her behavior at seventeen. He had pondered the question for some time before deciding to accept the invitation on Belinda's behalf. It had been Deirdre's family situation plus the knowledge that the visit was to take place in the restricted society of the country that had overcome his initial reluctance. Belinda would not be racketing around London in the sole charge of a young woman scarcely more seasoned than herself. The setting might be luxurious beyond anything Belinda had ever seen, but they would be leading a quiet life for all that, thanks to Deirdre's pregnancy and her husband's absence. Without a host there could be no lavish entertaining, but it would still be possible for Belinda to meet the genteel families in the area. Something might come of it; at the very least it would afford enough of a change that it would serve to counter her grief at her grandmother's demise. He had made the right decision.

A knock on the door interrupted Sir Walter's ruminations. It was Beddoes with the post that had been picked up at the receiving office. Glancing through the few pieces, Sir Walter was brought up short by an envelope postmarked from Northumberland and addressed to his daughter before he realized that it must be from Miss Fenton, who had been Belinda's governess for three years. She had become quite fond of Belinda and Mrs. Gordon while at Millgrove. Sir Walter was aware that Belinda had written to apprise Miss Fenton of her grandmother's death. This was undoubtedly a letter of condolence. He would send it off to Archer Hall when he wrote to Belinda.

The ticking of the ornate yellow Limoges mantel clock sounded loud in the sunny apartment as the critical moment

approached. The room's two occupants were staring with
equal avidity into the large rectangular mirror above the gilded
dressing table whose top was littered with bottles and jars.
Both women were in the full flush of youth and were possessed of more than ordinary good looks, though the obvious
attractions of the buxom blond abigail standing behind her
seated mistress paled in comparison with the latter's radiant
beauty. In this young woman every visible element appeared
to contribute its full share to the delightful total, from the
gleaming blue-black curls piled atop her head in luxuriant profusion to the slender ankle and dainty foot peeking out from
beneath her skirts. If any one feature could be said to be more
outstanding than the rest, however, the nod would have go to
her eyes, which were large, exquisitely placed, and of an in-
credibly vivid shade of blue rarely found in nature, and made
more startling by their frame of black lashes of enviable length
and thickness.

At the moment those eyes were fixed on her dresser's fingers, which hovered over the dusky curls, hesitating for anxious seconds before nestling a life-sized butterfly of gold
filigree work among the shining tresses. As the abigail withdrew her hands ceremoniously, both women released their
pent-up breaths in unison at the butterfly's successful landing.

"Oh, that is perfect, Meritt!" cried Lady Archer, using the
hand mirror she had been holding in her lap and angling it to
better gauge the effect of the ornament in a profile view. "Did
I not tell you this would add the perfect touch to my new gold
tissue gown? Now, do not forget this exact placement unless
you wish to see me go into strong hysterics," she exhorted the
dresser gaily, laying the mirror down on the dresser top with a
careless motion that knocked over a small perfume flagon,
which promptly rolled onto the floor, spilling its contents lib-
erally before the maid could retrieve it.

"Be quick, Meritt," her mistress said quite uselessly as a
strong aroma of crushed flowers rose to invade their nostrils.
"Phew, that is overpowering at close quarters. I don't believe
I care for that scent as much as I did when we bought it in
London. Throw it away—or you may have it if you wish," she
offered on a generous impulse, adding, "but don't wear it
around me."

"Thank you, my lady." Meritt slipped the restoppered bottle into the pocket of her apron. "Shall I arrange your hair for the day now?"

"Not yet. I'd like you to devise another style for evening first. This time keep it smooth on top and arrange the ringlets at the back of the head. I wish to assess the effect of a wreath of flowers totally encircling the curls."

"That is something we have done on several occasions before, my lady. It is excessively becoming to you."

"I have been wondering if it might not be deemed too *jeune fille* now that I am a married lady."

"Never that, ma'am. Wearing the hair all pulled to the back of the head requires a perfect brow and profile such as few females can boast. Only those fortunate enough to be blessed with such features should ever be coiffed so."

While she reassured her mistress on this vital point Meritt was removing the pins anchoring Lady Archer's hair on top of her head. She then proceeded to brush out the curls.

A knock sounded on the door to the sitting room connecting Lord Archer's and his lady's bedchambers. Lady Archer stiffened and her glance skidded away from the knowing expression reflected in her dresser's eyes in the mirror. "I'm not dressed to receive anyone yet," she said sharply as Meritt put down the hairbrush she had been wielding.

As the maid walked over to the door, Lady Archer scrabbled in the drawer of the dressing table to find a box of gray powder, which she hastily applied to her face with a wad of cotton, her ears straining to follow the low-voiced exchange going on out of her line of vision across the room. As her husband's neatly attired figure appeared in the mirror, she tossed the cotton pad into the drawer and shut it, turning on the bench when he sent his voice on ahead.

"Good morning, my dear. Meritt says you are not yet finished dressing, but I assured her I find a certain degree of dishabille rather attractive in a woman; in fact, quite ravishing in your case," he added, his eyes sweeping over the cloud of dark hair tumbled about his wife's shoulders before traveling down the length of the yellow silk wrapper of a cobweb delicacy that revealed the exquisite lines of her body. "I hope you won't consider me overcritical if I just hint that your use of French scent might be a bit on the extravagant side today, however."

"Meritt spilled some perfume on the floor earlier," said his bride. "It has made me feel ill—more than usually ill, I should say."

"Perhaps an open window might help," his lordship suggested, turning to the stiff-faced maid. "Meritt?

"You do look rather pale this morning, my love," Lord Archer continued, scrutinizing his wife's face as the abigail went over to the window to do his bidding. "I take it that is why you are still in your room at noon and why you did not feel able to respond to my earlier request to reserve a few moments of your time when it should be convenient?" Lord Archer's tones were sympathetic but his intelligent hazel eyes had not missed the pile of discarded garments strewn on the bed and the opened wardrobe spilling its colorful contents onto the floor.

"It was just that every time I tried to walk around, my stomach would begin to feel queasy again," Lady Archer explained, summoning a pathetic little smile to her lips as she made a gesture of resignation with shapely white hands adorned with several sparkling rings. "Then I'd have to sit down again. I simply could not face going downstairs and dealing with the housekeeper this morning, and the very thought of breakfast made me bilious." She gave a delicate shudder and gazed up at her husband imploringly.

"I quite understand, my love. Rather than subject you to the strain of coming down, shall we have our little talk here?" Ignoring the uneasiness that flitted across his bride's lovely features, Lord Archer turned to the abigail with a polite little bow. "If you will excuse us for a few moments, Meritt, your mistress will ring when she needs you again." He remained standing until the maid had closed the door behind her; then he pointed to one of a pair of elegant *fauteuils* covered in buttercup moiré. "I believe you will be more comfortable here than on that backless bench, my dear." He assisted her into the chair and seated himself in its twin.

"If you are meaning to scold me again about that diamond bracelet, Lucius, I think it is too bad of you. I have already promised I won't buy anything that costly in the future without telling you first. I did not realize I was being so extravagant. It was mostly that clerk's fault anyway. He kept insisting the bracelet was meant for me, had been destined for my wrist alone, and that its beauty was wasted on another female. In the end he simply wore me down with his arguments until I weakened and agreed to buy it."

"Calm yourself, Deirdre. This isn't about the bracelet. I hold myself largely to blame for not setting more explicit limits upon your spending right from the beginning. I should have realized that a girl used only to pin money to spend on fripperies would have little idea how to manage what must seem at first to be a fortune. Perhaps it was inevitable that you should have assumed your resources were inexhaustible. As I told you at the time, it is merely a matter of keeping a record of all your expenditures each quarter so you will always know what your current resources are. I have no doubt of your ability to grasp this vital principle of finance and am confident that you will study to do better in the future."

"And you are not going to make me return the bracelet?"

Lord Archer's smile was a shade wry. "No, I have decided to regard the bracelet as the price of fiscal experience, mine and yours."

"Oh, thank you, Lucius. You are the dearest and most generous husband." Deirdre clasped her hands together, her lovely face alight with elation for a moment until her eyes shifted under his. "Wh . . . what did you wish to speak to me about then?" she asked hurriedly.

"What I need to discuss with you is a letter I have just received from Sir Walter Melville thanking me for inviting his daughter to bear you company while I am in London this spring. Perhaps you can enlighten me on this subject since I was unaware of issuing such an invitation."

"Yes, of course. Sir Walter is my uncle—at least his first wife was my mother's twin sister. Belinda is the cousin I told you about who is like a sister to me."

"I comprehend the relationship, my love, and naturally your cousin is welcome in this house whenever you choose to invite her. But I thought you understood that an unmarried girl does not constitute a proper chaperone."

"I do not at all understand why a married woman should require a chaperone in her own house," Deirdre exclaimed hotly, her lovely eyes sending out blue sparks. "It must look to the world as if you do not trust me!"

"It is not a question of trust but propriety," Lord Archer said patiently. "You are very young and you are in a delicate situation. To leave you here without some older woman to look after you would be sheer neglect on my part."

"Nonsense, there is a houseful of servants to look after me, not to mention my cousin, who is an extremely capable and reliable person. She has just nursed our grandmother through her final illness."

"Nevertheless, I would feel more comfortable about leaving you in the care of my elder sister, Lady Ilchester."

"Do you care nothing about my feelings?" Deirdre cried passionately. "Lady Ilchester is nearly forty years old, old enough to be my mother. We have nothing in common; in fact, she heartily disapproves of me, you know she does. She disapproves of levity and laughter and any activity others find enjoyable. I should be made to feel like a child under the thumb of a strict governess in my own home!"

Lord Archer heard this unflattering depiction of his sister's character with no appreciable emotion. "It is true that Lydia's nature could never be called fun-loving, nor are her manners particularly conciliating. She cherishes strong moral principles and is a firm adherent of self-discipline, even asceticism, in her personal life, but she would never try to impose her standards on another. She is wise enough to make allowances for the fires of youth."

"If you can say that, you have not been much in your sister's company of late," Deirdre retorted with brutal candor, "And besides, you are a man. She would not try to subjugate you."

"Actually she did tend to take advantage of her superior years when we were children," Lord Archer admitted with a smile that gave life to his unremarkable features. He rose from his chair, saying reflectively, "It is not my desire to curb your innocent pleasures, my love. I realize, of course, that I am much too old and staid for you, but what is done is done. Your cousin arrives tomorrow. Shall we wait and see how matters go for a bit before deciding whether to ask Lydia to come to the Hall?"

"Thank you, dearest Lucius," said Deirdre, jumping to her feet. "And you are not too old for me," she declared, with a toss of black curls and an inviting smile as she placed both hands on his arm, hugging it to her breast.

The viscount looked down at his wife's upturned face for a second, a question in his eyes, before he bent his head and accepted the invitation, kissing her lips with a degree of ferocity that, unmet before, startled a murmur of protest from her. Instantly he abated the pressure, breaking off the kiss with an inarticulate apology. He avoided her eyes as he walked over to the connecting door, reminding her in even tones that he would be out on the home farm for the rest of the day, before disappearing into his own suite.

Lady Archer stood in the middle of the room, her fingers running along her tender lips, the remnants of shock in her eyes as she tried to reconcile the gentle careful lovemaking she had previously experienced from her husband with that brutal kiss. It took a minute or two before she could shrug off a mood of uneasiness and recall with elation that matters looked like falling out the way she had intended. Lucius had made a real concession in delaying his request to his dreadful sister. She must see to it that he had no cause to regret this concession.

Cautiously triumphant, Deirdre rang for her maid. In the interim she washed the gray powder off her face and wandered over to the bed to cast an appraising eye over the gowns scattered upon its surface. Most were brand new and she looked forward to wearing them. Her eyes narrowed as she held up a dress in a rusty shade that seemed less appealing made up than she had expected. She walked to the dressing table to study the effect of the color against her hair and skin. Yes, it definitely was not at all flattering to her.

When Meritt walked into the room a few moments later, neither woman made any reference to the unvarnished lie the viscountess had told her husband about the spilling of the perfume. They proceeded directly to the task of getting Lady Archer groomed and gowned for the afternoon. When this was completed to the critical satisfaction of both, Lady Archer prepared to go downstairs, leaving her maid to set the room to rights. With her hand on the doorknob, she said in an offhand manner, "By the way, Meritt, I have decided the rust-colored gown does not become me after all. You may have it."

"Thank you, my lady," said Meritt, tacitly accepting the indirect apology and handsome restitution as her due.

Chapter Three

It would have been impossible to say who was more impressed, maid or mistress, when the Melville traveling coach swept around the last gentle curve of the tree-lined avenue, exposing Archer Hall in all its sun-lighted glory to their eager view. Both girls' faces were unashamedly pressed against the carriage window, the better to take in the vast expanse of the entrance facade as they approached.

"Nine . . . ten . . . I make it eleven windows across that front, Miss Belinda, including the ones in those end wings what stick out some," Polly said, adding on a note of wonder, "and just look at those two flights of stairs going on up to a great door in the middle of the house. I never saw anything like that in all my life."

Neither had Belinda, but not for nothing had she enjoyed the freedom of her father's library for years. "That reflects the influence of an Italian architect named Palladio, Polly," she said casually. "All the most important rooms are on that middle level, where the windows are the biggest; it is called the *piano nobile*. This style used to be considered very grand a hundred years ago—actually it is still grand, of course, but I do not believe such houses are built any longer. Most people prefer less formality and more convenience in their homes nowadays. I think the reddish color stone is quite attractive, do not you, Polly?"

The tired horses had pulled to a stop by this time near the center of the building. Though she had not cared to confess her ignorance to the maid, Belinda had been wondering if they were expected to enter on the lower level or ascend one of the outside staircases to what would undoubtedly be a magnificent entrance hall. The sight of a tall, black-clad gentleman making a dignified descent down the right-hand staircase put her uncertainty on that point to rest.

"Is that his lordship?" asked Polly in an awed whisper.

"It is much more likely to be the butler, or perhaps his lord-ship's steward," Belinda replied, resisting an inclination to whisper herself.

This minor mystery was cleared up by the individual in question when he opened the door to the carriage a moment later.

"Miss Melville?"

At Belinda's soft assent, he inclined his head respectfully. "Welcome to Archer Hall, Miss Melville. I am Drummond, Lord Archer's butler. If you and your maid would care to fol-low me?"

Belinda accepted the hand extended to help her alight from the coach. She stumbled a little in descending, but the butler's strong clasp helped her regain her balance.

"One is apt to feel a little wobbly at first after hours in a swaying carriage," Drummond murmured kindly, earning a grateful smile from the embarrassed young woman before he rendered the same assistance to Polly, who popped out of the coach with the undirected abandon of a cork from a cham-pagne bottle.

Belinda took advantage of the few seconds' delay while Drummond directed her driver to the stables to marvel at the long vista of rolling parkland spreading out before her to a broken line of trees in the distance. Evidently everything at Archer Hall was on a grand scale.

She saw no reason to qualify that conclusion in the few minutes that elapsed before Drummond left the two women in a beautifully appointed saloon to the right of the entrance hall. At the butler's invitation to follow him they had as-cended the right-hand stairway that shared a landing and united with the left one halfway up. She would have liked to pause there to look over the park prospect with the additional height advantage they'd gained, but Drummond had kept going upward and the young women had followed meekly in his wake. Nor had he given them an opportunity to do more than suck in an excited breath at the imposing splendor of the two-storied entrance chamber with its huge columns of stri-ated alabaster before leading them directly into the saloon to wait in comfort while he informed his mistress of their ar-rival.

As Belinda's gaze lighted on her companion after conducting an initial rapid survey of the saloon, she saw that for Polly, at least, comfort in such surroundings was an impossibility. Evidently cowed by a surfeit of spendor, the normally chatty girl was perched gingerly on the very edge of the red velvet seat of a mahogany chair of the Queen Anne period, looking the picture of apprehension.

"Pray do not look so gloomy, Polly. There is nothing to worry about. Things might seem a bit strange here at first, but I am persuaded you will soon feel quite at home."

"I dunno, Miss Belinda. Everything is so grand in this place. I won't know how anything is done—"

"Probably much the same as things are done at Millgrove. In any case, recollect that you will not be a housemaid here; you will be my personal maid and take care of my clothes. No doubt Miss Deirdre's abigail will take you under her wing. Miss Deirdre will be here any minute. Try not to look as if you did not like her new home. You would not wish to hurt her feelings."

Belinda was still engaged in trying to cheer Polly when a step was heard on the marble floor outside the room where they waited. She jumped up and took a step forward, stopping suddenly when the newcomer turned out to be, not her cousin but a slim, elegantly attired gentleman in his midthirties. Not wishing to repeat Polly's misidentification, she stood silent, but her sense of awkwardness was soon put to rout when the man, who had checked slightly on sighting her, advanced into the room, smiling and extending his hand.

"How do you do, Miss Melville; I am Archer, Deirdre's husband. Welcome to Archer Hall."

"Thank you, sir. And may I offer my belated felicitations on your marriage?"

The shy smile Belinda offered in response faded as Lord Archer said, "Thank you. Before we go on to happier topics, I would like to offer my sincere condolences on the loss of your grandmother. Deirdre has told me that you were deeply attached to her and that you nursed her through her final illness."

"Yes." Belinda nodded sadly. "She was only in her midsixties, not really very old, but the untimely deaths of her daughters weighed heavily on her. After Aunt Laura died, she just seemed to lose heart."

"I regret that I did not bring Deirdre to see her grandmother immediately after our marriage. She could not have realized how very ill Mrs. Gordon was. I wish I might have met her."

"She desired to meet you too, sir," Belinda replied, appreciating the hint of apology in his forthright manner, "but at least she took comfort in knowing Deirdre was married."

At that moment Deirdre herself strolled through the doorway. Her eyes flashed from her husband to her cousin before she broke into a run and threw her arms around a surprised Belinda. "Darling Bel, you're here at last! But look at you," she continued, pulling back almost immediately and running an assessing glance over her black-garbed cousin, "so pale and haggard, poor dear, though I do believe you've put on weight since last we met."

"Gran kept forcing her meals on me," a red-faced Belinda explained with a lopsided smile, "so they would not discover in the kitchen how little she was actually eating toward the end. And after Nellie died last fall there was no one she could tolerate near her for long, so I rarely left her suite. It will be good to go for long walks in this lovely country through which we drove today."

"If you like to ride, Miss Melville, there are ladies' mounts at your service in the stables," Lord Archer said with a smile.

"Oh, Bel was never much good on a horse, were you, darling?" Deirdre put in gaily before Belinda could thank her host for his kind offer. "But what are we doing standing here without even giving you a chance to take off that frightful black cloak that I vow must have belonged to Gran? Come, I'll show you to your room."

Deirdre seized her cousin's hand and would have led her from the saloon posthaste if Belinda had not resisted the tug and planted her feet. "Wait, Deirdre. You remember Polly Watson, do you not?" she said, directing her hostess's gaze to the chair where the maid sat in anxious silence, staring at her mistress with pleading eyes. "She will be my abigail while I am here," she went on after a second when it became clear that Deirdre's careless nod in the girl's general direction was all the acknowledgment she intended. "She is a trifle intimidated by these surroundings. If you do not object, I'll keep her with me until your housekeeper or someone can introduce her to some of the other servants."

"Oh, very well, come along then," Lady Archer said, a trace of impatience in her fluting voice as she addressed the maid.

"Thank you for your kind welcome, sir," Belinda said over her shoulder as her cousin pulled her forward once more with no further ceremony.

The viscount's polite smile lingered until the young women disappeared through the doorway, then slowly gave way to a pensive expression as he exited the room himself in a less precipitate manner.

The bedchamber that Lady Archer showed her cousin into was on the other side of the entrance hall, one of a line of rooms that made up the master suite. "This is a poky little room, I'm afraid," she said, throwing open a paneled door and entering first. "All the best guest chambers are up on the next floor or in the wing at the back of the house, but Archer insisted that I put you close to me, rather than have you all alone upstairs, though I told him you would not care for that and would prefer the privacy and extra space. My dressing room is through that door and my bedchamber is beyond that. This was designed as a servant's room orginally."

Belinda stepped into the room assigned to her, unsure what sort of reply to make to these offhand remarks. It was evident from something in her cousin's voice that she had emerged the loser in a contest of wills with her husband over the room allocation. Knowing Deirdre of old, she was persuaded her objection to having her cousin placed near her was based on concern for her own, not Belinda's comfort, but prudence and civility would keep her silent on that head. Instead she said pacifically, "It is clear that it will add to Lord Archer's peace of mind to know I am within easy reach should you ever need assistance during the night. The room is perfectly adequate and the furnishing are lovely," she went on, affecting not to notice the discontented set of Deirdre's lips.

As she looked around the small but bright room, the latter courtesy of the enormous window that dominated the outside wall, Belinda found she did not have to pretend admiration. Someone—Lord Archer for a guess—had caused several choice items of furniture to be placed in the room. The Tudor bed with its exuberantly carved headboard and footposts against one wall had been lovingly preserved for centuries, and the dainty little escritoire decorated with designs of multiple veneers, placed next to the window, had never graced a servant's room. A walnut kneehole dressing table stood under an elaborate gilt gesso wall mirror and was flanked by an armless chair with cabriole legs and claw and ball feet. Belinda speculated that these pieces and a tall handsome walnut chest-on-chest in lieu of a wardrobe were probably the same vintage as the house and, like it, had been kept in prime condition. The rich jewel tones in the Persian rug under her feet attracted the eye, and a Dutch interior painting over the mantel was a joy to behold.

Deirdre listened to her warm praise of the room without comment, saying when Belinda paused for breath, "I have cleared a portion of one of the wardrobes in my dressing room for you, Bel." As her cousin slipped out of her cloak and gave it to a waiting Polly, she eyed the plain dark traveling dress beneath it with a disparaging expression and added, "Though if that is a sample of your wardrobe, you will drive me into a fit of the dismals. I hope you do not expect me to wear mourning with spring almost here and much of my trousseau unworn as yet, because nothing would persuade me into dead black, which does not become me at all. Gran would not wish or expect it anyway."

"I know she would not," Belinda said quietly, hearing the defiance in Deirdre's tones. "There was no time to have any new dresses made before I left, but Papa gave me some money, if you would not object to going shopping with me?"

"Now when did you ever hear me object to shopping?" her cousin asked with a grin. "We'll drive into Taunton tomorrow. You require smartening up if you are not to look the complete country mouse," she added as Belinda removed her black velvet bonnet. "We shall have to do something about your hair also. You look like a housekeeper with it all pulled back in a bun like that."

Belinda bit her lip at this unflattering appraisal but was saved from making an injudicious reply by the entrance at that moment of a footman bearing her trunk, and a large, neatly dressed woman whose own gray hair beneath a starched cap was arranged in the identical manner as her own. She avoided Deirdre's knowing smirk as her cousin introduced the housekeeper to her guest. Mrs. Curran's unsmiling acknowledgment was perfectly respectful though a bit daunting, but she unbent sufficiently to speak kindly to a nervous Polly, promising to return for the girl after she had unpacked her mistress's belongings.

"Meanwhile, Bel, you must come and see my quarters," Deidre said, almost before the woman had finished speaking. She led her cousin through the door that opened into the dressing room, waving vaguely to indicate the end one of a row of armoires as the place reserved for Belinda's gowns, but proceeding straight to the door on the other side of the narrow room, which she threw open, gesturing proudly toward the interior.

"I made Lucius promise that I might have a free hand in decorating my bedchamber," she announced when Belinda stepped into the apartment. "All the furniture I chose is in the French style, and I decided to do everything in yellow, which is my favorite color. It took simply ages to find the right pieces, and some of the fabrics had to be dyed several times to arrive at the desired shades, but I feel I have achieved a triumph."

Deidre turned expectantly toward her cousin as Belinda continued to sweep a fascinated glance around the opulently adorned apartment with silk-covered walls in a shade darker than the butter yellow ceiling of ornate, gilded plasterwork. The large room was crowded with sinuously curved chests, tables, mirrors, even an elaborate chaise longue strewn with plump pillows dripping with lace. Belinda's first impression was that every stick of furniture was gilded and that miles of watered yellow silk hung at the long windows and draped the huge scrolled bed. Her eyes met her cousin's, clearly anticipating encomiums, and she frantically sought phrases that would satisfy Deidre without putting her immortal soul in danger for lying. "A triumph indeed . . . and . . . and so . . . *sunny*," she offered, adding faintly, "I am overwhelmed," which seemed at last to appease her cousin's appetite for praise while not departing drastically from the realm of truth.

Deidre pointed to an enormous cabinet with glass doors on the fireplace wall. "What do you think of my collection of Dresden shepherdesses? Aren't they pretty?"

"Yes indeed," Belinda murmured, gazing at a half dozen shelves crammed with cavorting groups and single figures. "I was not aware that you collected porcelain, Dee."

"Well, I didn't before my marriage. Not all are Dresden; some of the pieces on the lower shelves are English—Derby or Chelsea—but I could not find enough Dresden ware to fill up the cabinet before we left London."

Belinda could find nothing to say to this beyond an incoherent murmur that the viscountess was free to interpret as admiration if she chose. To her relief, Deirdre soon grew bored with showing off her feats of decorating. To Belinda's chagrin, her cousin also seemed to become bored with her company; at least, she glanced pointedly at a lovely porcelain clock on the mantel and suggested that Belinda was probably fatigued from her journey and would welcome a period of rest before it was time to change for dinner. After a palpitating instant during which Belinda mastered her surprise, she accepted her obvious dismissal with a reasonable facsimile of smiling grace and made her way back through the dressing room to her own apartment.

No trace of the smile remained when she rejoined Polly, who was busy unpacking her mistress's trunk. Though she managed to respond coherently to Polly's chatter, Belinda's intelligence never became fully engaged in the task of deciding where to dispose of her belongings as she and the maid worked together before Mrs. Curran returned to escort Polly downstairs for an introduction to the servants' hall.

Left alone in the charming but still alien apartment, Belinda wandered about, pausing to admire a graceful silver candlestick and to run a finger over the beautiful marquetry patterns on the escritoire. The room was smaller than her bedchamber at home but the large window and high ceiling, painted white and more delicately ornamented in this room, ensured that she would not feel confined. In contrast to the flamboyant style of Deirdre's bedchamber, the atmosphere here was pleasant and restful.

She stopped in front of the fireplace and gazed for several minutes at the serene homey scene in the Dutch painting depicting two women sewing in the light from a lattice window while a baby slept in a cradle nearby. Her eyes lingered on the infant. Deirdre hadn't even mentioned her expected child, but neither had she herself offered her felicitations on this happy situation. Belinda bit her lip, a slight pleat forming between her brows. Deirdre's greeting had been cordial, in fact, surprisingly affectionate in tone, but in retrospect their initial meeting seemed oddly impersonal—her cousin might have been any hostess conducting a newly met guest to her room. Deirdre had controlled the conversation, if a description of her decorating efforts could be so designated, and then she had terminated it and the interview, giving Belinda no opportunity to introduce any subject of a more personal nature.

Belinda turned her back on the painting and cleared her mind of the lingering sense of dissatisfaction produced by the first meeting with her cousin. She and Deirdre had never been on terms of ceremony, forced for much of their lives as they had been by their mothers' closeness to tolerate each other's idiosyncracies. Despite past history, she must have allowed herself to expect something more from Deirdre in the light of changed circumstances. Resolving to suppress any such optimistic hopes in the future, Belinda eyed the inviting bed with its green-and-white toile covering. She decided that her cousin's suggestion of a rest had merit. As she slipped off her shoes, it occurred to her belatedly that Deirdre may have felt the need of a rest herself. As she recalled, Louisa had complained of a persistent fatigue during the early months of pregnancy. Berating herself for being too quick to judge harshly when it came to her cousin, Belinda eased herself down on the big bed, finding it blissfully comfortable.

Three hours later, refreshed from a nap and a bath, Belinda stood in front of the dressing table, examining herself with a critical eye, something she could not remember doing since Deirdre's last visit to Millgrove. Her cousin was correct; she had put on flesh recently, she conceded with chagrin as she stared at the dark blue dinner dress that had been her best last year and now felt uncomfortably tight. She resolved on the spot to limit her intake of food until that situation corrected itself. She was more then ever grateful that Papa had provided funds for a new wardrobe. She had not tried on the lighter weight gowns she'd worn last spring before packing in haste for the journey, and could only hope some could be let out a bit until she had acquired one or two new ones. As Polly fastened a superb double strand of pearls around her throat, Belinda turned her head to get a better look at the large, soft knot of hair at her nape. There was no denying it was a rather severe arrangement, but what else was to be done with a yard of nearly straight hair? Her father had resisted any suggestion from his wife that her stepdaughter might like to have her hair cropped in the current mode. Knowing he had always admired her mother's dark, smooth hair, Belinda had been content to tie hers back with a ribbon, then, as she got older, put it up in its simple knot. Deirdre's hair, arranged in an artful halo of ringlets today, had been wildly attractive, but her cousin's curled naturally. The thought of curl papers, hot irons, and hours spent having her hair dressed each day rather diminished her enthusiasm for trying something similar herself.

Belinda's thoughts were jolted away from her own unsatisfactory appearance by a knock on the dressing room door. Thinking it was her cousin come to escort her to wherever they gathered before dinner at Archer Hall, she opened a drawer in the dresser and extracted a black-bordered handkerchief. She was tucking it into her reticule when an unknown voice speaking to Polly caused her to look up. Her eyes met those of a boldly attractive young woman whose attire struck her as more fashionable than her own, though she wore a cap.

"I am Meritt, Lady Archer's dresser, Miss Melville. Her ladyship sends her compliments and begs you will not wait for her to go into the saloon before dinner as she is running a trifle late with her toilette this evening."

"I see. Thank you, Meritt," Belinda replied, conscious that her person was being thoroughly inspected by a pair of prominent blue eyes.

"Very good, miss."

Absolute silence held while the dresser retraced her steps. Not until the door closed behind her did Polly sidle closer to her mistress to confide in a near whisper, "I met that one in the servants' hall earlier, Miss Belinda. The other maids treated me as if I was important, being as I'm a lady's maid now, but not that one. Not half uppish she wasn't."

"Never mind her, Polly. You will have the other girls for companions. Is your room to your liking?"

"It's fine and bright. I'm sharing with one of the maids, but I've got my own bed and a small chest. All the female servants are down on the ground floor. The men, except for Drummond and his lordship's steward, Mr. Mackey, are out in the stable block."

"Well, try to be happy here, Polly. Do you know where the family gathers before dinner?"

"Yes, Mrs. Curran showed me the main rooms earlier."

"Good. It seems I'm to go down on my own, so if you will lead the way, I am as ready now as I'm going to be."

Actually, the time she spent with Lord Archer before Deirdre arrived passed very pleasantly. Although not timid by nature, Belinda was a modest young woman not in the habit of putting herself forward in company, so it was a tribute to her host's social expertise and light touch of the conversational reins that he was able to draw her out to speak about her background and the experiences she had shared with her cousin in their childhood. It was perhaps as well for her peace of mind that she remained unaware of how much her artless reminiscences altered and expanded Lord Archer's understanding of his beautiful bride. He was repaying his informant with a description of some of the villages in the area when Deirdre danced into the room looking utterly ravishing in a soft gown of yellow sarcenet over a white slip, her gleaming dark curls confined by a ribbon covered with brilliants.

"I'm sorry to be so late," she said, smiling radiantly at her husband and cousin. "Just everything seemed to go wrong this evening. Meritt couldn't seem to get my hair to cooperate, and I thought we'd never find the right combination of accessories."

"The results more than justify the time expended, my dear." Lord Archer's smile was indulgent.

"Yes, Deirdre, you look delightful," Belinda said in honsest admiration.

Deirdre's sparkling eyes, which had turned from her husband to her cousin, narrowed as they espied the pearls about Belinda's throat. "You are wearing Gran's pearls!" she stated in what Belinda could only call an accusatory tone. Having anticipated this reaction, she had discussed the matter of her bequest with her father before she left Millgrove, and now she said quietly:

"Yes, Gran willed her jewelry to me, but I know that she would want you to have the sapphire set; she always intended that to go to Aunt Laura. I have brought it with me for you."

"Oh, good." Deirdre turned to Lord Archer, explaining, "The sapphires are Gran's only really valuable jewelry except for these pearls, and my mother was the elder by fifteen minutes."

"I see." Lord Archer's gravity gave away none of his thoughts as he took in his wife's satisfied expression and the serene countenance of their guest. "I am persuaded it will be a happiness to you to possess something that belonged to your grandmother."

Deirdre nodded. "The settings are old-fashioned but the stones are very good. Something can be done with them."

Belinda was compelled to clamp her lips together to prevent them from assisting in the cry of protest that was reverberating in her head. She was relieved when Lord Archer, looking directly at her, said softly, "Here is Drummond to announce dinner, ladies."

Mindful of her promise to herself, Belinda took care to eat no more than half of what was on her plate during the meal that followed. She was aided in this resolve by her real interest in the historical murals painted on the walls of the long, formal dining room and also by the effort involved in acting as a breathless audience for her cousin's rambling accounts of various social triumphs from her London come-out during the past autumn. Once or twice when Deirdre's stories became too involved, her husband intervened with an item of local interest to help their guest become a bit more familiar with this corner of Somerset, but for the most part he gave an appearance of attending politely to his wife's monologue.

When the ladies left Lord Archer to his port at the end of the meal, Deirdre led the way back to the elegant saloon with the beautiful painted pianoforte where they had met before dinner.

"You enjoyed your time in London so much, Dee; it must be a great disappointment that you are feeling too unwell to accompany Lord Archer there this spring, though I must say you look remarkably blooming for all that."

Hearing the sympathy in Belinda's voice, Deirdre looked a trifle discomposed for a second, then said quickly, "I am disappointed, of course, but it is only when I am in the carriage for any length of time that I am really unwell. There will be plenty of society to amuse us around here."

"Still, it must be hard to be separated from one's husband when one is only a few months married."

"As for that, Archer and I are not one of those dreary couples who must be forever in each other's pockets." Seeing the shock on her cousin's face, Deirdre gave a trill of laughter. "When you have seen rather more of the world, you will learn that fashionable people have a different way of looking at things, and their ideas go beyond the provincial mentality of rural Gloucestershire."

Irked by her cousin's assumption of superiority, Belinda might have been goaded into a spirited defense of the mentality and morality obtaining in the provinces had not the viscount joined the ladies at that moment.

While Deirdre, at her husband's request, played and sang in her light, well-trained soprano, Belinda found herself studying Lord Archer unobtrusively. Though she would have denied having a preconceived idea of her cousin's husband on the incontrovertible grounds of never having spared a thought to his existence before her arrival in Somerset, the viscount was yet a surprise to her. For one thing, he was older than she would have expected, in his midthirties at least, and his appearance, while perfectly pleasant, was neither handsome nor dashing, qualities she would have thought indispensible in a man who would attract Deirdre. Similarly, his demeanor since her arrival had been restrained and quiet, his manners almost formal in their correctness, scarcely attributes that had previously appealed to her irrepressible cousin. She suspected a high degree of intelligence from the penetrating alertness in his clear hazel eyes, though their conversation so far had been the inconsequential sort initially embarked upon by strangers thrown into close contact. He projected a sympathetic aura that encouraged one to talk at length, but at this point she could not say with confidence whether it was genuine, or a skillful ploy to extract information. Nor could she tell by his manner toward Deirdre whether he was aware of the person she was beneath the prodigal charm and gaiety, or if her beauty blinded him to the defects of her character.

Belinda was no closer to a real understanding of Lord Archer's complexities three days later when he left on his postponed journey to London. She had found him a most considerate host and wonderfully easy to talk to, but she could not

have told whether he liked or approved of her. His pleasant facade might be concealing anything from a touch of ennui in
her company to an irremedial dislike of her person. Despite his
well-bred manners, his reserve was so impenetrable to her
searching intellect that she could not even discern the depth of
his feelings for his bride. There was nothing remotely lover-
like in his behavior or voice—indulgent was the strongest
word she could summon to characterize his attitude, though
once or twice she had intercepted a glance of brooding intensity directed at Deirdre when he did not know he was under
observation.

All in all, Belinda considered the viscount and his bride a
very unsatisfactory pair of newlyweds from a romantic per-
spective. She certainly need not have feared to play goose-
berry at Archer Hall. She did feel a bit guilty at taking up
Deirdre's time during her husband's final hours before em-
barking on a lengthy absence, but when Lord Archer had suggested they show their guest around the estate together on
Belinda's first full day, Deirdre had insisted that it was absolutely essential to set about readying a wardrobe for her
cousin that would not cover them with shame in the neighborhood. Seeing that Belinda was not at all disturbed by the implied insult, Lord Archer had accepted the supremacy of
feminine concern with appearance and had withdrawn his
offer to be their guide, an offer Belinda would have much preferred to accept.

Though she had been interested in the countryside through
which they passed and was pleased with the bustling town of
Taunton, that first day in her cousin's more or less exclusive
company had been less than a resounding success, apart from
the fact that their tastes differed and Belinda refused to order
anything made up that did not accord with the spirit of mourning. She embraced the triple flounce at the hemline that her
cousin assured her was all the crack in town this spring, but
would not be persuaded to adopt the low cut décollètage
Deirdre had worn at dinner, becoming though it undoubtedly
was to lovely shoulders. One of the two evening dresses she
ordered was of unrelieved black but the simple lines suited her
and the inserts of lace on the short puffed sleeves and along
the bottom of the skirt gave it an understated cachet that
Deirdre refused to recognize. She did admit, grudgingly, that

the gray silk with its black satin bands made the most of Belinda's eyes.

Deirdre's abundant gaiety since Belinda's arrival seemed slightly forced, assumed perhaps to conceal some private feelings she did not wish examined by others. If she were an ordinary bride the likeliest guess would be that she was putting on a brave show of nonchalance to cover unhappiness at the imminent departure of her husband. A lifetime's knowledge of her cousin, plus her observations of the couple, ruled out that explanation in Belinda's reckoning. Intuition told her that Deirdre was simmering with some hidden excitement and trying to mask her impatience with an assumed show of liveliness. She could make no sense of the situation, but it awakened an uneasiness in the back of her mind that threatened the surface pleasantness of her stay at Archer Hall.

Belinda's uncomfortable prescience received unwanted support at the relief she sensed in her cousin as Lord Archer's carriage vanished from sight after an unemotional farewell that had included both young women almost equally. Deirdre instantly declared that she was going to her rooms, and she headed back up the staircase on the words, avoiding her cousin's eyes.

Belinda certainly did not repine at this sudden gift of solitude. Almost all her time had been accounted for in company since her arrival and she seized this respite from enforced sociability to have a look around the extensive grounds of her host's estate. She turned her back on the house and strolled away with no distination in mind but with a glorious feeling of freedom that expanded geometrically as she increased her distance from the mansion.

Several hours later, Belinda approached the house from the back after a rambling walk that had taken her through magnificent gardens and a portion of the home wood out into open country. She had climbed several hills and gazed her fill at beautiful vistas in every direction, some of which included tantalizing glimpses of toy-sized villages nestling into folds of the green hills. The temptation to continue walking until she reached one of these villages was great, but fear of getting lost had kept her returning to an outlook from which she could keep Archer Hall in sight.

The calves of Belinda's legs protested as she climbed an inner staircase, proving what she had suspected during her hike; months of enforced idleness at her grandmother's bedside had made her muscles flabby. She was physically exhausted but mentally exhilarated by her hours in the crisp air and she smiled spontaneously at a young footman as she approached the central hall on her way to her room.

"Good afternoon. I'm afraid I don't yet know your name."

"It's Tom, miss, and I'm to tell you Lady Archer is expecting you in the crimson saloon. She is entertaining callers, miss," he added at her questioning glance.

Belinda hesitated, knowing she must look disheveled after hours of tramping over the hills. She had gone off without a hat and now put up a hand to her hair in an attempt to sweep back the tendrils that had escaped her chignon in the brisk breeze.

"Her ladyship said you was to join her immediately you returned, miss," the footman persisted, preserving an immobile visage.

Belinda sighed and began to remove the black shawl she had been wearing over a plain dark cotton gown.

"Perhaps if you was to keep that on, miss, it would sort of account for the windblown appearance," Tom hinted delicately, still wooden-faced.

Belinda accepted the suggestion with a grateful smile and headed on reluctant feet toward the reception room where she and Polly had been shown on their arrival. She was miserably conscious of her ruffled hair, and unaware that the same errant breeze had whipped some flattering color into her pale cheeks. She squared her shoulders and raised her chin in a precarious assumption of poise as she prepared to meet some well-dressed matrons who would take one look and condemn her—correctly—as an unfashionable country dowd.

To Belinda's surprise the crimson saloon contained no critical matrons but only two gentlemen who sprang to their feet at her quiet entrance. Her eyes flashed to her cousin, dainty and fresh in a raspberry pink gown as she sat on the sofa behind a table laden with the paraphernalia of tea drinking.

"Where have you been all these hours, Bel? You look like you've been climbing trees as you were used to do when we were children," Deirdre said on a trill of laughter.

"Not trees, just hills." Belinda came slowly forward, miserably aware of being under observation by three pairs of eyes. Through the partial numbness of embarrassment, she registered the comforting fact that the tall man closest to the door was regarding her in a friendly fashion before she shifted her eyes and found herself gazing into the amused face of . . . Apollo!

Chapter Four

Five years dissolved in an instant and Belinda was taken back to a dusty lane on her fifteenth birthday as her astonished eyes beheld a slightly older version of the man around whom all her romantic yearnings had centered in the intervening period.

"You!" she breathed, a smile of shining delight bursting over her face.

This radiance lasted until the horrified realization hit her that recognition had not been mutual. Deirdre's guest wore the stiff expression of a man trying to conquer embarrassment as he looked to his hostess for rescue. A hot tide of humiliation surged up from Belinda's throat, her step faltered, her lids descended protectively, and she nearly missed Deirdre's introductions as she battled to regain her composure.

"This is my cousin, Miss Melville. Bel, may I present Captain Anthony Wainright and our closest neighbor, Sir John Hanks?"

Deirdre's voice seemed to rise from the bottom of a well. Belinda was dimly aware that the other man stood off to the left near where she had halted as she sketched a shaky curtsy to Captain Wainright without meeting his eyes and turned blindly to offer a hand to Sir John. The blood had receded from her head as fast as it had risen, leaving her drained and weak. She identified gratitude as one component of her churning emotions when the man who clasped her trembling finger unobtrusively guided her down onto the nearest chair before releasing her to take the chair beside her, all the while delivering himself of the sentiments suitable to the occasion in a deep, slow voice that had a calming effect on her jangled nerves, though she did not take in what he actually said. As for Apollo—Captain Wainright—the sense of his polite acknowledgment had not penetrated to her clouded intelligence, though the indifferent tone in which it was uttered had added to her distress.

By the time the gentlemen took their leave, Belinda had mastered her initial agitation to the extent that she was able to participate in the parting ritual in an acceptable fashion, although she had certainly not contributed anything resembling conversational brilliance up to that point. Sir John's gentle questioning had extracted a potted biography from her, and they had exchanged a few observations on the local topography. Deirdre had monopolized Captain Wainright, who had appeared more than content with that situation. He had addressed precisely one remark to her during the call, an obviously dutiful inquiry into her impressions of the local scene, which she had answered in the briefest style included in civility.

How many times during the long, lonely years had she dreamed of meeting this man again? Now it had happened, but far from being a celebration and a renewal, the occasion most closely resembled the death of a loved one. A sensation similar to the chill emptiness that had assailed her when her grandmother left Millgrove for the last time spread through Belinda as she watched the man she had christened "Apollo" walk away so uncaringly. She shivered, unconsciously rubbing her right hand up and down her left arm, which was pressed tightly against her rib cage as she did so.

Belinda had time neither to disguise nor analyze her emotions before Deirdre whirled on her the instant the door closed behind Drummond and their visitors.

"What ails you? You look positively green." And in the same breath, "What did you mean by the mawkish look you gave Captain Wainright when you first came in? Do you two know each other? Why did he not acknowledge it?" she demanded.

"I got chilled during my walk this afternoon," Belinda replied, as she debated what to say to allay her cousin's suspicions while preserving her own privacy. "At first glance, C . . . Captain Wainright"—the name stuck a bit in her throat—"did remind me of someone I once . . . knew. I was mistaken," she added, her voice firmer as she uttered the literal lie that was, sadly, true in the deepest sense.

"Who is this person? Why have you never mentioned him before?"

"I knew him only briefly and it was a long time ago. Hence the mistake. I'm tired, Dee," she said abruptly, desperate to gain seclusion. "I walked for hours and my feet hurt. I'm going to lie down for a bit before dinner."

It was plain that Deirdre would have liked to pursue the subject of her cousin's former acquaintance more thoroughly, but Belinda gave her no opportunity. She gathered up her shawl and walked out of the room, her slow, heavy movements lending authority to her claim of fatigue.

Rest was impossible, of course, in her shaken state, but Belinda took off her shoes to massage her aching feet while she sat back against pillows piled on her bed, reviewing the wreckage of her girlhood dreams. Though she chided herself for the intensity of her reaction to what was no more than a minor embarrassment—a man who had met her once for five minutes nearly five years ago had failed to remember or recognize her—she could not fully argue away a poignant sense of loss. Like the books in her father's library, her memories of Apollo and the fantasies she wove around his person had peopled her imagination. His exciting image had helped to ward off occasional bouts of something she could only describe as a loneliness of the soul, when her spirit longed for communion with another, just one other being who would discern her thoughts almost before she knew them herself and would be content to share his with her.

Belinda's face grew hot once more at the memory of her gaucherie this afternoon and her fingers ceased their healing motions. Her cousin wasn't the most observant creature in the world when it came to other people's concerns. If Deirdre had described her expression as "mawkish" when she looked at Captain Wainright, what must the man himself have thought? His quick glance at his hostess had been an appeal for help. Coupled with his careful avoidance for the rest of the call, it was proof positive that her unguarded warmth had embarrassed him at the very least. She writhed in remembered humiliation, her hands going up to cup and cool her heated cheeks as she winced mentally at the impression she had given to everyone present. With his handsome face and strong, manly physique, Captain Wainright must be quite used to having females flutter about him seeking his attention. He must have considered her uncommonly forward. With this in mind, the thought of seeing him again made her distinctly queasy.

Oddly, this feeling of dread did not extend to Sir John Hanks even though he had been the one person aware of the full extent of her distress this afternoon. The discreet strength of his supporting arm, his calm incurious expression and subsequent easy undemanding conversation spoke of a tact and kindness that had warmed and sustained her throughout the ordeal.

In an effort to banish the hurtful memory of Captain Wainright's avoidance of her, Belinda summoned up a mental picture of Sir John. It was a blurred image at best since most of her intelligence had been concentrated on maintaining a fragile composure while she tried to master her emotions. She would venture to place his age at some few years in advance of Captain Wainright, who looked to be in the midtwenties, though conceding that in making this judgment she might be influenced by Sir John's air of quiet assurance. The dominant physical impression had been of a very tall, reed-thin man with unexpected sinewy strength in his arms. His face was rather long with hollow cheeks and a thin, straight nose below a broad forehead. She remembered his eyes best, large and dark and full of intelligence allied with some quality that invited confidence. Having already benefited from what she instinctively knew was a kind nature, Belinda indulged the hope that in Sir John Hanks she may have found one friend in Somerset.

Two days later Belinda had the satisfaction of seeing that hope closer to being realized when she met Captain Wainright and Sir John at a small dinner party given by Lord and Lady Barton, longtime friends of her cousin's husband.

The days in between had passed pleasantly enough but had left her oddly unsettled, though she'd have been hard pressed to put her finger on the cause of this elusive feeling. Another neighbor, a Mrs. Hamilton, had called with her daughter the morning after the gentlemen's visit. Drummond had tracked Belinda down in the rose garden, where she was engaged in conversation with Lord Archer's head gardener, who was pruning the newly greening bushes. Entering the gold drawing room a few moments later, she found a fresh-faced young girl peppering Deirdre with questions about the delights in store for her in London, where she was soon to embark on her come-out, while a well-dressed matron looked on with an indulgent eye.

After introductions had been made and both visitors had commented on the strong resemblance between the cousins, Miss Hamilton fixed her large blue eyes on Belinda and returned to the subject that totally occupied her mind at present.

"Have you had a London Season, Miss Melville?"

"I'm afraid not," Belinda said, sorry to be disappointing the eager girl. "Until I set out on this visit to my cousin I had never traveled more than twenty miles from my home."

"Oh." Miss Hamilton looked rather blank for a second; then, catching her parent's censorious eye, blushed and tried hastily to make amends. "There will be a lot of social activity right here this spring, I daresay. I understand the Bartons will not be making the journey to London this year, and we saw Sir John Hanks and his guest in the village yesterday, and Sir John said he would be remaining on his estate for the next few weeks at least." She gave a rapturous sigh. "His friend, Captain Wainright, is the handsomest man I ever laid eyes on. I vow if this weren't my first Season nothing would induce me to leave the neighborhood while he is staying with Sir John. He has such a delightful manner about him and such a winning smile, does he not, Mama?" Without waiting for her parent's probable agreement, the young girl rattled on, "Such a strong military air as he has, though he was not in uniform, of course, having sold out, I believe, after the victory in the Peninsula, but it is—"

"That will do, Sarah," Mrs. Hamilton said, squelching what promised to be an even longer rhapsodic description of the ex-soldier's manifest attractions. Turning to her hostess, who was regarding the girl with a condescending little smile, she said, "One trusts that exposure to a wider society will have the effect of overcoming the deplorable tendency in very young girls to judge a man solely by his looks, which are no credit to him at all. We are setting out for London tomorrow, and I would consider it extremely remiss of me as a neighbor to depart without offering to carry a message to your husband for you, my dear Lady Archer. Lord Archer told Mr. Hamilton that you have been feeling rather unwell lately and not up to the rigors of traveling. I am sorry to hear of your indispostion."

If Mrs. Hamilton hoped to secure an admission of her condition from Deirdre by this circumlocution, she was doomed to disappointment. Ignoring the second part of her guest's speech, Deirdre gave her a bland smile. "How kind of you to undertake to be the bearer of messages, Mrs. Hamilton. If it would not be an inconvenience, I wish you would tell my husband that Belinda is settling in well at Archer Hall, and that we go along quite comfortably here."

"And of course I shall be only too happy to convey your fondest love," Mrs. Hamilton put in archly, apparently considering the trivial message somewhat inadequate to the occasion.

"If you think it appropriate," Deirdre agreed, adding with matching archness, "Fortunately, I have the Royal Mail at my disposal for the conveyance of more personal sentiments."

Listening to the purring exchange of meaningless discourse between her cousin and Mrs. Hamilton, Belinda wondered if exposure to grand society had the effect of stripping people of sincerity in a quest for wit or cleverness. Would this attractive, bright-eyed girl return from her Season with her endearing openness replaced by a hard patina of worldliness?

Belinda pondered the subtle changes in her cousin during a long, solitary walk that afternoon. That there was a difference in Deirdre was beyond question, but she found it difficult to pin down, finally concluding that the change was not in her basic character or personality. She saw no evidence that marriage had made her beautiful cousin softer or less selfish, but something had taught Deirdre to better disguise her determination to get her own way in all things. Her pleasure-loving nature remained unchanged, but her natural liveliness was accompanied these days by a pretty charm that had not been much in evidence during their youth. It was undoubtedly appealing, especially to men. This new manner seemed to be reserved for times when they were in company, however, which lent credence to Belinda's gloomy conclusion that *au fond* Deirdre was the same unlikeable creature she had always been.

Reflecting with shame on the lack of generosity in her judgments at this point, Belinda berated herself soundly for the familial disloyalty of her thoughts, especially since she was accepting Deirdre's hospitality. She resolved to do her utmost to make her visit pleasant for both of them, which meant resisting the critical habits of a lifetime. It would be nice if they could become better friends one day. Deirdre was the only relative she possessed who was close to her in age and association.

Unfortunately for Belinda's good resolutions, she could discern no like desire in her cousin to forge a more amicable relationship. Deirdre spent most of the day in her apartment, having breakfast in bed and emerging only when callers were announced. At first Belinda attributed this seclusion to the nausea that often accompanies the early months of pregnancy, but when she extended sympathy and offered to read to her cousin while she rested, Deirdre rejected it out of hand, claiming she was involved in planning her wardrobe for the next few weeks. Rebuffed in her attempts to be more companionable, Belinda was left to her own devices, no real hardship since she was taking fierce pleasure in the freedom to roam about outdoors after being cooped up during her grandmother's final illness.

The women spent their evenings after Lord Archer's departure in the small saloon, where there was also a fine pianoforte, indulging in sporadic conversation interspersed with music. Deirdre had a pretty voice that had been well trained and Belinda could coax music out of the most indifferent pianoforte. The splendid instruments at Archer Hall were a joy to play. The hours the cousins devoted to making music together were by far the most agreeable of the day. Their conversations—if indeed that lofty term could be applied to the glancing verbiage that passed between them—were not nearly so harmonious in tone. A lifetime of enforced intimacy had not resulted in any measurable degree of spiritual rapport though they certainly knew each other thoroughly.

It was this intimate knowledge of her cousin's mind that gave rise to the vague presentiment of trouble that nibbled away at Belinda's serenity.

Something about the situation at Archer Hall was not as it should be. Belinda reached this disquieting conclusion indirectly, alerted by a nuance in her cousin's manner that did not ring true. Deirdre was going out of her way to be pleasant to her guest, reining in her tongue from giving vent to sarcastic remarks and eschewing for the most part her usual pose of superiority, but she was incapable of concealing the effort this policy cost her. Occasionally her eyes would flash with the old impatience, her lips would part as if to utter a scathing remark, then be firmly pressed together as Deirdre censored the impulse before changing the subject. This deliberate policy, in combination with her uncharacteristic desire for seclusion, aroused a reluctant curiosity in Belinda about the reason behind her cousin's forbearance. It was basic to Deirdre's makeup that everything she did was calculated to advance her own interests. For some reason as yet obscure it suited her purpose at present to keep Belinda comfortable but at arm's length. From Belinda's point of view the result was eminently satisfactory, if only she could have dismissed the nagging little suspicion that something unsettling lurked in wait for her.

Belinda looked forward to the dinner party at the Bartons' both to increase her acquaintance in the locality and to give her thoughts a new direction. At the very back of her mind, barely admitted to consideration, was the hope that Captain Wainright would be among the Bartons' guests. The first of her new gowns had been delivered, a soft, smoky gray creation trimmed with three bands of black satin at the bottom of the skirt and again on the puffed sleeves. It fit better than her old gowns and the flowing lines helped disguise the few extra pounds she had gained during the sedentary winter.

Polly was eager to experiment with her mistress's hair after observing Lady Archer's profusion of dusky curls. Finding Belinda lacking the courage to cut drastically, she'd had to content herself with gathering the smooth length on the crown instead of at the nape and forming a number of fat curls, which she arranged to fall in graceful array from the top knot. A spark of excitement glowed in Belinda's eyes and her lips curved spontaneously at the sight of the resultant transformation, but her mild pleasure in her appearance did not survive the entrance into her bedchamber of her cousin, resplendent in a superb gown of shimmering blue silk that matched her eyes and set off to perfection her grandmother's sapphires.

Though admiration was generally meat and drink to Deirdre, tonight she brushed aside Belinda's sincere compliments, saying rather pettishly, "This dress was a mistake; it makes me look nearly shapeless, but it was the most logical choice to wear with the sapphires. I shall have another deep blue dress made immediately to set them off."

The young women entered the waiting carriage in a silence that lasted until Deirdre said with an elaborate casualness that did not accord with the intent look in her eyes, "By the way, I do not wish word of my condition to get about the neighborhood yet, so do not speak of it this evening."

"No, of course not," Belinda promised, but she looked rather puzzled. "I would have thought the mere fact that you did not accompany Lord Archer to London would have been sufficient reason for the news to have spread abroad already."

This idle remark was received by Deirdre as though it were an unpleasant surprise. "What do you mean?"

Belinda blinked at the sharpness of her cousin's tone. "I . . . I just assumed that with you so recently married everyone would naturally expect that you would go with your husband unless . . . unless prevented by illness or . . . or something of the sort," she stammered in the face of Deirdre's frowning concentration on her response.

Deirdre pressed her lips together and lapsed into a brooding silence while Belinda puzzled over her cousin's strange mood. It must be related to her condition, but she could not recall that her stepmother had been given to such odd humors while she was increasing.

It was a relief to pass under the Tudor arch of a brick gatehouse some few moments later. Belinda gazed at the welltended park as the chaise negotiated the curving carriage drive leading to the Barton's house. A spark of anticipation had her sitting straighter and she put her cousin's moodiness out of her mind.

Dinner was served in the vast chamber that had been the great hall of the original castle around which the Barton's house had spread in a haphazard fashion over generations. Sixteen people were easily accomodated at a long table surrounded by what seemed like acres of space. Huge candelabra on strategically placed columns did their best to dispel the shadows in the far reaches of the room, a necessity despite the immensely tall leaded windows running the entire length of the long outside wall. Here and there the flickering candlelight produced a dull gleam where it reflected off metal surfaces of armorial weaponry displayed on the other walls.

Belinda was intrigued by the romantic setting, much more so than by the food, which was uniformly cold by the time it arrived, suggesting that the kitchens were some distance away. She hoped for the Bartons' sake that their family dining quarters were more advantageously situated, but at least the congealing offerings on her plate did not tempt her to swerve from her resolve to partake abstemiously until she lost those unwanted extra pounds.

The food being of minimal interest, Belinda's attention was free to wander at will around the table, catching snatches of soft conversation that gave rise to ephemeral thoughts too unformed to withstand the next breath of sound. As she had secretly hoped, Sir John Hanks and his guest were among the company. Captain Wainright had given her a civil smile and greeting before she was led off by her hostess to be presented to the three local families who made up the balance of her table. In their number were four members of her own generation accompanying their parents, three twittery young ladies and a tongue-tied youth who was cast into a pitiable state of confusion upon learning that he had the honor of escorting Miss Melville into dinner instead of his sister or a girl he had known from the cradle. It took half the dinner hour of a bland monologue leavened with occasional questions, all expressed in a soft, low voice, but ultimately Belinda had the pleasure of seeing young Mr. Crandall conquer his shyness to the extent of describing his studies as he prepared to go up to Oxford. His excitement at the prospect seeped through his hesitant speech and he became expansive about his expectations in the face of her quiet encouragement. Never again, she judged, would he be quite so terrified in the company of a strange female.

When Mr. Crandall turned to respond to his sister on his right, Belinda happened to cross glances with Sir John Hanks, whose approving smile she appreciated but felt she did not entirely deserve since her kindness to her young dinner partner had contained an element of self-interest. Concentrating on the awkward youth had helped to keep her eyes, which seemed to have a mind of their own, from straying to that area of the table where Captain Wainright was being well entertained by her cousin, judging by his rapt expression.

The program after dinner consisted of conversation among the ladies until the gentlemen joined them, at which point music became the preferred entertainment. Lady Barton, a vivacious redhead whose high-waisted gown of emerald silk could not disguise her advanced stage of pregnancy, came bustling over to Belinda, smiling widely.

"Miss Melville, your cousin tells me you are a talented performer on the pianoforte. Would you give us all the pleasure of hearing you play?"

Belinda blinked in surprise at the unexpected request, but it would not have occurred to her to be other than accommodating to her hostess, and she rose immediately. "Of course, ma'am, but it will have to be something from memory as I have no music with me."

While Lady Barton was assuring her that they had a formidible collection of sheet music, Belinda spotted some upraised eyebrows being exchanged among the ladies present and she felt her cheeks grow warm as she followed her hostess over to the instrument. Should she have demurred until other ladies had performed? Or perhaps it was considered more becoming to make a show of rating one's ability too low to please before acceding to a request? At home she was so long acquainted with all the local families that no formality obtained in their social intercourse. She could only pray for Deirdre's sake that she had not appeared forward in this strange company.

Belinda's doubts soon stopped pricking at her in her pleasure at producing music. Her performance of a Beethoven sonata was received with gratifying applause that appeared sincere. She allowed herself to be persuaded to play a second short selection but firmly declined to remain longer at the instrument, giving way to a young lady who played some lively marches as accompaniment to her father's rollicking bass voice. Deirdre and another young lady then sang for the company before the tea tray was brought in.

It was shortly before the Archer carriage arrived that the pleasant evening was spoiled for Belinda. Lady Barton had led her over to a large burled walnut cabinet in an alcove screened by palms and other greenery, exhorting Belinda with smiling good nature to rummage through the sheet music kept there and borrow anything she might like to play during her visit with her cousin. Excited by such an unexpected windfall of delight, Belinda was kneeling before the open cabinet studying some old songs by Bononcini she'd unearthed when she gradually became aware of masculine voices on the other side of the plants.

"—an enjoyable evening despite the cold food," a pleasant low voice was saying. "It is a rare treat indeed to find real musical talent combined with delightful physical attributes as personified by Lady Archer and Miss Melville."

"Oh, come, Jack, you cannot be serious in comparing Lady Archer and that dumpy little cousin of hers in the same breath. You might as aptly couple Botticelli's Venus with a Rowlandson caricature!"

"You are unduly severe, Tony," protested the first voice, "especially in view of the strong resemblance that exists between the ladies in question."

"Even granting a superficial family likeness, there is still no basis for comparison. Lady Archer is all exquisite modeling and vivid coloring—deny if you dare that there could exist in all England another pair of eyes of such an extraordinary deep blue, another smile of such brilliance, or a face of such astonishing perfection—"

"Cease!" the first man importuned with a note of amusement in his voice. "There is no doubt that Lady Archer is a very beautiful young woman, but it may surprise you to learn there are those who find large eyes of soft silver gray equally appealing, and some who might even choose a pair of sweetly curved lips over the most brilliant smile in the world."

"Creatures of such perverse tastes must be rare indeed," the other retorted in teasing accents that faded to nothing as the two men walked away.

On the far side of the screen of plants a white-faced Belinda glanced down at the cruel indentations made by her fingernails on the palms of her hands, insensible of physical discomfort as she struggled to her feet from the crouching posture she had involuntarily assumed upon realizing that the unseen men were discussing *her*.

With fingers that trembled so much she might with reason be described as "all thumbs," Belinda put back the pile of music she had removed from the cabinet, keeping a few sheets—she no longer cared which—to justify her absence. She fought to impose blankness on her features, desiring at the moment only to present a composed appearance until she could attain the privacy of her own room. Until then she would not think about anything, she vowed. She would make her mind a complete blank.

Chapter Five

"Sir John and Captain Wainright are coming to take us riding at ten," Lady Archer announced from the doorway of the dressing room that communicated with her guest's bedchamber.

Belinda, viewing with disgust the results of a disturbed night in shadowed eyes and pallid skin, started and knocked a hairbrush off the dressing table with her elbow. She turned her head and gazed at her cousin, who had come only one step into the room. "You said nothing of this plan on our way home last night."

Deirdre shrugged. "My mind was on other matters."

Apprehension was written plainly on Belinda's face. "I . . . I haven't been on a horse since I arrived in Somerset."

"In addition to my two hacks, Archer keeps a placid old mare in the stables for his sister's use," Deirdre said. "Blossom will give you no trouble, an armchair ride, I promise you."

"I'm not sure I can keep up with you, Dee. You were always a much better rider."

"You may suit yourself whether or not you join us," Deirdre said shortly, turning back into her dressing room.

Belinda sat unmoving for several minutes after her cousin left, a troubled look on her pale face while she considered the situation from all angles. She thought there could be no objection to the riding party as proposed by the gentlemen, but it might well be another matter if she cried off. Certainly an unmarried woman could not jaunter about the countryside with two men unrelated to her without calling down criticism upon her head, but was Deirdre in the same case? With two escorts, no one could accuse her of making assignations, but people were apt to be more conservative in country circles. The free and easy manners obtaining in London did not sit well with country folk. There might well be some eyebrows raised and tongues set wagging if Deirdre were to comport herself with such a lack of circumspection.

Belinda sighed and turned back to the unrewarding study of her reflection in the mirror. In the light of the conversation she'd inadvertently overheard last night between their proposed escorts she dreaded meeting Captain Wainright again, knowing she would feel self-conscious and awkward in his company. How could it be otherwise when each time their eyes met she would be reminded that he considered her person unworthy to be mentioned in the same breath as that of her lovely cousin?

No amount of rationalizing, of reiterating what she'd always known—that Deirdre was an exceptionally beautiful girl—of reminding herself that beauty was in the eyes of the beholder and that Sir John had spoken of herself in most complimentary terms had served to alleviate the pain caused by Captain Wainright's low opinion. For nearly five years she had indulged the sentimental habit of summoning up a mental image of the man she had dubbed "Apollo" to comfort her lonely hours. She had imagined numerous situations where they met again, and naturally the essential ingredient, the one circumstance that never varied, was his unbounded joy in her existence. The mirror girl's mouth twisted into a self-mocking grimace as she picked up her brush and began smoothing the tangles from her hair. The irony of the situation was not lost on her. The dearest wish of her heart had come true, but in a fashion that bade fair to keep her in a continual state of chagrin.

Belinda's movements reflected her extreme reluctance for the upcoming appointment as she submitted silently to Polly's attentions. She barely glanced in the mirror before accepting the crop and gloves the maid had ready for her. What was the point? If her appearance last night in a new gown and modish coiffure had been so inferior to her cousin's, this old gray habit, ill-fitting and threadbare, would undoubtedly confirm Captain Wainright's poor opinion of her attractions. She summoned up a shadowed smile for Polly as she passed out of the bedchamber but her thoughts were anything but pleasant as she crossed the central hall on lagging feet.

Unexpectedly catching sight of her downbent head and drooping lips in a pier mirror, Belinda was brought up short and her pride, dormant of late, rose up in protest. What kind of supine creature was she to permit the careless opinions of near-strangers to destroy her sense of her value as a human being? Why, she would be tacitly accepting the shallow scale of values that placed accidental physical qualities above character in estimating a person's worth. Her father and Miss Fenton would be disgusted with her. Her chin came up, her spine straightened, and Belinda entered the small saloon with a calm little smile upon her lips, despite an uncomfortably rapid pulse.

It was fortunate that her head was still full of this stern lecture on the unimportance of fine feathers because the contrast between her appearance and the others' was every bit as marked as she had feared. Belinda's heart dropped but her chin did not as she took in Deirdre's dashing habit and tall hat inspired by military uniforms, both in a rich burgundy gabardine that enhanced her vivid coloring. The gentlemen were equally *point de vice* with their well-cut coats and pristine white tops to their boots.

Belinda's smile did slip a bit and her eyes flew to the mantel clock as Deirdre jumped up from her chair, exclaiming, "At last! What took you so long?"

It was only one minute past the hour, but Belinda had opened her lips to apologize for her tardiness when Sir John said with an easy smile, "I hope you will pardon the eagerness that brought Captain Wainright and me to your door well in advance of the hour agreed upon, Lady Archer. We have been anticipating the pleasure of a ride in such delightful company."

Deirdre's silvery laugh tinkled. "That particular excuse will always secure your pardon, as you very well know, Sir John, but I can see we must be on our guard against accepting Spanish coin, must we not, Bel?"

Untutored in the gentle art of graceful flirtation, Belinda was at a loss to know how to respond, settling for what she hoped was a noncommittal smile.

Like Sir John, Captain Wainright had gotten to his feet when Belinda entered the saloon. Now he possessed himself of Deirdre's crop, which she had laid on the sofa. This served as a signal for the other three to start toward the doorway.

Belinda had no trouble picking out her mount when the quartet descended the left-hand staircase of the main facade a few moments later. Blossom, a hefty chestnut, was unconcernedly cropping the grass along the edge of the gravel drive

while two grooms kept three restive thoroughbreds in order. A
little sigh escaped her lips as she gauged the old mare's docile
temperament. Sir John, noting that her eyes had lightened from
pewter to silver, concealed a smile and tossed her up into the
saddle, personally adjusting the stirrup to her liking. Her
cousin, who had had the same service performed for her by
Captain Wainright, was as eager to be off as her impatient
steed, a handsome black gelding with a white patch over one
eye. Deirdre looked magnificent atop the large horse, as sleek
as the powerful animal she controlled with no apparent effort.
Captain Wainright's eyes were full of admiration as he edged
his sidling bay closer to her while Sir John swung himself into
the saddle of another fine bay stallion.

For a time the four riders kept together as the men discussed
the direction they should take with Lady Archer. Belinda, her
attention directed toward becoming familiar with her mount's
gait and responses, let the conversation flow past her. When
she had assured herself that she and Blossom had arrived at a
good understanding, she began to listen with more interest but
soon discovered that Deirdre was controlling the conversation,
gaily chattering about persons with whom she had associated
in her brief London sojourn. The gentlemen laughed apprecia-
tively at her amusing descriptions, obviously recognizing the
people she had singled out as butts for her witty derision.
Since all were unknown to Belinda, she was effectively si-
lenced, but she had little inclination to participate in what
amounted to wholesale character annihilation, no matter how
amusingly done. Besides, she was acutely self-conscious in the
company of the man who had made it abundantly plain that he
considered her a nonentity. She exercised conscious control to
prevent her glance from straying to his magnificently muscled
form astride an equally impressive steed that she thought
might be the same big bay he'd ridden in Gloucestershire five
years before. She tried to content herself with the benign
warmth of the sun and the earthy scents rising into the crisp air
as they passed through a grove of fine old trees.

Growing bored with their sedate progess, Deirdre proposed
a gallop over the pastureland that spread out to their left as
they emerged from the trees.

Captain Wainright eyed Belinda's mount dubiously. "I do
not wish to appear to criticize Lord Archer's stables, but do

you really believe Miss Melville will be able to persuade that slug to anything faster than a gentle canter?"

As Deirdre's laughter chimed out, Sir John came to Belinda's rescue. "Why do not you and Lady Archer have a gallop?" he suggested to his friend. "I'll confess to being so lazy as to prefer ambling along this delightful path if Miss Melville will give me the honor of her company."

"Capital," Deirdre declared, taking her cousin's agreement for granted. "Shall we give them their heads, Tony? My Conquistador is eager to stretch his legs."

She was off on the words, the black gelding leaping forward at a touch of her heel.

"I'd best see that she comes to no harm," Captain Wainright said quickly. With an apologetic glance at the other two he spurred his mount after the black.

Sir John had to hold his big bay on a tight rein to prevent him from heading in pursuit. Swiveling his head around, he noted the strained look on his companion's face.

"Do not be anxious for your cousin's safety, Miss Melville," he advised kindly. "It is obvious that she is an excellent rider—and an intrepid one."

The slight dryness of tone in this last description was lost on Belinda, who continued to gaze after the fast-disappearing figures of Deirdre and Captain Wainright. "Yes, Deirdre has always been utterly fearless on a horse, but . . . " Her voice trailed off and she bit on her bottom lip, for she could not divulge that the source of her concern was her cousin's unborn child. "Shall we quicken our pace a little?"

"If you think your . . . *flower* has another pace," Sir John agreed, and this time she heard the dryness in his voice and chuckled.

"Don't malign poor Blossom," she said sternly, struggling to keep her lips from curving upward. "She cannot help her unfortunate name, nor is it her fault she is old and unloved, is it, old girl?" She patted the chestnut's neck affectionately. "She may surprise you yet."

"Anything is possible in this vale of tears," Sir John agreed with equal gravity.

They set off across the field at a good canter, with the mare needing only occasional prodding to maintain the pace. An easy silence existed between the riders, interrupted now and then as one or the other made an observation on the passing scene. Belinda, away from the inhibiting presence of Captain Wainright, relaxed her guard and actually began to enjoy the rare experience of being in the saddle. The undemanding amiability of her attractive escort was largely responsible for this pleasant state of affairs, so she was all the more unprepared when out of the blue he said:

"Had you met Captain Wainright before that afternoon in Lady Archer's saloon, Miss Melville?"

The question was so unexpected and the tone in which it was asked so casual that Belinda was struck dumb for the moment. She could feel herself growing hot as she played for time. "Why . . . why, what can you mean, sir? Has Captain Wainright said any——"

"Tony has said nothing at all on that head; it was simply an impression I received from your reaction when you first saw him that day."

For the first time in her life Belinda wished she shared Deirdre's nonchalant attitude toward producing a lie when it served her purpose better than the truth. She wanted badly to protect her secret, but all she could do was take refuge in continued silence while she groped for inspiration.

"Please forgive my monumental impertinence, Miss Melville." Sir John's voice broke into her chaotic thoughts. "Curiosity has always been my besetting sin, but I wish I had bitten off my tongue rather than distress you."

Belinda's eyes flew to meet those of the man riding beside her. The honest regret she saw there and the kindness she had discerned from the beginning of their acquaintance suddenly liberated her from the burden of guarding her secret. She could trust this man not to ridicule her foolish disappointment. Drawing a determined breath, she said, "There is no call to apologize for expressing a natural curiosity, sir. As you have surmised, Captain Wainright and I have met before, but he plainly does not recall the event, and I *beg* you will say nothing to him about it . . . *ever*."

"You have my word on that, Miss Melville," he replied, his soothing tone a complete contrast to the intensity in hers. "When did this meeting take place?"

It was an odd relief to relate for only the second time in five years, the events that had made her fifteenth birthday so memorable. She was even able to make an amusing story of her grumpy stone-kicking and its unexpected aftermath, but as

with her report to Miss Fenton five years before, she withheld
the fact that she had been kissed by a complete stranger, who
had carelessly bestowed upon her the flattering epithet "flower
face" before riding out of her life. It was not Captain Wainright's fault that a besotted adolescent had tethered him tightly
by the ropes of her romantic imagination.

"A charming story," Sir John said lightly, "and how woefully typical of my sex to blithely dismiss the small things that
make life pleasant while intent on keeping our eyes and minds
fixed on the great adventures we hope lie ahead. Though, if I
may be permitted a word in undeserved defense of my gender,
the feat of memory required in this instance was much greater
for Captain Wainright. I am persuaded his appearance has altered little, whereas *you* have turned from a caterpillar to a
butterfly in the intervening years, if you will permit the flight
of fancy." Belinda's widened eyes revealed that this concept
was new to her, but Sir John went on without pause. "Your decision not to recall the incident to Captain Wainright is most
generous. In your desire to spare him embarrassment, you
have thereby denied yourself the pleasure of reliving a shared
memory."

Having given his companion much to think about at her
leisure, Sir John abandoned the subject of the prior meeting.
His questions were so casually put that Belinda found herself
telling him about the entrance of her stepmother into her life
and the subsequent joy of welcoming two lively little boys to
the family. By the time they came up to the others a good understanding flourished between them and Belinda was completely at ease in his company.

The sight of her cousin sitting on a stone wall with Captain
Wainright in close attendance as they gazed over a gently
rolling landscape that ended at the channel dimmed Belinda's
smile somewhat. Deirdre looked enchantingly flushed, her
cheeks and lips glowing with healthy color, her eyes darkly
blue as she welcomed them gaily while Captain Wainright
went to get their mounts, where they were tied to nearby trees.

"Hello, laggards. Is this not a glorious view we have found
for you?"

Sir John responded appropriately while Belinda's eyes
strayed to the man leading the two thoroughbreds towards
them. "Hello, Titan, how are you, boy?" she said, bestowing a

pat on the big bay's handsome nose as Captain Wainright threw Deirdre up onto Conquistador's back.

Belinda's words had been very softly spoken, but Titan's owner peered up at her, his eyebrows raised in query, "How did you know my horse's name, Miss Melville?"

"You must have mentioned it earlier," she said easily. "It suits him. How old is he?"

"He's eight, and I've owned him since he was a yearling."

"He is beautifully mannered and looks very strong, a handsome animal," Belinda said.

"He's all that and more. He was my best friend in the Peninsula, weren't you boy?" Captain Wainright gave Titan's neck an affectionate pat before mounting. He sent Belinda a smile that set her pulses fluttering. "It is clear that you have a discriminating eye for horseflesh, Miss Melville, which makes it all the more shocking that you should be mounted on such a slug."

Belinda smiled back. "A discriminating eye and a good seat do not invariably go together, Captain."

Deirdre's laugh rang out. "Too true. My cousin spent more time on the ground than in the saddle when we were learning to ride, did you not, Bel?" She made an observation on the view and they remained lazily chatting in the lovely spot until Sir John reminded his guest that they were promised to friends for lunch. The men also had plans for the following day, but it was agreed that they would repeat the pleasant riding experience the next day but one.

When Belinda entered her room on their return to change out of her habit, a welcome surprise in the form of a letter from her father awaited her. She stripped off her gloves and pounced, making the agreeable discovery that the envelope also contained a communication from her former governess. She tossed her hat onto the bed and dropped into the chair near the dressing table to savor a momentary sense of being close to the people she loved. Her lips curved gently as she read her father's rambling account of the ordinary early spring activities on the estate, the sprucing up of the home garden, and the early sowing of the fields. A number of the cottages needed repairs and some roofs must be replaced after the hard winter. She was sorely missed by everyone, especially her little brothers, who had been out of sorts since her departure, moping about the house in a fashion totally at variance from their usual high-spirited behavior. Their mother was beginning to wonder if they were sickening for something, but Papa expected a few warm sunny days with the new life in barns and fields would soon see them restored to their mischievous selves.

Belinda blinked rapidly once or twice to clear her vision as she reread the affectionate messages from various members of the household faithfully passed on by her father. It was stupid to feel so alone and bereft when she was sitting in the lap of luxury, so to speak, and enjoying a more active social life than she had ever experienced. There were two more dinner parties scheduled for the following week, and one of the young ladies she'd met at the Bartons' had hinted that her mama was planning a small dance in the near future. In addition, two most attractive men had placed themselves at their service for riding parties. Good manners demanded that she try harder to appreciate the efforts of those in Somerset to entertain her. She must conquer the persistent sense of alienation that dogged her footsteps here.

Belinda shook off her spasm of homesickness and turned her attention to the letter from her old governess. She had developed a strong respect and personal liking for Miss Fenton in the three years that lady had resided with the Melvilles, particularly after her mother's death, and she liked to think her feelings were reciprocated. Their close association had ended a few months after her stepmother arrived at Millgrove when an unexpected legacy had removed the necessity of earning her living from Miss Fenton's shoulders. She had inherited a modest villa in Northumberland, which she had subsequently described in detail by letter. Pupil and teacher had kept up a regular correspondence over the years, and Belinda felt almost at home in the town where Miss Fenton now resided, so compellingly did the latter depict the characters and scenes of her new life.

Belinda's fingers were not so quick as usual when she opened the letter from her governess because today's epistle would be largely a dutiful, though sincere expression of condolence on her grandmother's death. She could already feel her throat tighten and her eyes misting as she began to read.

The mists cleared when she got to the second paragraph, however. Miss Fenton, commiserating with her young friend's inevitable low spirits, was suggesting that a period of time in the salubrious air of the north might be just the thing to bolster her health and restore tranquility to her mind even if more positive emotions were not yet possible. Belinda's eyes sped past the delicate expression of temerity at proposing to deprive the Melvilles of their daughter's companionship and assistance and fastened on to Miss Fenton's warm assurances of the delight she herself would derive from the opportunity to renew their friendship, this time on an adult basis.

The excitement in Belinda at this surprising invitation lasted until she had reread the affectionate sentiments with which Miss Fenton had closed her letter; then the glow of anticipation died out of her face. It was out of the question, of course. Much as she would love to head northward to her friend and the simple, useful life she led, she was bound to Deirdre at present. The lack of affection between them was unfortunate but irrelevant. Her grandmother would have expected her to assist her cousin in any way possible; her father, who bore no love for Deirdre, felt that his daughter's place was with her cousin at present; and what was more to the point, Lord Archer was trusting her to hold a watching brief over his volatile wife. Perhaps in a few weeks Deirdre would be well enough to join her husband in London, thus freeing her cousin to accept this invitation, if they could spare her a bit longer from home.

Bolstered by deferred hope, Belinda gathered her writing materials together and sat down at the escritoire by the window to compose a reply that would nicely blend gratitude and pleasure at the invitation and regret at being forced to decline, while holding out the possibility of a later acceptance should Deirdre's indisposition be short-lived.

Over the next twenty-four hours Belinda found Deirdre more snappish than usual. She peremptorily vetoed every suggestion her cousin put forth for spending an entertaining hour or two, electing to remain in her rooms during the early part of the day. Belinda was happy to go off on her own after a nearly silent luncheon with a seemingly abstracted Deirdre. Whatever unfathomable reason lay behind her cousin's present restlessness was none of her concern, she assured herself, setting off to enjoy a peaceful walk wherever her feet took her.

It was getting on for late afternoon when Belinda approached Archer House from the back, circling the stable block to enter a lovely little garden that Lord Archer's father had enclosed for his wife when her health began to fail. She came through a wooden gate in the brick wall and strolled toward a fountain pool of green marble in the center of the garden. She bent down and dipped her fingers in the pool.

"*At last*! I had begun to fear that you—why, Miss Melville—"

Belinda's head had spun around at the first words, and now she straightened up, noting as she did so that the lowering sun shone fully on the man's uncovered head, turning the golden waves into an aureole. She was also aware that her heart was beating erratically beneath her shawl, but she remained quite still, keeping her expression pleasantly neutral. "Yes, Captain Wainright?" she said encouragingly to the now silent man. "You had begun to fear . . . ?"

Captain Wainright, who had halted his impetuous progress on recognizing her, was some dozen feet away, having come presumably from the wrought-iron settee near the door that led into the late Lady Archer's garden room on the ground floor. He put on a smile to cover his embarrassment and walked toward the waiting girl.

"I hope you are not inclined to treat trespassers too severely, Miss Melville. Jack had some business to attend to, so I came over here in hopes that you ladies would take pity on me and offer me a cup of tea. I was enticed off my course by a remembered glimpse of this delightful garden when we were riding yesterday."

"I am persuaded my cousin will be happy to oblige, sir—"

"Aha! Unless my eyes deceive me, I believe I have interrupted a tryst. Shall I go away again?"

The laughing voice startled both Belinda and Captain Wainright, neither having heard Lady Archer come into the garden from the house.

The gentleman's sky blue eyes were eloquently admiring as he smiled at his hostess, whose face was vibrant with a demure mischief as she drifted toward them in a ruffled gown of white muslin so fine as to appear nearly transparent where the sun's rays touched it.

"I was just explaining to Miss Melville that I came by hoping to enjoy a cup of tea in charming company and couldn't resist taking a peek at this lovely garden."

Deirdre's sapphire eyes laughed directly into the man's as she took his arm. "Such eagerness calls for a personally conducted tour, don't you agree, Bel? Be a dear and order tea to be sent to the small saloon while I bore Captain Wainright with the names of all the plants in the garden. You will have only yourself to thank, sir, if you get more than you bargained for."

On this playful threat, Deirdre turned her back on her cousin, pulling the willing man along in her wake. He cast a look of rueful apology at Belinda before bending his head to attend to the exaggeratedly pedantic tone in which Deirdre began her promised lecture.

Belinda stared after the engrossed pair for another second or two before she headed over to the door to the garden room, a faintly uneasy expression marring the smoothness of her brow.

Chapter Six

The twinge of uneasiness that had disturbed Belinda on observing her cousin's casual appropriation of Captain Wainright in the garden had matured into a persistent jabbing by the time the gentlemen called for them the next morning. The captain had remained drinking tea with them a scant half hour, but this provided sufficient opportunity to confirm her growing suspicion that he was besotted by her cousin's beauty. He made a couple of conscientious efforts to remember his manners and include Belinda in the conversation—a fine point of civility with which Deirdre did not trouble herself—but his eyes slid past her immediately to fix adoringly on his hostess's vivid face once more. This was enough to ensure Belinda's personal unhappiness but was actually the least of her problems.

Alone in her room, a concentrated period of reflection on the meaning of the scene in the garden had brought her to the unwelcome and decidedly uncomfortable conclusion that the meeting had been planned by the pair. Hers had been the only accidental presence in that particular spot.

Deirdre's self-indulgent nature was well known to her family, but it had still come as a profound shock that she, a newly married woman, might be engaged in a full-blown flirtation, complete with clandestine meetings. Belinda had struggled against acceptance, but what other explanation could account for Captain Wainright's hasty words, uttered before he had known she was not Deirdre? He had started to say that he'd feared she wasn't coming. If Deirdre had never appeared, one might perhaps argue against Captain Wainright's presence in the garden at that moment being prearranged, but Deirdre *had* shown up less than a minute later. In the light of what Belinda now knew, her cousin's joking reference to interrupting a tryst was exposed for a colossal piece of impudence.

"Oh, I'd like to *smack* her one!" Belinda had cried aloud, jumping out of her chair in her frustration.

This yearning for the simpler, unsanctioned methods of childhood, was brief. Once she'd walked off her rage in a few rapid circuits of the bedchamber, curtailed by the painful impact of the corner of the desk against her thigh, Belinda had been able to bring her intelligence to bear on the problem. For problem it most assuredly was, she acknowledged soberly, rubbing the sore spot on her leg with her fingers as she sank into the desk chair.

Deirdre's nature was devious, but the person she fooled most completely was herself in deeming her self-serving machinations undetectable by others. She often committed the twofold error of overestimating her own cleverness while underestimating that of the rest of mankind. Much of the blame for this deplorable tendency could be laid squarely at her father's door. Hobart St. John had been Deirdre's first conquest, so thrilled with his beautiful little daughter that he laughed at her baby willfulness and eagerly became her dupe, closing his eyes to her deceitful little ways.

Belinda shook off this mental digression and concentrated on listing her observations of Deirdre's recent behavior. She'd noticed changes in mood right from the beginning of her stay, but now she tried to focus only on events since the first meeting with Captain Wainright. At that and each subsequent meeting, the two had spent a disproportionate amount of time tête-à-tête, but except for the Bartons' dinner party, no one would have witnessed this save Sir John Hanks and herself. A worried crease appeared between her eyes as she considered the garden assignation. That was probably agreed upon during the private gallop, but if not, then some form of written communication must be employed, and that meant widening the circle of persons aware of their secret. Servants' gossip spread with the rapidity of a fire in a haystack, and what servants knew eventually became known to their employers. Deirdre undoubtedly considered she was being very discreet, but she was courting disaster and must be warned. It was a foregone conclusion that she would fiercely resent any criticism or advice from her cousin. Cold perspiration appeared on Belinda's forehead in anticipation of the scene that would follow such temerity on her part. Perhaps if she simply kept her eyes open she might be able to forestall any plans for future assignations. For the moment she would refrain from confronting her cousin.

This compromise carried Belinda through most of the riding party the next morning, though her enjoyment of the exercise was largely spoiled in advance. As before, Deirdre and Captain Wainright went off on a gallop together, but this time Belinda did not achieve her former pleasant sense of camaraderie with Sir John. She was too busy speculating whether or not he was aware of the attraction between the other two and if he condoned the situation or merely turned a blind eye. Perhaps he had even connived at the affair. The three had often met in London last autumn, judging by their conversation. Perhaps everyone in that elevated stratum of society winked at such indiscretions. She was woefully conscious of her own lack of experience in this realm of male and female association.

It was when she and Sir John were coming up to the others that the situation took a new and frightening turn. Deirdre and Captain Wainright had evidently turned around at some point and were coming back toward them at a strong gallop. Suddenly Belinda became aware of a stone wall some distance ahead and, almost instantaneously, that her cousin meant to jump it. She hissed in a breath that dragged harshly across the back of her throat as Conquistador gathered his muscles and sailed over the wall. At the last instant a rear hoof caught the top of the wall and he stumbled on landing. Deirdre came partway out of the saddle, but she and the horse managed to right themselves with no harm done to either.

At first Belinda went limp with relief but then her jaw stiffened with the effort of holding in the rage that raced through her veins at Deirdre's unconcern for her own and her child's safety. She said nothing at all when Deirdre made light of Sir John's expressed anxiety and relief, but the fulminating gaze she fixed on her cousin's face caused a startled look to appear in Captain Wainright's eyes for a second. Like the others, he had been momentarily frightened for Deirdre's safety, but now he was bubbling over with admiration for her courage and riding ability.

"The sound of Conquistador's hoof on that stone wall nearly stopped my heart," he said, his voice roughened, "but, by Jove, that was the coolest piece of riding I've ever seen from a lady, not to mention the most skillful."

Belinda did not join Sir John in echoing these sentiments, nor did she say a word when the gentlemen's invitation to ride again on the morrow was accepted by her cousin for both of them. She was keeping her powder dry but she had taken a firm resolution in the instant when her cousin looked to be heading for a serious fall.

Belinda lost no time in carrying out her intention when they parted from the men at the front entrance to Archer Hall. She ascended the staircase in her cousin's wake, ignoring Deirdre's bright chatter. When her cousin would have parted from her at the entrance to her own suite, Belinda pushed wide the door and gestured her inside, following immediately.

Deirdre's eyes ran over her face and she emitted an exaggerated sigh as she pulled off her gloves. "Very well, I can see that you are just bursting with righteous indignation, so go ahead and relieve your mind of its burden." When Belinda did not speak for a moment but continued to examine the impatient face of the other as if seeking some clue to the workings of her mind, Deirdre shrugged and added, "You should know that Conquistador is a superb jumper. That stumble would not happen again in five hundred jumps."

"Dee, you could have been seriously injured and might even have lost your child."

Deirdre's eyes shifted away as she unstrapped her shako hat. "Nonsense, everyone takes a tumble now and again. I know how to fall without hurting myself."

"That is really beside the point at this stage. You were fortunate today, but you know you should probably not even be riding at this juncture."

"Don't be ridiculous. I've been riding all my life; it is as natural to me as breathing."

"Well, at least let there be no more jumping or galloping. It is too dangerous in your condition."

There was a pause and Deirdre's eyes and lips narrowed. Each word hit the air with the impact of a pebble on a marble floor. "I have no intention of plodding along like an octogenarian. I shall continue to gallop and jump as usual. If you do not wish to witness this, you may stay at home."

"I cannot let you do that, Dee," Belinda said quietly. "I would be unworthy of Lord Archer's trust if I permitted this rashness to continue."

"You cannot stop me," Deirdre retorted. "Do you plan to go running to my husband behind my back with tales like some little spy? It would be just like you!"

Belinda blinked at the ferocity in her cousin's voice. Her chest heaved as she fought down her own anger. "I see no need to carry tales to Lord Archer, but I shall stop you from behaving in such a reckless manner. All I have to do is acquaint Captain Wainright with your condition. I assure you he will not wish to have that responsibility on his conscience."

"You can't do that!"

"I promise you I can and I shall—tomorrow morning." Belinda spun on her heel and would have left the room without another word except that Deirdre leapt forward and grabbed her arm, whirling her around.

"You can't do that, Bel," she repeated. Her voice was controlled but her eyes were glazed with what Belinda could only call fear—or desperation.

"Why can I not?" Belinda searched her cousin's face, at a loss to explain the sudden frission of alarm that crawled up her spine.

Deirdre's eyes were wide with distress and she bit her lip nervously, saying in a monotone, "Because it isn't true."

This time the silence dragged out excruciatingly as Belinda's gaze never left the twitching features of the other girl which now reflected hopelessness as well as defiance. "What are you talking about? What isn't true?" The reluctant words came off her tongue as if someone else had planted them there and compelled her recital.

"I am . . . not . . . increasing."

"How can you not be?" Belinda protested, fighting not to believe what Deirdre's subdued manner told her was true. "Why am I here if you are not increasing?"

"It was the only thing I could think of . . . the only way I could avoid going to London with Archer. And you are here because otherwise Archer would have invited his horrible sister here to make my life miserable. I couldn't have that."

Belnda's brain was still reeling, trying to assimilate the stark statement. "How could you hope to get away with such a hoax? Sooner or later the truth is bound to come out!"

"No, you are wrong, Bel. I have thought it through carefully. Eventually I'll simply report a miscarriage. My maid is the only person except for yourself who knows I am supposed to be increasing. I can trust her completely. She is devoted to me, and I pay her very well for her discretion."

"What about the doctor? Lord Archer will certainly consult with your physician. How can you hope to hoodwink him?"

"Naturally I will wait until the right time of the month to stage the miscarriage. My maid will send for the doctor after it is over. Why should he suspect anything?"

Belinda stared in appalled fascination at the girl she had known all her life. Deirdre was calm now, her eyes clear and untroubled as she explained her plan to end the deception. Finally there was no escaping the essential question. "How could you do something so cruel to your husband?" Disgust at the callous trickery came through in her voice, for Deirdre instantly became defensive.

"I'm not being cruel to Archer. Besides, I told you—it was the only way I could stay here this spring. It was Archer's fault anyway. He insisted on a quick wedding, and he whisked me away from London the instant we became betrothed to go to see his sister in Yorkshire. I never really had a chance to say good-bye, so a few weeks ago when Sir John mentioned that Anthony was coming to make him a visit, I felt that my prayers had been answered."

"Are you telling me you created this elaborate hoax of being *enceinte* so you could flirt with another man behind your husband's back? Of all the *contemptible, selfish, egotistical*—and you had the gall to drag me away from my home to assist you in your depravity!" Belinda's voice had risen as her anger burst forth, but now she sucked in her breath and said with determined calm, "I'll have no part in this disgusting affair. I'm going home tomorrow if I have to go on the common stage."

"Wait, Bel, it's not like that! I'm in love with Anthony and he loves me. He asked me to marry him before Archer proposed. I had not given him my answer when Archer hurried me away from London. I was desperate to see Anthony again . . . to explain—"

Belinda's step had halted at Deirdre's dramatic announcement and a spasm of pain contorted her features, but when she turned to face her cousin a second later she was composed, though paler than usual, and her eyes were the dark gray of thunderclouds. "To explain what—that though you loved him, you preferred to marry a richer man? An act of supererogation surely. Even the greatest slowtop in the world will have figured that out by now."

"Don't be so sarcastic. You don't know what it was like!" Tears glistened on Deirdre's long black lashes. "My father—everyone—expected me to make a brilliant match. How could I tell them I wished marry a younger son with no real prospects, who was about to sell out of the army?"

"You could not," Belinda said dampingly, "because you *didn't* wish that. You *wished* to marry a title and a fortune, and that is what you did. As a point of interest, did Captain Wainright formally ask your father for your hand?"

Deirdre hesitated, debating, Belinda was certain, whether or not her cousin would swallow the lie. "I couldn't let him be humiliated by being refused," she said finally, her expression sulky. "Where are you going?"

"To my room to pack."

"You cannot desert me, Bel! Archer will send his dreadful sister here like a shot if you go. I couldn't bear it!"

"Then I suggest you stage your 'miscarriage' without delay and join your husband in London."

"I can't do that for nearly three weeks! Please, I beg of you, stay until then."

"A pity, but I refuse to be put in the position of trying to explain to Lord Archer how his wife's scandalous behavior became the talk of the county."

"I won't do anything to cause a scandal, I promise you, Bel."

Her hand on the door, Belinda surveyed Deirdre's anxious face, wishing she could trust her word. "You have already contrived one secret meeting with Captain Wainright—no, don't perjure your soul by denying it," she said with a weary shake of her head. "I was there; I heard his unguarded admission. Suppose it had been someone other than myself who happened into that garden yesterday, a servant or perhaps a visitor whom I might have conducted there unknowingly. There would already be gossip circulating about you two. If I agree to remain here, Dee, it is with the understanding that there are to be no more assignations with Captain Wainright, not even for the desirable purpose of requesting him to leave the area. You must promise this."

"Very well." Deirdre's lips were pressed together in a tight line.

"And we'll begin by canceling tomorrow's riding session."

"We can't do that—we've already agreed to it. It would be vastly uncivil to cancel."

"You agreed to it, I didn't. Three times in one sennight is demonstrating just the sort of particularity that will be noticed in the community."

"Who is going to know about it?" Deirdre demanded furiously. "You are being ridiculous."

"The servants will certainly know that the gentlemen from Hilltop House have come here three times this week; in fact, depending on where Captain Wainright left his horse yesterday, they may know it is four times in a sennight. You may lay the blame on me if you wish. Say I have the headache. No one would expect you to go off on a pleasure outing leaving me to suffer alone," she added with heavy irony, knowing Deirdre would have had no qualms about doing just that.

Belinda sought the haven of her own room at that point, having no stomach for more wrangling. The sense of unreality that had permitted her to discuss the unspeakable with some measure of detachment had faded, leaving her mind throbbing with pain and fury. She had let her cousin feel the weight of her anger at being used as an unknowing pawn in her despicable deception. And she didn't regret it, she raged, hurling herself across her bed, remembering at the last instant not to let her riding boots touch the coverlet. She remained in the awkward position for a time, almost reveling in the rush of anger that propelled the blood through her body in pounding surges, but the strange elation was short-lived, leaving her feeling drained and weary. Of what use was it to rage and protest and condemn? The dirty deed was done. Her own ravaged pride was the first but quite possibly the least serious of the potential consequences of Deirdre's atrocious self-indulgence.

Belinda rolled off the bed, pulling off her flattened hat as she did so. She must forget about herself, put her own foolish yearnings aside permanently, and concentrate on steering Deirdre through the next few weeks without causing a scandal that would hurt her husband and shame her family. At present Lord Archer was unaware of his bride's lack of affection for him—at least, she amended, recalling those intelligent and-piercing hazel eyes and his guarded manner—he had no public reason to doubt Deirdre's affection. She, a mere connection by marriage, could not afford to concern herself with his ultimate and inevitable disenchantment. The most she could hope to achieve was to prevent a public disclosure of Deirdre's desperate deception, and gossip about her and Captain Wainright, a not inconsiderable feat, she acknowledged with a sick feeling in the pit of her stomach.

Of crucial importance was the removal of Captain Wainright from the Somerset scene. Deirdre could send him away if she would, but she had borne a charmed existence to the present and would not easily be persuaded that her cleverness at getting her own way had its limits and that the situation was in danger of slipping out of her control. The idea of sacrificing something she desired—and it was patent that she reveled in Captain Wainright's blind adoration, begging the question of love on either side—was not a concept that would appeal to her. Short-term pleasures would always take precedence over the possiblity of adverse consequences in the future. In any event, Belinda had no intention of wasting breath in this doomed missionary work because Deirdre's word could not be trusted under the most favorable of circumstances, let alone when it was given reluctantly.

The thought of approaching Captain Wainright herself caused Belinda to experience distressing physical symptoms which convinced her that she could not carry it off. She squirmed at the expectation of having those electric blue eyes gazing on her with anger or disgust or, even more to be dreaded, humiliating knowledge of her secret feelings for him. She simply couldn't do it, she realized, wiping clammy palms down the sides of her skirt and conscious of dampness beneath her breasts.

The same distressing physical symptoms occurred, though to a lesser extent, when Belinda accidentally met Captain Wainright during one of the walks that provided the happiest hours of her visit to Archer Hall. It was the second day fol-

lowing Deirdre's appalling revelations, and racking her brain
in the meantime had produced no practical ideas for dealing
with the situation. Belinda was rather aimlessly roaming
about, concerned more with visions of direful consequences
than the charm of the countryside when her eyes were drawn
to a huge oak tree atop a flattened hill. She'd admired the
solitary giant on earlier walks but the steepness of the hill
had dissuaded her from taking a closer look. She gazed
fixedly at the majestic oak for a moment and decided impul-
sively that a physical challenge was what she would most
like today.

A half hour later Belinda reached the top of the hill, slightly
short of breath and flushed with triumph as she looked back
the way she had come. Verdant fields spread beneath her, ter-
minating in woods to her right. The village was on her left,
picture-pretty under an almost cloudless sky. Her eyes traced
the road leading to Archer Hall before coming to linger in admiration on the village church, its windows gleaming jewel-
like in the sun.

It wasn't until she turned her back on the lovely prospect
that Belinda realized that she was not alone on the hill. She
stopped in consternation as a man got to his feet from where
he had been propped against the trunk of the oak and strolled
toward her.

"I'm sorry if I frightened you, Miss Melville. I should have
made my presence known immediately, but I did not wish to
spoil your first glimpse of this marvelous view."

"That was very considerate of you, Captain Wainright," Belinda said gravely. "This is a heavenly and peaceful spot."

He halted a pace away from her and gazed into the distance.
"Yes. Up here it is difficult to imagine that evil and ugliness
can exist in the world, much less war."

His hatless profile was clear and perfect except for a suggestion of grimness about the set of his mouth as he ceased
speaking. Belinda was dismayed to discover that her heartbeat
was racing once more. She bitterly resented this weakness, especially since she was aware that *her* presence made scarcely
any impact on Captain Wainright's consciousness despite his
polite conversation. She noted that he was holding a slim vol-
ume in his left hand, his place marked by the index finger. Angling her head she read the title with some surprise. Raising
her eyes she found him regarding her neutrally, and she

blurted into the lengthening silence, "You are reading poetry up here?"

"Yes," he admitted, pulling a wry face, "though I would be grateful if you did not find it necessary to inform the world of my aberration."

"Your secret is safe with me," she promised lightly, her pulses racing as he flashed her a grin of sheepish complicity. "I'll leave you to your reading."

"Please do not let me chase you away. That was a prodigious walk for merely a moment's enjoyment of the view."

Reading good manners but nothing more personal in his protest, Belinda smiled and shook her head. "I have been gone longer than expected and must not tarry, lest my cousin worry about my absence." She pronounced the lie unblushingly and took her leave after an exchange of courtesies.

It had been a pleasant encounter but Belinda acknowledged on the trek home that she had squandered her opportunity to plead with the man to leave Somerset. She was never going to be able to muster the requisite nerve to raise the issue, so she had better concentrate on trying to control Deirdre's actions.

This proved no easy task. At a dinner party the next evening, Belinda found herself wedged in the middle of a group of young people while Deirdre ignored her eloquent glances and carried on a private conversation with Captain Wainright under the interested eyes of Mrs. Crandall, a lady whose sharp tongue was legendary. Remonstrating with her cousin on the drive home achieved nothing save the exacerbation of Deirdre's temper. She flatly refused to accept that Mrs. Crandall's pointed interest indicated a need for greater circumspection in her response to the captain's persistent attentions.

The young women did not exchange another word that night, and the coolness between them was not eased the following afternoon when Mrs. Crandall and her son were ushered into the small saloon where Captain Wainright and Lady Archer were practicing duets at the pianoforte while Sir John and Belinda argued vigorously over their favorite composers. Nothing could have exceeded Mrs. Crandall's amiability as she begged her hostess and the captain to sing the piece they were working on, but Belinda, sandwiched between Sir John and her young friend from that first dinner party, misliked the speculative gleam in the lady's rather protuberant blue eyes.

At another dinner in the area two days later there was no lessening in Deirdre's and Captain Wainright's marked preference for each other's exclusive company or in Mrs. Crandall's avid interest in the pair. Trying to maintain an air of unconcerned enjoyment when she was constantly revolving aspects of the situation in her mind seeking a solution that continued to evade her, was taking a toll on Belinda's nerves. It required a sustained and enervating resolution to keep a pleasant expression pasted on her face, and even more effort to keep her eyes from straying to where her thoughts were riveted.

At her side, Sir John's voice, gently insistent, brought Belinda's head around. "Mr. Crandall is interested in your impressions of our rolling hills, Miss Melville," he said with a warning look that told her she'd been guilty of inattention.

"I am enchanted with the scenery hereabouts, sir," she responded, smiling at her host, her voice and eyes aglow with the conviction of her feelings. "Each hill beckons me to climb it, and I become intoxicated with the glorious views and the lush greenness on all sides. I never tire of exploring and am only afraid lest I shall have missed some small corner when my visit is over."

"That was a neat recovery," Sir John said in a low voice a few moments later when a smiling and satisfied Mr. Crandall had turned to answer a question from another guest, "but I sense that you are rather *distraite* this evening. If there is any way in which I can be of assistance to you, I hope you know it would be my great pleasure."

"Th . . . thank you, you are very kind, but there is nothing . . . " Belinda's voice trailed off and her confusion increased as she gauged the depth of her companion's sincerity.

"Let me apologize in advance for any indelicacy, but would I be correct in ascribing your abstraction to concern over that situation?"

Belinda's gaze unerringly tracked the slight angle of his head to where her cousin and Captain Wainright sat with their heads close together. "No, of . . . of course not—at least, I am persuaded it is merely my rural upbringing that finds any— these matters are doubtless looked at differently in London circles?" Her eyes begged for confirmation.

"It is true that women, married women at least, have more freedom to form friendships with men in town, where people mingle in great numbers in a circumscribed area. There are so many more opportunities for meeting—perfectly unexceptionable, most of them."

"Then . . . then you would say I need not worry that their obvious partiality for each other's company will give rise to unkind gossip?"

Sir John hesitated, then said with discernible reluctance, "I would like to be able to reassure you except that I have noted Mrs. Crandall's rather pointed interest in them of late."

"Is Mrs. Crandall a gossip?"

"Worse than that, I'm afraid. She and Lady Ilchester, Archer's sister, are bosom bows. They were childhood friends who have remained in close contact through the years."

Chapter Seven

"It has been over a sennight since you promised to send Captain Wainright away, Dee, and still he lingers on in Somerset," Belinda said out of a dead silence. "He is at every social event we attend and pops up every time we go into the village, not to mention calling here nearly every other day. Something has to be done."

Deirdre's eyes widened at her cousin's outburst. "How could I promise to make him leave Somerset? He is free to go or stay anyplace he pleases. I promised not to meet him alone and I have refused all his invitations to go riding. What more can I expect?" she finished, her countenance portraying innocence wrongly accused.

"You know very well that he would leave in an instant if you made it clear that you do not welcome his attentions."

"But I *do* welcome his attentions, my dear cousin, as *you* very well know," Deirdre retorted in a purring voice.

The girls were taking tea together in the sitting room located between the viscount's and his lady's bedchambers in the master suite. Here too Deirdre's taste had reigned, but the intense, ubiquitous yellow of her boudoir had been diluted to advantage by cream colored walls and an Aubusson rug whose background color was a creamy white. Belinda liked the cozy room but she found the sight of her cousin curled up on a French chaise longue covered in yellow satin irrationally irritating. Deirdre had been idly sewing crystal beads onto a blue headband she planned to wear with her new sapphire gown but had abandoned the boring task, declaring that her maid would finish it for her. An unbiased observer would have been charmed by the picture she presented of indolent grace, but Belinda's eye was not unbiased.

"Why must you delight in playing with fire?" she charged. "Is another man's hopeless devotion so vital to you that you would chance a scandal that would produce an estrangement from your husband?"

She had succeeded in removing the smug expression from her cousin's lips. "You don't understand," Deirdre cried with equal irritation. "Anthony makes me feel so alive and desirable, and he is so handsome that every female in the room wishes he would distinguish her with his attention. I become weak in the knees when he looks at me in a certain way. The thought of never seeing him again is pure torture. Oh, why do I bother trying to explain it to you—you don't know what it is like to be in love!"

"Neither do you!" Belinda snapped, reaching for her cup and biting back the tirade on her cousin's selfishness that was clammering for release. The cold tea succeeded in cooling her heated temper so that she was able to keep her voice even as she suggested, "I apprehend you would elect never to see your husband or his fortune again rather than undergo this torture you just mentioned?"

"Don't be so sanctimonious!" Deirdre flashed back. "Can't you see that I don't yet *know* what I want?"

"Yes, you do; you want what you've always wanted— everything—but you have not yet been able to discover how to have two mutually exclusive things without payment in some unpleasant form being demanded." Belinda's movements were slow and discouraged as she set down her cup, shaking her head in wonder. She got to her feet, muttering, "I keep asking myself why I am still here."

"We've been into all that before. You are here to help me. You know Gran would have expected it." Deirdre's voice rang with impatience. "Why can you not relax in this luxury and simply enjoy the opportunity to experience some society that is far superior to anything you'd find in that dreary community around Millgrove? If you play your cards right, you might even succeed in getting an offer of marriage. Sir John appears to be somewhat taken with you. He is a rather charming man, quite clever, I believe, and witty in a quiet way that should appeal to you. Also, Hilltop House is a very pretty property. I am persuaded he is a far better catch than you ever dreamed of, and with my help you could very likely snare him. Where are you going?"

"To my room," Belinda said, pausing near the door to the corridor. "You snared an even better catch and what has been the result? Less than five months married and you are so dissatisfied with your bargain that you are prepared to risk your marriage and your reputation in pursuit of a romantic excitement you don't find with your husband."

Belinda intended to sweep out of the room on this Parthian arrow, but her grand gesture was foiled when she flung open the door and was forced to execute a quick side step to avoid plowing smack into Drummond, whose upraised hand was poised to knock. Her evasive action brought her almost nose to nose with a woman whose piercing hazel eyes and sharply etched features were so reminiscent of Lord Archer that she did not require confirmation from Deirdre's horrified expression, glimpsed as she turned back to Drummond, to tell her that the dreaded Lady Ilchester was no longer safely tucked away in Yorkshire. Swift upon this realization came the frightening question of what, if anything, the woman might have overheard of the revealing conversation she and her cousin had just concluded. Belinda's eyes winged to Drummond, but the butler's countenance was even more wooden than usual.

"I beg your pardon if I startled you, Miss Melville," he said. "I did not know anyone was near the door. I was about to announce Lady Ilchester."

The scene at the door had given Deirdre time to recover her composure. She took two small steps forward, saying, "Lady Ilchester, this is a surprise. I had no idea you had formed the intention of paying us a visit."

"It was a decision taken on the spur of the moment," Lady Ilchester replied, sweeping across the room, two fingers extended to her sister-in-law. "I was experiencing a mood of nostalgia for my old home and friends in Somerset and concluded it would be treating you like a stranger to stand upon ceremony and wait for a diffident bride to issue formal invitations. And, speaking of invitations, I see I must remind you that I have invited you to use my given name, my dear sister."

"Of course . . . Lydia. May I present my cousin, Miss Melville? Bel, this is Archer's sister, Lady Ilchester."

Belinda, cringing inwardly at the lack of cordiality in her cousin's manner, could not help but sympathize with Deirdre's reluctance to welcome this assertive and, very likely, domineering woman under her roof. She made certain her own response to the introduction was accompanied by a cheerful smile and struggled to maintain it under a prolonged assessment from the older woman's searching eyes that bordered on rudeness, though her greeting was perfectly civil.

Lady Ilchester signaled the end of these formalities by turning toward the butler, who had remained by the door awaiting orders. "After that dusty drive I am simply perishing for a cup of tea, Drummond."

"You may remove the tea things and bring a fresh pot, Drummond," Deirdre said quickly, establishing her position as mistress. "Won't you be seated, Lydia? I believe you'll find this chair comfortable." She indicated an armchair with the curving lines that proclaimed its French origin and, abandoning the chaise longue, seated herself on the sofa behind a tea table of similar workmanship, directing a hesitant Belinda to a place at her side with an imperative gesture. "Sit here, Bel."

"You are looking remarkably well, Deirdre," Lady Ilchester said, showing good teeth in a brief smile as the two young women lined up on the sofa across from her chair. "This is a pleasant surprise. I understood that you remained in Somerset because you were too unwell to travel."

"I still get dreadfully ill if I drive for more than a few miles, but I feel quite well most of the time, except in the mornings, of course."

Lady Ilchester's thin, arched brows climbed higher. "My dear Deirdre, the sort of queasiness to which I apprehend you refer is not an inevitable consequence of your condition. I for one never experienced this discomfort when I was increasing, but I am delighted to find you unexpectedly robust—it augurs well for your being able to join your husband in London in the next fortnight or so. It would be a pity to miss the entire Season. Archer tells me you were quite enchanted with the social whirl during your come-out last year." Another brief smile meant to indicate understanding played across Lady Ilchester's lips without being reflected in her eyes.

Belinda felt Deirdre stiffen beside her at being described as "robust" so was not surprised at the resentment in her voice as she demanded, "Did Archer send you here to check up on me?"

"I have had no communication with my brother in recent weeks," her sister-in-law replied evenly, "but I fear I do not perfectly comprehend what you mean by 'checking up' in any case. Given the closeness of our relationship, I would consider myself derelict in familial duty were I to overlook any opportunity to assure myself of your well-being, especially in your delicate situation."

"Speaking of my . . . situation, Archer and I have decided for the present not to tell anyone of it . . . anyone at all."

Belinda stirred uneasily at the steeliness of her cousin's tone and noted the narrowing of Lady Ilchester's eyes before she replied, "Naturally I shall respect your decision, though I confess I see no reason to keep secret what everyone must discover shortly."

Drummond's arrival bearing a tray at that moment was greeted with relief by at least one of the ladies present. The atmosphere of bristling animosity eased somewhat as the tea-pouring ritual progressed. Belinda took advantage of the others' preoccupation to study Lord Archer's sister.

Deirdre's virulent dislike had prepared her for a veritable dragon of a female and, on the surface at least, had been misleading. Lady Ilchester was the mother of two sons, the elder of whom was in his third year at Cambridge, so she could not be far off forty. Thanks to a trim figure and firm, clear skin that showed no aging lines around eyes or mouth, she appeared several years younger. Though not a beauty or even a former beauty, her well-defined features and rich brown hair, untouched by gray, would be judged attractive by most. She was dressed in an elegant mauve wool pelisse and matching hat, the graceful lines and unwrinkled perfection of which, even after long hours of traveling, endowed her with a look of cool distinction that, in Belinda's opinion, Deirdre, with her penchant for frills and furbelows, might do well to emulate.

The initial impression of an attractive personality began to waver and disintegrate, however, once Lady Ilchester launched into speech. Her voice, crisp and well modulated, was not unpleasant in itself but contained a suggestion of a superiority that was off-putting, despite the careful civility of her words. Belinda acknowledged a reluctance to accept Lady Ilchester's explicit posture of good will toward Deirdre as a true reflection of her sentiments. After all, the woman would have to be stupid to fail to perceive Deirdre's ill-disguised antipathy, and perceiving it, would have to possess the all-forgiving nature of a saint to return benevolence for dislike. Absent any evidence of saintliness in Lady Ilchester's manner, her words could be taken in the best light as indicating a desire to avoid raising Deirdre's hackles. If this was true, they had failed miserably in their intent.

Belinda stared glumly into her teacup, certain that the already strained situation at Archer Hall had been aggravated tenfold by the unexpected arrival of Deirdre's sister-in-law. Unless—a happy thought struck her—Lady Ilchester's critical presence exercised a restraining influence on Deirdre's reckless encouragement of Captain Wainright's attentions. Fear that Lydia might report any such observations to her brother might keep Deirdre from committing the sort of indiscretions that all Belinda's importunities had failed to curb.

Over the next day or two a praiseworthy pretense of amity prevailed among the ladies of Archer House. Deirdre had extended a small olive branch after tea that first afternoon by asking her sister-in-law's preference as to the quarters she would occupy during her stay. Lady Ilchester had replied that unless Miss Melville would be inconvenienced, she would choose the set of rooms she'd occupied as a girl. Deirdre's sweet apology for not having as yet begun to refurbish this suite was brushed aside by Lydia with a laughing disclaimer that she actually preferred them shabby and familiar. In her turn the older woman diplomatically refrained from voicing any criticism of her hostess's decorating feats, though Belinda detected with secret amusement a desperate mental scramble to come up with sufficient encomiums to please Deirdre without irreparable surrender of all regard for veracity. For her part, Belinda acquiesced in her cousin's pleas that she curtail her solitary rambles for the present to play the vital role of buffer between the sisters-in-law.

In the time-honored fashion, word of Lady Ilchester's arrival quickly spread around the countryside with the result that the ladies received a number of callers on the following day. When Sir John and Captain Wainright were announced in midafternoon, the saloon echoed with feminine voices and laughter comingled with the clatter of porcelain cups and plates. Mrs. Crandall and Lady Ilchester were sitting with their heads close together at a little distance from an array of ladies clustered around the sofa from which Lady Archer was dispensing tea and cakes with her cousin's assistance.

Drummond's announcement of the gentlemen produced an immediate cessation of speech as a half dozen heads turned toward the door. Captain Wainright looked faintly alarmed at the gauntlet awaiting them, but Sir John exhibited no such qualms as he headed toward his hostess, saying with exaggerated humility, "May two thirsty males beg pardon for our presumption and throw ourselves upon your charity, Lady Archer? We are on our way back from Taunton and our tongues are hanging out in a fashion reminiscent of George Crandall's hound dogs."

A little ripple of appreciative laughter rose from the assembled ladies, for Sir John, with his rare ability to enter into their concerns wholeheartedly, was as popular with his female neighbors as with their husbands. Greetings were called out and some of the women shifted about to make room for the new arrivals in their midst after Captain Wainright had been presented to Lady Ilchester.

Having taken note of the slight but discernible chilling in Lady Ilchester's manner when she acknowledged this introduction, Belinda could not help speculating anew that, despite her facile explanation, the woman's unexpected visit was a direct result of some communication from her childhood friend Mrs. Crandall concerning her young sister-in-law's friendship with the ex-soldier. From the way Deirdre avoided Captain Wainright's glance during the next half hour, Belinda could tell that her cousin had come to the same conclusion, although she had dismissed the idea of unpleasant repercussions originally when Belinda had passed on Sir John's information about the long-standing friendship between the two women. Never before had Deirdre ignored Anthony Wainright in company, but except for an initial nodding acknowledgment, she gave the impression of being unaware of his presence today. That gentleman had been neatly pinned between a garrulous matron and her simpering daughter the entire time, a piece of good fortune that helped Belinda master for the moment the escalating sense of forboding that had gripped her since Lady Ilchester's arrival on the scene.

Covertly glancing about the room, she was struck by the degree to which present appearances were misleading. Though Mrs. Crandall and Lady Ilchester continued to converse privately, Belinda sensed that the attention of both was currently shifting between Deirdre and Captain Wainright. Of the latter pair, Deirdre was giving a charming performance as a happy hostess interested solely in her guests' pleasure, but the captain grew increasingly restive under the efforts of the ladies near him to monopolize his attention. Trapped behind the tea table, Belinda was in no position to rescue him, not that he had any reason to regard her company as more entertaining, she reminded herself wryly. She had certainly not exhibited any sparks of wit or wisdom in his presence to date, quite the contrary, beginning with her fervent reaction to her first sight of him in this very room.

Belinda was trying to send a silent signal to Sir John, who was entertaining several of the women with an amusing story of an embarrassing slip of the tongue he'd made in the presence of the Prince Regent, when Captain Wainright took matters into his own hands. He excused himself from his captors and sauntered over to the sofa where Lady Barton was making her adieus to her hostess. When she withdrew to follow Drummond downstairs to her waiting carriage, he executed a smiling bow and pulled some sheets of paper from inside his coat, which he extended to Deirdre.

"Lest I forget, Lady Archer, this is the song I promised to bring you." His words, dropping into one of those periodic lulls that can occur in a room full of conversation, were audible to all.

"You are confusing us again, Captain," Deirdre cried gaily, scarcely missing a beat. "It was my cousin to whom you made that promise, do you not recall? Here is the music you wished to try, Bel," she added, taking the sheets from the captain's hand as he slowly released his grip on them. She handed them to the silent girl beside her, saying with a teasing smile, "Aren't you going to thank the captain prettily for his pains, Bel?"

"Yes, of course," Belinda said, glancing quickly from the unsmiling man to the music score Deirdre pressed upon her.

"Thank you very much, sir. I shall look forward to learning this piece."

"You will have to play it for Captain Wainright at our next meeting to show your appreciation," Deirdre said before leaning to her right to speak to someone behind the captain. Thus dismissed, the latter took the hint and retired with an unintelligible murmur.

With Lady Barton's exit the general exodus had begun, and all the guests took their leave within the next few moments. Deirdre allowed Captain Wainright to take her hand for the briefest of farewells, while waxing effusive in her parting remarks to others. Watching dispassionately from her place on the sofa, Belinda mused that it was just like her cousin to overplay her part. Lady Ilchester walked out of the room with Mrs. Crandall, the last to depart, leaving the cousins alone in a silence that thickened as Deirdre waited with wary eyes to be brought to book by Belinda. The latter was in no humor to pronounce an "I told you so," however. Actually, she had been encouraged by Deirdre's avoidance of the captain to indulge a faint hope that they might scrape through the ticklish situation unscathed, but she had no wish to engage in pointless discussion. She shrugged her shoulders and started toward the door.

"Just a moment, Bel. May I have my music, please?"

Belinda turned her head and said offhandedly, "Since you have just committed me to learning this piece before we meet Captain Wainright again, that would be ill-advised on my part."

"Nonsense. I just said all that stuff because that poisonous Lydia was watching Anthony and me like a hawk all afternoon. Detestable woman!"

"I am well aware of the reason behind your playacting, but *you* would do well in future to remember that words have consequences. You may have the song after I have learned it."

Belinda left her cousin biting her lip in impotent frustration, but her satisfaction in this small victory was short-lived. Her shoulders slumped forward as she made her way to her room carrying the sheet music. The longer she remained in this house the less she liked herself. Dealing with Deirdre brought out a side of her nature that she devoutly hoped existed nowhere else, a competitiveness and mean-spiritedness that overcame her better self periodically. She was already ashamed of the pettiness that had insisted on keeping the gift Captain Wainright had meant for Deirdre. As if she would ever desire to possess something that was intended as a tribute to another woman's charms, she thought, tossing the music onto the bed with an angry motion and stalking over to the window to stare out at nothing. It enraged her to be used so cavalierly by her cousin, but when she calmed down enough to put her personal indignation aside, what remained was simply the knowledge that she could not refuse to get Deirdre out of trouble—she was, like it or not. part of her family. Of course it would be pleasant to be *asked* and even nicer to be thanked for one's sacrifices, but gratitude from Deirdre was worthless anyway, always expedient rather than heartfelt. The brutal truth was that her cousin was incapable of caring about anyone's sensibilities except her own. It had been thus since childhood, the only difference at present being that she had acquired a patina of charming manners that disguised this deficiency from those who did not know her intimately.

Did Captain Wainright see Deirdre as a model of feminine perfection, Belinda wondered a moment later as she smoothed the corner of the music sheets that had turned under as a result of her rough handling. It must be wonderful to know the man one loved thought one a perfect being. Fortunate Deirdre to have two men feel this way about her.

At this point in her reverie the fog of romanticism cleared away from her thought processes and she paused in the act of putting a weight on the music to flatten the creased corners. Somehow she could not reconcile Lord Archer's penetrating intelligence with the mindless adoration Captain Wainright lavished on Deirdre. Could love blunt the critical faculties of even the most cerebral of humans?

Polly's arrival at that moment to assist her mistress in dressing for dinner prevented Belinda from wandering down this intriguing philosophical avenue, and the next few days provided little opportunity for pursuing philosophical questions of any nature. Deprived of her customary riding exercise in the wake of Lady Ilchester's horrified reaction to this activity by one in her delicate condition, Deirdre commanded her cousin's presence nearly around the clock in order to keep her sister-in-law at arm's length. For the most part she played the role of carefree young matron quite successfully, but Belinda could sense the effort required to disguise the moodiness that was part of her character. Deirdre's had always been a mercurial nature, swinging from excitement and optimism to petulance and low spirits with seemingly little external cause, and she was ill-equipped to present a sustained picture of contentment. Lady Ilchester's relentless observation of her brother's wife demanded the exercise of more control than Deirdre had ever needed to impose on her temper before. Belinda found the older woman's chilling correctness, unleavened as it was by any touches of spontaneity or humor, uncongenial at best and positively unnerving at those times when she sensed Deirdre's simmering frustration. She silently applauded her cousin's efforts but waited in fearful expectation of the inevitable breach in her heroic self-control.

Captain Wainright did not call at Archer Hall during the two days that elapsed before the Prescotts' ball, but Belinda suspected the besotted pair had been in communication. She had knocked and entered her cousin's bedchamber unexpectedly one morning to return the music he had given Deirdre, and had seen her stuff a sheet of paper into the drawer of her dressing table, where she sat while Meritt brushed out her dusky curls. It had always stood to reason that the maid was the conduit between the frustrated lovers since she enjoyed her mistress's confidence, but Belinda's heart dropped to her shoes at the probability that Deirdre had broken her promise not to communicate with the captain. Her lips parted involuntarily but she pressed them together again. What was the point in raising the question? Deirdre would surely deny it, and besides, the letter, if that was what the paper was, might be from her husband. Even if it was from Captain Wainright, that did not necessarily mean she intended to reply to it. Lady Ilchester's watchfulness might well have convinced her of the danger of any further contact. Belinda averted her eyes from the drawer even while this rapid assessment took place. She would not speak in Meritt's hearing in any case, she vowed, as her gaze caught the maid's in the mirror for an instant. Perhaps it was her imagination but she always fancied she detected secret amusement on that pert and pretty face.

"Here is the new song," she said. "Where shall I put it?"

"I'll take it, thank you," Deirdre replied, holding out her hand. "By the way, Bel, you may have the blue dress I wore to the Bartons' dinner. I never liked it on me. My new one is finished and is much more becoming. The old one is over there on the bed," she added, inclining her head to indicate a heap of sapphire silk, "but don't wear it to the Prescotts' ball tomorrow because I plan to wear the new one myself."

"Thank you, it's a lovely gown," Belinda said quietly, trying to conceal her reluctance to accept her cousin's careless generosity as she picked up the garment on her way back through the dressing room between their bedchambers.

Belinda would not have worn the vivid blue dress so early in her mourning period even without Deirdre's proscription, so she experienced no pangs of deprivation as she donned her gray silk the next evening. In the scant three weeks of her stay in Somerset, she had dropped more than half a stone of weight and was quite naively pleased with the suggestion of interesting hollows beneath her cheekbones. The loyal Polly was loud in her praise of her mistress's appearance and outdid herself in creating a high knot of glossy curls through which she threaded a velvet ribbon.

Lady Ilchester, quite regal in a burgundy satin gown complemented by an imposing headdress featuring dyed-to-match plumes, glanced from one young woman to the other as they waited for the carriage to arrive. "You two are amazingly alike when Miss Melville dresses her hair on top of her head," she observed on a note of surprise. "I had not really noticed the degree of resemblance before."

"Perhaps my cousin has told you that our mothers were twins," Belinda said to fill in the gap caused by Deirdre's movement toward the mantel to check the time.

"I believe she did." Lady Ilchester followed Deirdre with her eyes. "My dear Deirdre, that is the second time you've walked over to that clock. Drummond said the carriage would be outside in five minutes and he is generally very reliable about these matters. You seem rather anxious to arrive at what is merely a small country dance attended almost entirely by persons you see every week."

"If I am anxious, my dear Lydia, it is because I dread the ordeal of driving in a closed carriage. The sooner the trip is over with, the sooner I shall be able to relax. Thank goodness it is less than four miles to Singleford."

Her cousin had had a plausible explanation ready for her behavior but her nerves did appear to be on the stretch tonight. A
little twinge of premonition scuttled up Belinda's spine as an
image of Deirdre's hands hiding a piece of paper in the drawer
flashed across her mind's eye. Her own anticipation of a pleasant evening dimmed forthwith as she soberly gathered up her
reticule and shawl in response to Drummond's announcement
that the carriage had arrived at the front steps.

Chapter Eight

Belinda was enjoying herself.

She had decided on the drive to Singleford, the Prescotts' modern red brick house with lovely arcaded wings, that worrying about her cousin's possible indiscretions would achieve nothing except to call her own nervous state into question. The sensible thing to do was to dismiss all speculation from her mind and concentrate on savoring the rare treat being offered. Also, it had occurred to her that she was no longer alone in trying to prevent Deirdre from committing some impulsive action under the influence of Captain Wainright's ardent persuasion that she would regret in the clear light of morning; there was an unwitting ally now in Lady Ilchester, whose critical vigilance could be depended upon to cut off avenues of opportunity for injudicious behavior.

Consequently, Belinda acted upon her own advice and, beyond keeping an unobtrusive eye on her cousin's whereabouts, gave herself over to the pleasures of dancing to astonishingly good music performed by a group of young musicians Mr. Prescott had discovered in Taunton.

The girls had been taught to dance by their mothers when they were quite young and the experience had provided one of the more pleasant memories of their times together before Belinda's mother's health had failed. Her grandmother had played the pianoforte for the lessons which, looking back, seemed to have been punctuated by carefree laughter as the sisters recreated their experiences during their London Season for their wide-eyed daughters, interrupting the instruction sessions to exchange half-forgotten stories of their trials and triumphs in the ballrooms of London. As was their habit all their lives, one twin would begin to articulate a thought which would then be completed by the other, whereupon both would dissolve into shared laughter, looking for the moment too ab-

surdly young to be the parents of adolescent daughters. She
and Deirdre had relished those sessions which were unique in
being devoid of the squabbles and competitiveness that distinguished their normal relationship.

Remembrance of past pleasures combined with anticipation
had set Belinda's eyes aglow and lent a becoming tinge of rose
to her cheeks as the ladies from Archer Hall were welcomed
by their hosts. There were probably no more than sixty or sev-
enty persons attending, not all of whom expected to participate
in the dancing, but to a girl accustomed to small gatherings
where she had known all those present from the cradle, this
was every bit as exciting as a London party.

Within moments of their arrival, a veritable swarm of young
men buzzed around the cousins requesting dances. Belinda's
card was soon filled, as was Deirdre's. Following Captain
Wainright's progress to Deirdre's side, Belinda noted that her
cousin tucked a tiny piece of paper into one of her gloves after
he bowed over her hand. A quick glance assured her that Lady
Ilchester had not been in a position to witness this bit of folly.
Belinda closed her eyes for an anguished second, wishing with
all her might that she were still in that state of happy ignorance. An educated guess would be that, a tryst having been
previously agreed upon, the time and location were being con-
veyed to Deirdre by this means. She dismissed as useless any
idea of confronting Deirdre openly; prevarication was second
nature to her cousin, right behind determination to have her
way in the face of all opposition. Preventing the assignation
would be a matter of sheer blind luck, considering that Belinda
was committed to being on the dance floor for large segments
of time. So was Deirdre, of course, but promises would not
prevent her from disappearing at the moment appointed by
Captain Wainright. As she saw it, the best Belinda could manage was to plan to stick as close as possible to her cousin between dances and hope to block any attempt to vanish.

As the musicians struck up for the first dance Belinda gave
a mental shrug, acknowledging the feebleness of her strategy.
While her partner crossed the floor toward her, however, she
could not refrain from leaning closer to her cousin and whis-
pering urgently, "Do not do it, Dee. Don't try to meet him secretly; you will be found out."

The flicker in Deirdre's eyes might have been guilt or surprise, but she deigned no response, turning a shoulder on her

cousin while summoning up her famous smile for Lord Barton, who had engaged her for the first number.

Despite the underlying anxiety, Belinda could not help giving herself over to pleasure in the next hour or two, betrayed by youth and her love of dancing.

One of her partners early in the evening was Sir John Hanks, who bowed gallantly at the end of their dance together. "May I say what a great pleasure it is, Miss Melville, to take the floor with such a graceful and accomplished dancer?"

"Thank you, you may indeed, sir," Belinda replied, smiling delightedly up at him. "I do enjoy it so."

Sir John continued to gaze at her sparkling face until a shade of self-consciousness appeared thereon, causing him to say in hasty explanation, "You seem a different person tonight, as though your spirit had been set free. The resemblance to your cousin is really uncanny when you smile that way."

Even as he spoke, the brightness dimmed and Belinda, instantly recalled to the potential disaster lurking beneath the festive atmosphere, glanced rapidly around the ballroom until she located Deirdre laughing and flirting with three young gentlemen. Returning her attention to her late partner with relief, she flushed a little at the curious look he bent on her but was spared awkward explanations by the timely arrival of her next partner.

An hour later Belinda's cheeks were still flushed, now from exertion, as she parted from young Mr. Crandall after a sprightly country dance. She headed in the direction of the room set aside for the ladies in which to refresh themselves. She put up a hand to her topknot as she went, checking that the pins were still secure after Mr. Crandall's energetic swinging. A tiny smile played about her lips. If Sir John thought *she* was a different person on the dance floor, how would he describe the shy Crandall lad under the influence of a lively reel performed by an enthusiastic group of musicians?

Belinda paused, blinking at two paneled doors in the corridor she had entered upon leaving the ballroom. Was the ladies' retiring room the second or third door on the left? Frowning a little in her effort to remember, she proceeded to the last door and opened it.

Her mistake was immediately apparent. This chamber was dark, illuminated solely by moonlight beyond the pair of French doors in the end wall to the right. On the point of re-

treating, Belinda hesitated, irresistibly drawn as iron to a mag-
net to the silvered scene beyond the walls. She crossed the
threshold, closing the door softly behind her, and glided over
to the glassed doors which gave on to a small walled garden.

She laid a hand on the door frame and gazed out into the
starry night. By daylight this would be a pleasant little private
place in which to escape, perhaps to read beneath the leafy
bows of the shade tree a dozen feet from the doors. Tonight it
was a place of magic, bleached of its daytime colors. A white
iron bench gleaming silver in the moonlight invited lovers to
add the warmth of their human emotions to the cold purity of
the moon's radiance. It was a sublimely romantic setting . . .
and somehow melancholy.

Lost in a private reverie, Belinda was unaware that her profile gleamed pearl-like in the moonglow while the rest of her
remained in deep shadow. Nor did she realize that her solitude
had been compromised until an impassioned voice at her
shoulder said, "Darling, these past days have been interminable! I—*damnation!*"

This last imprecation was uttered a fraction away from her
lips before the urgent hands that had pulled her shrinking form
up against his body pushed her away again, releasing her
shoulders so abruptly that she staggered before regaining her
balance.

"I beg your pardon."

The harshness of the tone in which it was pronounced viti-
ated the man's apology, which might have been for unaccept-
able language, rough handling, or the original mistake in
identification.

Gathering her composure about her to disguise her shaken
state, Belinda said, "This is the second time you have mistaken
me for my cousin, Captain Wainright." Into the palpitating silence that continued, she added, "Or is there more than one
woman with whom you plan—rather inefficiently, if you will
forgive my mentioning it—romantic assignations?" She regretted the taunting words the instant they left her tongue and
steeled herself as he drew himself stiffly upright.

"That, Miss Melville, is none of your affair, but you may
rest assured that *darkness* is the only conceivable condition
under which I could ever mistake you for your cousin. Please
excuse me."

She had asked for that in all fairness, Belinda reminded herself as Captain Wainright strode from the room, but admitting that her own attack had invited retaliation did not lessen the pain caused by his deliberate insult. She was shaking all over and hugged her arms against her ribs, her fingers pressed tightly into the soft flesh above her elbows. She had known he disliked her from the start—this last evidence was superfluous. She did not care two pins for the good opinion of someone with the poor taste to set Deirdre up as his feminine ideal, and the moral turpitude that enabled him to seek to ruin another man's wife. He was nothing but a profligate and she detested him!

The warmth engendered by these vitriolic sentiments combatted the sick coldness that Captain Wainright's angry words had brought on her and ultimately restored Belinda to a semblance of her usual self. There was no longer any trace of rose in her cheeks and the earlier brightness had vanished, but otherwise she looked normal as she mustered the assurance to reenter the ballroom.

The last dance before supper had already begun when she reached her anxious partner hovering in the opening to the ballroom. She offered a hasty apology accompanied by a warm smile for the tall lanky young man she had met only that evening, and they joined a set. Belinda had her share of feminine pride and had determined on her way back that her only course was to show the offensive Captain Wainright that his unfavorable opinion had no power to dim her spirits. This she set about doing, greeting her partner's sallies with sparkling animation and such flattering appreciation that the youth could be pardoned for any inflated ideas he might have acquired of his own conversational prowess by the time he returned her to Lady Ilchester. She had not been so engrossed by her own performance that she had failed to discover that her cousin and Captain Wainright, part of another set nearby, appeared to be conducting an unusually earnest conversation for a dance floor. Doubtless he was relating the unpleasant little episode to Deirdre, but Belinda refused to admit any feelings of humiliation to her consideration and redoubled her efforts to entertain her own partner.

They shared a table with Lady Ilchester and the elder Crandalls in the supper room. Deirdre and Captain Wainright, entering well behind them, had attempted to head in another direction but were swept up by Sir John, who was escorting Lady Barton, and propelled into their midst. The enlarged party was still small enough to discourage any private discourse.

Belinda was determined not to commit the error of avoiding Captain Wainright, and thus possibly giving rise to curiosity and speculation among the others. She kept what she trusted was a pleasant expression plastered on her face and forced her glance to linger as long on him as on the others of the group. It was a secret satisfaction to discover in the course of the repast that the former soldier appeared to have to struggle to maintain an equally carefree manner as irritation bubbled to the surface occassionally when their glances crossed.

As frequently happened these days the conversation soon turned to the subject that had all of England in thrall since Bonaparte's escape from the island of Elba, where he had been exiled after the defeat in the Peninsula the previous year. The deliberations of the Congress of Vienna had been disrupted, and Wellington had promptly set off for Brussels to take command of the Allied Armies.

Not everyone was convinced that the specter of renewed fighting threatened the hard-won peace. Mr. Crandall shared the views of a number of persons who believed Napoleon had run his course.

"The French themselves have suffered enough under his rule that they will have no stomach for another war," he predicted with a conviction that did not find response in the younger men who had faced the French Army.

"I believe it would be foolhardy to underestimate Bonaparte's influence with the men," Sir John cautioned. "They march into battle shouting *'Vive l'empereur!'* According to rumor, the Bourbons are still unpopular, even ruling under a constitution. If the returned soldiers are as disaffected as their British counterparts at the difficulty in making a living in peacetime, they might flock to Bonaparte's side."

"But has not Napoleon proclaimed that he does not wish to wage another war?" Lady Barton interjected.

"He really has no choice, ma'am," Captain Wainright replied. "The other nations have branded him an outlaw and will act to prevent any attempt on his part to overthrow the restored monarchy."

"Then . . . you are saying that war is inevitable?" Mrs. Crandall said, aghast.

Captain Wainright hesitated a second, his eyes flashing past Deirdre's white face to focus on the older woman. "I fear I do believe that there must be a confrontation sooner or later."

"Your gloomy forecasts will prove wrong," Mr. Crandall insisted, "if the Bourbon regime can stop Bonapart before he has a chance to enlist many malcontents under his banner. Recollect that the army is now in the service of King Louis."

"I hope you may prove correct, sir," Captain Wainright said, but his face showed his low expectation of this desirable outcome.

Lady Barton introduced a more cheerful topic at this point and the rest of the supper hour passed pleasantly enough, although Belinda's heightened awareness seemed to be shared by Lady Ilchester, who waged a subtle but determined battle to engage Captain Wainright's attention and prevent any private conversation between him and her sister-in-law. These efforts were successful, thanks to the gentleman's faultless manners. It seemed *she* was the only female who ever had cause to complain of Captain Wainright's manners, Belinda reflected with unhappy perception, although Deirdre's pouting mouth gave every indication that her swain's exemplary courtesy was not an unmixed blessing in her eyes.

Belinda's dance with the captain occurred near the end of the evening. Sick anticipation of the upcoming ordeal had cast a pall over the festivities since their unfriendly encounter and she had seriously considered crying off. The problem with this appealing course of action was that the insufferable man would know that any excuse she offered was a lie. Some source of stubborn pride within her, of whose existence she had been previously unaware, gushed forth unquenchably, refusing to sanction this tempting avenue of escape. Though honesty compelled her to admit some slight provocation on her part, his behavior earlier had been ungentlemanly in the extreme. If anyone deserved to find the scheduled dance untenable, it was he.

As the unsmiling man approached, Belinda imposed a serenity she did not feel over her features, acknowledging his stiff bow with the barest nod.

The interval Captain Wainright and Belinda spent together on the dance floor was fraught with tension. The gentleman went through the motions of the dance with a jaw set tightly over clenched teeth, his eyes fixed somewhere beyond his partner. The lady performed her part with exquisite grace, a little smile playing over her lips to show suitable enjoyment to the world. Their hands met frequently as dictated by the movements of the dance, their eyes never. In the quarter hour of the dance, not a syllable passed between them until on being returned to Lady Ilchester's side, Belinda smiled sweetly at her silent escort and said, "That was most enjoyable, sir. Thank you."

She could only trust that Lady Ilchester had missed the incendiary look in Captain Wainright's eyes as he swept her a rudimentary bow and took himself off. Still holding on to her smile, she sank into the nearest chair, grateful for its support of her trembling limbs. Now that the ordeal was behind her—and it had been every bit as horrible as she'd feared—Belinda felt drained of all strength, as physically spent as if she'd run a mile. She had maintained her carefree pose vis-à-vis Captain Wainright, and part of her was fiercely triumphant at this accomplishment, but when all was said, she could not deny it was a hollow triumph. He had offered no apology for his incivility. She had denied him the satisfaction of seeing her wounds, but the knowledge that he had deliberately inflicted them and felt no remorse even when the heat of the moment had abated was the deepest cut of all.

Severe self-discipline got Belinda through the rest of the evening, which now seemed interminable, without betraying her misery. At last the carriage was called. She was about to follow her cousin and Lady Ilchester to get her wrap when a masculine voice said, "May I have a moment, Miss Melville?"

Belinda's eyes had been trained on Lady Ilchester's back and she was startled to find Captain Wainright at her side. She stiffened, but before she could remount her defenses he went on in low urgent tones, "I wish to apologize for that scene earlier. It was an awkward situation to say the least, but that was no excuse for losing my temper with you or for my offensive remarks, which were totally uncalled for."

Belinda, studying his set features, felt an unaccountable lightening of her own misery as she detected both unhappiness and regret in his eyes. "That is generous of you, sir. For my part, I must own that I did offer some provocation."

"You certainly don't mince words," he agreed, the ghost of a smile tugging at the corners of his mouth, though his eyes remained somber. "I wish——" he began, but at that moment Lady Ilchester came up to them with Belinda's cloak and the opportunity was lost.

On the drive back to Archer Hall Deirdre seemed to be suffering an irritation of the nerves that made her more abrupt than ever in her responses to her companions. Belinda threw herself into the breach, drawing Lady Ilchester out about her youth in Somerset. The woman spoke well and recounted several amusing stories involving some of the people who had been present at the Prescotts' ball. Belinda tried to stay attentive, but her mind was such a jumble of undifferentiated fears and feelings that she was grateful for the deep shadows within the carriage that provided a measure of visual privacy at least.

The virtual privacy of her bedchamber was even more of a blessing than usual that night, though she could not with accuracy have described her sleep as restful. Gazing at the shadows under her eyes the next morning after a restless night of interrupted sleep and vague, troubling dreams, Belinda longed for the sight of those dear faces at home, and the comfort of their uncomplicated affection. Archer Hall had been bearable at first when she'd had just her cousin's difficult personality to contend with. The arrival of the man whose deified image she had kept in her heart for five years had produced a sense of excitement and anticipation in the beginning. From the moment she'd experienced the first suspicion of the attraction between him and her cousin the situation had begun to deteriorate, her own faint hopes had crumbled to dust, and an apprehension of danger and disgrace had replaced the mild promise of those early days. The advent of Lady Ilchester, alien of personality and eternally on the alert for something to criticize, had exacerbated the tension to a level that threatened to burst the bonds imposed by common civility that permitted disaffected persons to rub along together with the appearance of harmony at least. The terrifying conviction that she was trying to outrun an avalanche already set in motion had taken hold of Belinda last night in the aftermath of the abortive tryst between the frustrated lovers, and she dreaded what the next days would bring, having no longer the least conceit that anything she might do could affect the eventual outcome in a positive manner.

Relations between the sisters-in-law had rapidly descended from a high of spurious cordiality to a snappishness on Deirdre's part that would have sent any guest with nice sensibilities packing in a trice. Lady Ilchester's eyes became even more icy and watchful and from her tongue came the occasional reference to unnamed persons who failed to properly appreciate their great—and presumably undeserved—good fortune.

Belinda's own nerves were reaching screaming pitch two days after the Prescott ball when Deirdre rose abruptly from the table near the end of a more than usually awkward dinner hour, declaring that she had a fiendish headache and intended to go straight to bed. Lady Ilchester offered a special tisane made by her abigail that was efficacious in curing headaches brought on by an irritation of the nerves. This offer was promptly repudiated by her sister-in-law with no pretense at a conciliatory speech.

"Thank you, but I never quack myself and I have a rooted objection to trying any potions, lotions, or medicaments prescribed or brewed by persons not in the medical profession. All I need is a good night's uninterrupted sleep. Good night."

She swept out of the room on the words, her slender figure trailed by two pairs of feminine eyes. Belinda swallowed nervously at the inimical expression she had glimpsed in Lady Ilchester's clear hazel orbs. She produced a hasty comment on a new veal dish the cook had sent up that contained an elusive seasoning. The older woman responded smoothly, and the meal progressed to its finish in simulated amity.

Upon entering the saloon after dinner, Belinda offered to play the pianoforte, an offer she was grateful to have accepted, for Lady Ilchester was not overly fond of instrumental music. With this in mind, she kept to the more melodic pieces and the two women passed the evening avoiding the necessity of making stilted conversation.

She was climbing into her bed when Belinda recalled a message from the head gardener that she had neglected to pass on to her cousin, thanks to that unscheduled departure from dinner. It could certainly wait until morning. She glanced at the clock and saw that it was barely ten. Deirdre was most likely already asleep, but if by any chance the headache had been real, perhaps she ought to check on her. Deirdre did indeed eschew most medications, but she had always found it soothing have her hair brushed when she had the headache. If Deirdre was comfortable and relaxed she might be more receptive to the reiterated advice her cousin felt it her duty to proffer respecting the making of secret appointments with Captain Wainright. She had been evading any private conversation since the ball.

Belinda hesitated, looking longingly at the smooth linen sheets Polly had turned back which invited her repose; then she straightened her back and went to fetch her black velvet robe.

Leaving her own door open, she crossed the dark dressing room and tapped softly on the door to Deirdre's room so as not to awaken her if she were sleeping. Receiving no answer, she peeked inside. The first thing she noticed was the lighted lamp on the bedside table; the second was the empty bed. Her seeking eyes moved to the open door to the sitting room at the same time she became aware of Deirdre's voice coming from the room beyond. Thinking her cousin had rung for her maid because she felt unwell, Belinda hurried forward, only to freeze in consternation as a man's low accents mingled with Deirdre's.

Oh, dear God, how could she? The silent cry of agony reverberated in Belinda's brain as she identified the masculine voice as that of Anthony Wainright. She couldn't recognize the words but the urgency in his tones came through clearly.

"No, no, I cannot, I tell you!" Deirdre's shaky, high-pitched notes were more distinct. "I'd be ruined; we'd both be ruined!" Her next words were muffled, as if she were crying.

Belinda came out of her temporary paralysis, taking an impulsive step forward before stopping short, appalled that she could even consider confronting the pair in the sitting room. If their honor was not strong enough to prevent whatever they were contemplating, it was ludicrous to suppose they would take any notice of her pitiful importunities.

Belinda had taken a hesitant step toward the dressing room while contradictory impulses battered her senses. An instant later she was frantically speeding back to her own quarters as the voices in the other room came closer. Grateful for the deep shadow in this corner of the the room and the thick carpet underfoot, she had just reached the dressing-room door when two figures appeared in the sitting room doorway.

"How can you argue with this?" Captain Wainright said softly, their outlines merging as he took Lady Archer in his arms.

"I cannot—no, we must stop . . . ohhh . . . do that again . . . "

Belinda, closing the dressing room door behind her with infinite care, mercifully saw and heard no more.

Chapter Nine

A haggard but resolute Belinda confronted her cousin while the latter was sipping chocolate, propped up on a mound of pillows in her bed the next morning. Deirdre, vital and fetching in a frothy silk confection in her favorite yellow, looked anything but pleased when her cousin walked into the room after a perfunctory tap on the door. She instantly went on the offensive.

"If you have come to read me a lecture for leaving the table last night, you would do well to save your breath. That woman is impossible! Her superior airs and implied criticism truly give me the headache every time I am forced to endure her company for more than a few minutes."

"I am not here to lecture you, merely to let you know that I plan to leave this house as soon as arrangements can be made for the journey—tomorrow if possible."

The cup stopped on the way to Deirdre's mouth and her eyes rounded. "But you can't do that! You would not be so cruel as to leave me alone with Lydia! Besides, you promised to stay at least until I can stage a miscarriage."

"You made certain promises too, in case you want reminding. Since you have seen fit to break them, I feel equally free to regard our agreement as void. I am going home."

"What are you going on about this time?" Impatience rang in Deirdre's voice but something akin to fear dwelled in the deep blue eyes as she put the cup back on her tray and pushed it aside.

"Do not fence with me," Belinda snapped, her nostrils flaring in contempt. "I came into this room last night to see if you needed anything, just in time to see you kissing Captain Wainright in that doorway!"

"And, being the little prude you are, immediately thought the worst! It may interest you to know that Anthony was not in

my bed last night; in fact, I sent him away less than two minutes after he kissed me." At Belinda's unladylike snort,
Deirdre said earnestly, "I know it looks compromising, but
Anthony has been begging me for weeks to run away with
him, and I have been nearly out of my mind trying to decide
what to do. Now that peace has been signed with the Ameri-
cans, he wishes to go to America, where no one knows us and
start a new life. Archer would divorce me eventually, and then
we would be able to marry."

"When do you plan to leave?"

The dryness in Belinda's voice went unremarked as Deirdre
said seriously, "I had almost decided it was all too difficult to
attempt when Anthony told me at the Prescotts' ball that he intended to go back into the army if I refused to go with him. I
felt I could not bear it if he were to be killed, so I said perhaps
I would go after all. When we met last night in the garden I
was to give him my answer, but we argued for simply ages and
came inside when it began to get cold. It was odd but the more
he tried to persuade me we could make a good life together
without anyone knowing who we were, the more convinced I
became that the truth would come out and there would be a
frightful scandal and no one would receive me. Also, I do not
believe I am really cut out to be the wife of a poor man, even
though I am madly in love with Anthony. In the end, I told
him I just could not go through with it and I sent him away."

Belinda pressed her lips together and willed herself to remain silent.

"You must believe me!" Deirdre cried. "Everything I have
told you is the truth!"

"No one seeing what I saw last night would believe you,"
Belinda pointed out coldly.

Deirdre made a gesture of dismissal with her hand. "That is
beside the point. No one else saw us together. I sent Meritt to
bed early last night. Please, Bel, you cannot desert me now
just when I have finally decided that I wish to continue with
my marriage. I'll make it up to you. I'll take you to London
with me, and Archer shall find you a husband."

A scathing rejection of this handsome offer was on Belinda's tongue, but before she could give voice to her sentiments there came a sharp knock on the sitting-room door.

Without waiting for any acknowledgment, Lady Ilchester,
her back ramrod straight and an expression of rigid distaste on

her face, strode into the room, stopping a few feet from the elaborately draped bed.

"Were it not for an inconvenient but ingrained sense of justice," she began without preamble, "nothing would induce me to expend breath on a female who would betray her husband of a few months in his own house, but I could not reconcile it with my conscience to fail to inform you that I intend to send a detailed report of your perfidy to my brother without delay."

"Wh . . . what are you talking about? Have you gone mad?" gasped Deirdre, sitting straight up away from her pillows, one hand at her throat.

"Do not bother to play the innocent with me, for I cut my wisdoms long ago and I'd have had to be blind to miss the blatant public flirtation you have been carrying on with Captain Wainright since my arrival in Somerset. That would have been sufficient to prove you unworthy of the honor my brother bestowed upon you in marrying you, but to invite that man into your bed is to put yourself forever outside the knowledge of decent women!"

"It's not *true*!" Deirdre protested, falling back against the pillows, her skin drained of all color.

"You only compound your crime by denying it," Lady Ilchester said with an expression of icy disdain on her patrician face. "You were seen embracing him in this room by my maid, whom I sent to you with a tisane for your alleged headache after I dismissed her last night. Unfortunately, she did not have the sense to come back to me immediately so I might have averted this disgrace, but that is past mending. She told me what she saw when she came to me this morning. She has been in my employ for over twenty years, and she is *not* a liar."

"Not a liar, but mistaken, ma'am. It was not Deirdre but I who was kissing Captain Wainright in that doorway last night."

Belinda's quiet words, spoken while Lady Ilchester drew breath to continue her attack on her sister-in-law, caused that lady to turn an angry glare on the girl whose presence she had ignored to that point. "A very touching display of family unity," she said in sneering tones, "but your lies are wasted. There was enough light for my maid to clearly identify the female in Wainright's arms. You were wearing the sapphire dress you wore to the Prescotts' ball," she said to Deirdre as if to clinch the matter.

"*I* was wearing my own sapphire gown which is somewhat similar to my cousin's," Belinda replied, assuming a composure she was far from feeling.

"You cannot shield your cousin from the consequences of her treachery by trumped-up tales," Lady Ilchester declared.

Seeing that she was about to renew her attack on Deirdre, Belinda darted into the dressing room, calling, "Wait!" over her shoulder. She returned a moment later with the sapphire gown her cousin had given her, which she thrust under the woman's nose.

"This is what I was wearing last night when your maid saw us."

Though she certainly examined the gown closely enough to differentiate it from the one Deirdre had worn to the ball at Singleford, Lady Ilchester pronounced herself unimpressed by this material evidence. "An attempt to throw sand in my eyes," she snapped, giving the silk a disdainful push with one long-fingered hand. "What would you—or rather, what would a *respectable* female be doing embracing a strange man in another woman's bedchamber in the middle of the night?"

Belinda's quixotic lie had indeed been the result of an upsurge of family feeling at the sight of Deirdre's ashen desperation, and had been given impetus by her own appalled fury at the virulent dislike on Lady Ilchester's face when denouncing the girl her brother had married. Her lips parted but her brain was reeling and she made no sound.

Deirdre, however, had used the time provided by her cousin's intervention to recover her wits. "Belinda and Captain Wainright had come to my room to tell me they wished to marry, and to ask me to intercede for them with my uncle," she announced calmly.

It was fortunate that Lady Ilchester swung her attention back to her sister-in-law at Deirdre's first words, for the frantic protest on Belinda's face would have given the lie to this interpretation instantly.

"In the middle of the night, having met the man in a clandestine fashion somewhere after stopping to change her clothes? You must think you are dealing with a half-wit," Lady Ilchester said with contempt. "Enough of this persiflage. There is one sure way to get to the bottom of the affair. I shall send for Captain Wainright and ask him point-blank which of you he intended to ruin by his disgusting behavior." She spun on her heel and headed for the sitting room, only to be arrested by Deirdre's voice, every bit as cold and determined as her own.

"I am the mistress of this house, and anyone who enters it does so at my pleasure. I'll send for Captain Wainright myself and I shall be present when you put your insulting question to him. You might also wish to explain to him just when and how it came about that a proposal of marriage is now tantamount to ruining a girl."

"It remains to be seen how eager he will be to marry a female so lost to all sense of propriety as to indulge in the sort of behavior your cousin does not scruple to claim as her own," Lady Ilchester retorted, sweeping out of the room.

"I hate that vicious creature!" Deirdre declared as the door slammed behind her sister-in-law. "She would be thrilled if Archer divorced me, but she shan't succeed in this attempt to discredit me. Anthony will not betray me. What's the matter with you?" she added in alarm, sliding off her bed to shore up her cousin's suddenly sagging form. "Sit in this chair. You're not feeling faint, are you? I'll get you some water."

Belinda allowed herself to be pushed onto an armless boudoir chair and meekly accepted the glass of water Deirdre put into her hands, though she made no effort to drink any. Sheer panic stared out of the eyes she raised to her cousin's. "What am I to do, Dee? I tried to help you, but I only succeeded in ruining my life."

"Do not let that horrid female frighten you, Bel. She cannot hurt you."

"You told Lady Ilchester that Captain Wainright wishes to *marry* me! You cannot expect the man to swear to that. It must be obvious to anyone with two eyes that he has taken me in dislike, and for my part, I find him completely without principles or honor."

"Once you claimed you were the one that wretched maid saw, the story about wishing to marry was the only one that could account for the presence of the two of you in *my* bed-chamber. Do not put yourself in such a taking. Anthony will certainly not fail me. It is not as if you two will have to go through with a marriage. Betrothals can be ended quietly these days without arousing talk."

"Are you mad? You heard Lady Ilchester's description of my character. She intended to write an account of what her maid saw to your husband. What is to prevent her from doing the same with my parents even if Captain Wainright upholds this story you have concocted? How will I ever be able to look my father in the eye again?"

"If that happens, you may explain the whole situation to Uncle Walter," Deirdre replied, adding impatiently, "Look, Bel, I cannot explore all the possible ramifications with you right now. I must get word to Anthony before that poisonous Lydia tries to summon him behind my back."

So saying, Deirdre grabbed a frilly wrapper in the same yellow silk as her night rail and shrugged into it as she headed into the sitting room where her gold-and-white-painted desk stood.

Belinda, mouth agape, jumped out of her chair and took two steps in pursuit before halting uncertainly. What could she hope to accomplish? Her own impulsive declaration had provided Deirdre with a way to save her skin, and her cousin was not about to relinquish control of the situation. Other people's problems and objections never weighed heavily with her when she had it in mind to carry out a plan to her own advantage, as was clearly the case here. Unhappily for Belinda's peace of mind, she could not so easily dismiss Deirdre's vital concerns in order to protect her own interests, especially after having come to her rescue just now.

As she wandered back to her own room, a troubled Belinda acknowledged that she would not have been so quick to act on Deirdre's behalf had she been fully awake to the extent of the sacrifice that might ultimately be demanded of her. She was no saint, and she didn't even *like* her cousin. What was more, she passionately disapproved of Deirdre's recent conduct. If she were indeed the adulteress Lady Ilchester accused her of being, then she would have earned society's condemnation, but there was no denying the conventional punishment was extremely harsh. Was Lord Archer as vindictive a personality as his sister, or would he be more inclined to forgive this lapse on his bride's part? Since the only person who knew about last night's compromising situation was his own sister, he would be spared the humiliation of having his wife's conduct become a public scandal, assuming he could control Lady Ilchester's malevolent tongue. Would this circumstance incline him toward leniency, or would his pain at Deirdre's disloyalty make him revengeful? Belinda did not flatter herself that she had developed any insights into Lord Archer's complex character during their brief acquaintance.

Belinda shook her head as if she could physically clear away the mass of confusion therein. She glanced down when her fingers felt wet, surprised to see that she was still clutching the water glass Deirdre had given her when the full impact of her rash action had hit her with overwhelming force. She drained the glass now, grateful for the relief to her parched throat. If only she could as easily rid herself of the dull headache that was beating behind her eyes. All this speculation about Lord Archer's reaction was most likely pointless. Deirdre was supremely confident that Captain Wainright would support her story of worried young lovers seeking intercession on their behalf.

As she placed the empty glass on her dressing table, Belinda's sombre eyes met those of her pale image in the mirror over the table. Whether Anthony Wainright still loved Deirdre enough to sacrifice himself to save her from disgrace or was so angry over her rejection of his wild plans for their future together that he would like to see her suffer as he had done mattered little to Belinda's unenviable position. Whatever the outcome, humiliation was to be her lot. She had winced at the thought of facing her father, but she would a thousand times rather face her father, who loved her, than look once into the aloof blue eyes of the man who considered that she could not hold a candle to her vain, shallow, and selfish cousin.

It had been a mistake admitting Anthony Wainright into her thoughts, for she could already feel the accelerated beating of her heart and a preliminary quiver in her extremities. She knew with dreadful certainty that she would be unable to impose a passable tranquility on her traitorous body at the moment Lady Ilchester posed her incriminating question to the unsuspecting captain.

Or would he be unsuspecting? Belinda's eyes involuntarily sought the door to the dressing room she shared with her cousin, narrowing as it occurred to her that Deirdre's superb confidence surely included the knowledge that she would be able to alert her lover to the situation awaiting him at Archer Hall. Ultimately it made no difference to her own craven desire to be elsewhere when Captain Wainright gave his response.

It was too warm in her room; she was having difficulty breathing. What she needed was a long tramp in the brisk spring air, Belinda decided. Putting this hastily conceived plan into execution on the spot, she bent down to take off her soft house shoes and padded over to the dressing room to get the sturdy half boots she wore on her walks.

Belinda's cowardly attempt to absent herself from the upcoming scene of human drama was thwarted at the outset by Deirdre, who, having finished her note to Captain Wainright, entered the dressing room at the moment her cousin was extricating her boots from an armoire. After several minutes' exposure to the rough side of Deirdre's tongue, Belinda reluctantly conceded that her presence was essential to what her cousin termed "the happy resolution" to the threatened unpleasantness, although she was personally persuaded that such a goal was impossible of achievement except from Deirdre's narrow point of view, which embraced only her own self-interest.

The opportunity for this happy resolution did not come about immediately because, as the groom who had been the bearer of Deirdre's summons reported an hour later to his mistress, the gentlemen were out riding when he arrived at Hilltop House. It was midafternoon when Captain Wainright was shown into the small saloon where the three women sat as three separate islands of industry working on their individual pieces of fancywork with varying degrees of application and success. Belinda's work would not have withstood even the most cursory inspection, while Lady Ilchester sat in frigid serenity at a tambour frame, setting stitches in a floral-patterned seat cover with the rhythm and efficiency of a machine. Neither she nor her sister-in-law deigned to glance in the other's direction. From time to time one or the other would address a remark, mostly rhetorical, to Belinda who, far from being grateful for the recognition, tended to react like some wild creature poked with a stick, jumping at the sound of each voice, her nervous state clearly apparent.

Deirdre, maintaining a pose of uncaring insouciance as she worked on a little neck ruff, was not best pleased with her cousin's inability to ape her own performance. The looks she sent the hapless Belinda as time crawled by were increasingly annoyed, but her voice was all tender solicitude as she said after a rather more prolonged silence than usual, "Do not fret about your father's reception of Captain Wainright, Bel. It is true that he is only a second son, but he is not entirely without prospects, and my uncle is a reasonable man. Besides, that modest legacy from his maternal great-aunt—that you told me about—" she added smoothly as if sensing Lady Ilchester's quickened interest, "is bound to improve his position in Uncle Walter's eyes."

A quickly smothered "Ouch!" was Belinda's only verbal response to this latest audacity as she pricked one of her ten thumbs in her agitation, but her eyes cast a smoldering glare at her cousin over the bleeding finger she was sucking.

Deirdre, pleased that bottled-up irritation had lent her pasty-faced cousin some much needed color, sat back, a satisfied little smile playing about her lips.

It was at this fraught moment that Drummond announced Captain Wainright.

Three pairs of feminine eyes instantly focused on the tall, handsome man, late of His Majesty's victorious army, walking into the room with the stern resolution of someone facing a well-concealed battery of field artillery.

Captain Wainright was dressed with his customary neatness, which did credit to a military background. Not a wrinkle marred the fit of his coat of blue superfine across his broad-shouldered frame or the impeccable buff pantaloons stuffed into mirror-bright, tasseled Hessians. Not a wavy hair on that golden head was out of place, and his intricately tied cravat was a work of art. Belinda registered these details on one level while part of her mind shrank back from the rocky set to his jaw and the veiled danger in steel blue eyes that swept over the women in turn before settling on his hostess.

"I must apologize, Lady Archer, for keeping you waiting so long, but Jack and I were out when your note was delivered this morning. I came as soon as I could since I understand there is some . . . confusion about my presence in this house last night."

"I see my sister-in-law has already regaled you with her version of the affair, which is no more than I expected," Lady Ilchester said before Deirdre could open her mouth. "That being the case, all I require of you is an answer to the following question: Which of these young women were you embracing in Lady Archer's bedchamber last night after the household had retired?"

In the folds of her embroidery Belinda's fingernails were cutting into her palms as she ceased breathing. She suspected that, despite the fixed smile on her lips, her cousin was doing the same as she kept her eyes on the waxy tautness of Captain Wainwright's classical features.

"It was Miss Melville, of course," the ex-soldier replied in an uninflected tone that sealed Belinda's fate without so much as a glance in her direction.

"I see." To Belinda's hectic fancy, Lady Ilchester's face had briefly worn an expression of fierce triumph before assuming a mask of cool arrogance once more. "May I assume then that the rest of their story is also true—that you and Miss Melville, having met somewhere else by pre-arrangement, entered Lady Archer's bedchamber to tell her of your desire to marry and to seek her intercession with Miss Melville's parents?"

"Yes . . . you may," Captain Wainright answered in that same deadened tone.

Belinda, staring blindly at the heap of sewing in her lap, wondered if she were the only one to detect a tiny hesitation before he crossed his Rubicon. Her spirit writhed beneath the accumulated humiliations. How he must detest her for being the agent, however involuntary, of separating him forever from the girl he had pursued beyond the tolerance of society. Though it was Deirdre who had demanded his sacrifice, Belinda knew she would pay a high toll for her part in the sorry conclusion to the affair. She could not even deny that it was justice of a sort, for it was she who had given Deirdre the means by which to save herself from disgrace.

Lost in her melancholy musing, Belinda was brought back to the painful present by Lady Ilchester's clipped tones addressed to herself. "While I can never condone behavior that reflects so badly on your upbringing, I must concede that your recent escapade has succeeded in its object of making a marriage with Captain Wainright mandatory."

Shame color dyed Belinda's cheeks and she flinched from this cruel analysis, but it was Deirdre who protested vehemently, "You have no right to assign devious motives to the unwise but impulsive behavior of a young girl in love."

"A woman of your experience, ma'am, must be aware that impetuous young men have been leading innocent girls astray from time immemorial," Captain Wainright said, entering the lists. "It is safe to assume that it is always the male who is to blame in the case of a proper young lady temporarily forgetting the dictates of her upbringing."

This cynical championship did nothing to remove the sting from lady Ilchester's charge for Belinda, nor did it appear to inspire the older woman to take a more charitable view of the case. "What is done is past mending," she said briskly. "Please, Captain Wainwright, sit down. We all seem to have forgotten our manners." As Captain Wainright with tangible reluctance seated himself in a chair close to the sofa where Deirdre sat, she added, "It is time we got down to practical matters."

"What practical matters?" Deirdre demanded.

"Why the matter of securing the consent of Miss Melville's parents before the betrothal is announced, of course."

"Oh, yes, eventually," Deirdre agreed. "But there is no call for unseemly haste."

"On the contrary," her sister-in-law riposted, "there is every need with a couple who have demonstrated such unseemly haste that they must resort to secret rendezvous and midnight calls for assistance."

The two individuals most concerned had taken no part in this dialogue, but now Captain Wainright intervened, saying, "Naturally it is my intention to call upon Sir Walter Melville in the very near future."

Lady Ilchester signified her approval with a regal nod. Captain Wainright stood up, indicating his intention to bring his visit to a close, whereupon her ladyship said graciously, "I see no reason why Miss Melville should not accompany you to the door, sir. No doubt she will have messages she desires you to convey to her parents."

"I . . . I think I should go home." Belinda's agitated statement, scarcely above a whisper, was her first contribution to the meeting.

Her suggestion was immediately vetoed by Lady Ilchester. "I fear it is quite out of the question for a young woman to travel with a male escort unrelated to her by blood or marriage."

"Besides, Bel, you promised you'd stay with me until I am well enough to go to London," Deirdre put in hastily.

Belinda shot her cousin a fulminating look, then started in surprise as Captain Wainright, who had approached her while her attention was diverted, took her hand to raise her to her feet. "Come, we have much to discuss."

Stunned by the rapidity of events, Belinda allowed herself to be led out of the room, not even hearing Captain Wainright's adieus to the other ladies. Her docility ended on the other side of the door, however. She seized her grim-faced escort's arm and said frantically, "You cannot go to see my father!"

"Do you have a better suggestion?"

"Yes, just go away . . . disappear," she said wildly.

Captain Wainright bowed ironically, detaching his sleeve from her grip. "I would be delighted to obey you, ma'am, except that among the three of you you have put that option beyond me. My honor demands that I save your reputation."

These callous words had the unexpected effect of restoring Belinda's cringing spirit. A flame of anger ignited in her veins and sent the heated blood pounding through her body. Her eyes sparked fury and she fairly spat at him, "Honor! If you knew the meaning of the word you would not have been in my cousin's bedchamber last night, and I could have gone home and tried to forget that I have been an unwilling witness to a flagrant, protracted, and thoroughly despicable attempt at seduction."

"Attempt?" he repeated in a silky tone strongly at odds with the cold rage that gave her the impression that his features were hewn out of granite.

Belinda was not in the least cowed, but her own useless anger had burned itself out as quickly as it had arisen. She glanced briefly at the man who might have meant so much to her had a kindlier fate prevailed and said quietly, gazing into the distance, "I was there when Lady Ilchester threatened to write to her brother about what her maid reported to her. Even if Deirdre is guilty, I could not stand by and do nothing when she looked so desperately afraid, so I told Lady Ilchester I was the one you were kissing. Naturally she did not believe me at first, but Deirdre had given me her other blue gown and by the time I produced it to support my claim, Deirdre had worked out the story of our wishing to marry and coming to see her for help. It was too late to deny my words then."

She took a deep breath and let it out in a sigh, missing the shame and regret that crossed his countenance before he said in tones from which the animus, indeed all feeling, had vanished, "I beg your pardon, Miss Melville. I should not have ripped up at you for trying to help your cousin."

"It doesn't signify," she said with weary tolerance, "but is there no way to keep this from my family?"

"If I read that beldam's character correctly, she will make it her business to air the situation to all and sundry unless a betrothal is forthcoming. It is the only way to keep your name from being smirched, and for a betrothal, your father's consent is essential."

"Then I must write to him and explain how this came about."

"I gather your father would otherwise take the same line as Deirdre's esteemed parent—out for much bigger game for his lovely daughter," he said with a bitter twist to his mouth.

"No, of course not, but neither will he be eager to bestow my hand on someone of whom he has never heard, and who has known me for less than a month, if I do not explain that it is to be a temporary expedient."

"Temporary? You cannot be that naive! Under the unsavory circumstances obtaining, any betrothal between us is temporary only in the sense that it is to be shortly followed by a wedding!" he said on a laugh that contained no humor, adding, "My dear good girl, I would suggest that you consider carefully before deciding just what you wish your parents to know of our situation before you make me the bearer of any messages to them. I will call on you tomorrow before setting off for your home."

Before Belinda could muster up any arguments, or even catch her breath, Captain Wainright had made her an elegant bow and swiftly headed for the stairway.

Chapter Ten

When Deirdre entered her sitting room a half hour later, Belinda stopped her frenzied pacing and pounced. "Where have you been? What took you so long?"

"Lydia was sitting in the saloon looking like a cat that had got at the cream after you left. I was not about to give her the satisfaction of thinking she could chase both of us away," her cousin replied with a toss of her head. "Where did you get to anyway? Do not tell me it took you all this time to bid Anthony a fond farewell?"

Belinda missed the suggestion of pique beneath the careless question. "Of course not," she said bitterly. "He bolted away before I could persuade him to tell my father the truth. Dee, he is talking as if Lady Ilchester can compel us to go through with a marriage ceremony, but that is not so, not even if my reputation is lost and I can never go to London."

Deirdre looked closely at her cousin's resolute expression and said curiously, "Most females would not regard a lost reputation as a fate to be preferred to marrying Anthony Wainright."

"They would under these circumstances! What girl would wish to wed a man who was in love with another female?"

Deirdre shrugged. "Love does not always last forever. Many girls would take a chance of worming their way into his affections eventually."

"Well, I am not among them. You must see that it will be best if I go home at once. You can send a guard with Polly and me."

"No! I need you here to keep Lydia away from me and convince her that I have suffered a real miscarriage. There are only a few days to go now."

"All you ever think of is your own convenience!" Belinda cried angrily.

"How are you different?" Deirdre shot back. "Moaning about your lost reputation! Go ahead and tell Uncle Walter the whole story if you must. He never approved of me anyway." She cleared the pettishness from her voice and her manner became coaxing once more. "Please, Bel, be reasonable. By the time Anthony returns from Gloucestershire I should be past the danger of discovery. A speedy recovery and I'll be ready to join Archer in London, which will rid me of Lydia's unwelcome presence. You may accompany me or return home as you choose. A betrothal can be announced to pacify Lydia, and you may terminate it at your convenience. Tell Uncle Walter whatever you deem necessary to make him consent to the betrothal."

"You make it sound so simple," Belinda said, her features wan, "but Captain Wainright seems to feel his honor requires that he marry me to save my reputation."

"It need not come to that. Once you go home the people here will forget about an engagement, and most likely no one in Gloucestershire will even know about it."

Belinda did not share Deirdre's optimism but she could see nothing to be gained from further argument. She made a little gesture of resignation with her hands and went off to compose a letter to her father.

This turned out to be a far more difficult task than she could ever have conceived of before the recent harrowing events. She began confidently enough with her customary affectionate greetings to all and then came to a full stop, absently brushing the feathered tip back and forth across her lips while she stared into space and contemplated the best way to phrase what she wished to convey.

A half hour later when the ink was long dry on her pen and no new words had been added to the sheet of paper in front of her, she acknowledged this as a singularly unproductive approach. She threw the pen down in disgust and began pacing. It was another half hour before she was brought to admit that she did not know precisely *what* she wished to convey to her parent. She had raged aplenty at Deirdre for her selfishness and lack of consideration for her husband, but now she found it difficult—nay, nearly impossible—to set down in writing an unvarnished account of her cousin's behavior leading up to the current crisis. Everything looked so much worse somehow, inscribed in sharp, black letters on white paper, comprising words and charges that could never be mitigated or retrieved, words that would henceforth take on a life of their own apart from the persons to whom they referred. Similarly, her hand refused to pen the words, accurate and truthful though they were, that would forever condemn Captain Wainright as a profligate in her father's estimation.

Belinda wrestled with this problem for the rest of the day, but her insights always stopped short of revealing her own motivations to her understanding in a clear light. Consequently, the letter she handed Captain Wainright the next day when he called to tell the ladies of his plans to leave for Gloucestershire early the following morning was very short. She despaired that it was totally unsatisfactory as far as communicating any sense of the actual situation, but she had been unable to achieve a compromise that would inform without predisposing her father against the man who sought his daughter's hand in marriage.

Captain Wainright made no attempt to be private with her on the occasion of his leavetaking. He greeted the three ladies with a smile that lacked spontaneity and refused all refreshment, remaining only long enough for Belinda to retrieve the letter from her room and give him more precise directions for locating Millgrove. True, he kissed her fingers upon his departure, but since he also treated Deirdre to this charming ritual, Belinda took no comfort in the gesture. In fact, inadvertently having caught sight of Lady Ilchester watching them with a satisfied expression that had nothing of kindness in it, Belinda found her fragile composure threatened still further. She was reminded of the look of something close to malicious triumph that had appeared on Lady Ilchester's face when Captain Wainright had declared that she, not Deirdre, had been the recipient of his amorous advances. A shiver ran up her spine at the memory.

In the days that followed Captain Wainright's departure for Millgrove, Belinda's state of mind could scarcely be said to approximate that of a girl on the brink of betrothal. Under Deirdre's continual prodding she made a valiant effort to appear carefree when in Lady Ilchester's company, but she evaded that joyless circumstance whenever possible despite her cousin's pleas not to be left alone with her sister-in-law. She increased the duration of her solitary rambles, sometimes covering long distances at a prodigious pace designed to outrun her fears and misgivings about the future. On occasions she merely climbed a nearby hill from which there was a serene and homely vista, sitting with her back against a tree while she tried to regain the equanimity she had formerly considered an intrinsic part of her nature.

These precious interludes of privacy came to a halt on the third day of Captain Wainright's absence when Deirdre popped into Belinda's bedchamber after lunch to announce that she was going to undergo the supposed miscarriage that night. The imminence of yet another opportunity for their deception to be exposed added to Belinda's tribulations, but in this instance her fears were proved groundless.

Belinda's demeanor when she told Lady Ilchester of the alleged mishap the next morning was appropriately, and quite legitimately, saddened—if not for the stated reason—and she withstood a barrage of questions with a gentle dignity, patiently reiterating that it had been her cousin's expressed wish that she not disturb her sister-in-law during the night. She acquiesced readily to Lady Ilchester's demand to send immediately for the doctor, knowing this to be an unavoidable part of the unfolding drama, but she successfully repulsed all the older woman's attempts to see her sister-in-law, repeating with polite firmness that Deirdre had desired her to admit no one but the doctor to her presence. Short of physically challenging the young woman seated outside her cousin's door, Lady Ilchester was unable to impose her will to gain admittance. This minor triumph bolstered Belinda's courage and permitted her to contain her apprehension during the physician's visit.

It had been a tremendous relief to learn that Dr. Simmons was unacquainted with Lady Ilchester, having recently replaced the old practitioner who had formerly attended the inhabitants of the Hall until his retirement. A brisk, almost brusque man in his forties with a bristling moustache, Dr. Simmons was unimpressed and certainly not intimidated by her ladyship's haughty manner. He brushed aside Lady Ilchester's high-handed assumption that she would accompany him into the patient's bedchamber, asking shortly, "Is anyone with her now?"

"Yes, her maid," Belinda replied.

"That will do then. Ladies, if you will excuse me, please."
With that, Dr. Simmons strode into Deirdre's bedchamber,
leaving one fuming and one thankful woman outside.

The minutes dragged by in such an atmosphere of unspoken
animosity that Belinda was surprised, on glancing at the clock,
to see how few had actually passed when the doctor came out
of Deirdre's room. His professional demeanor had not notice-
ably softened as he said to the waiting ladies, "These things
happen sometimes, but there is nothing wrong with Lady
Archer that a few days rest and coddling won't mend. She is a
strong healthy young woman, and I see no reason why she
should not successfully bear children in the future. I have a
rather urgent case several miles away, so I will bid you ladies
good day and show myself out." If he heard Lady Ilchester's
imperative voice calling to him a second later when she recovered her wits, he did not allow it to slow his purposeful
progress to the door to the hall, through which he soon vanished.

Limp with relief, Belinda dropped back into her chair and
imposed a mask of polite attention over her features, though
she heard little of Lady Ilchester's subsequent harangue
against the doctor's rough manners, suspect professional com-
petence, and obvious lack of breeding.

Deirdre, freed from her last concern in the affair, was in
tearing spirits, and Belinda had to remind her on more than
one occasion in the next day or two that her eagerness to be
up and doing accorded ill with the grief she was presumed to
be feeling by the tiptoeing members of her attentive household.

Belinda's relief at the successful resolution of the problem
had been fleeting, swamped in a tidal wave of revulsion for the
sordid experience, comprising equal parts of resentment toward her cousin for bringing her into it, and self-disgust for
her on complicity and deceit. And underneath this was the
gnawing anxiety concerning her future. All in all, she was
hard-pressed to be civil in the face of Deirdre's grating cheer-
fulness. The warm appreciation of the household staff and so-
licitous neighbors who called, for her supposed devotion to her
cousin, nearly overset her precarious composure as she battled
the sensation of being gradually smothered in a blanketing fog
of deception.

It did not help that her thoughts strayed to Gloucestershire often enough that she lost track of the conversation with embarrassing regularity, frequently responding at random to her companions' remarks. She had no difficulty envisioning Captain Wainright riding up the curved drive of Millgrove or ringing the old-fashioned bellpull at the front entrance. She could even imagine him sitting in the worn brown velvet wing chair near her father's desk in the library, but there her imagination faltered to a dead halt, leaving him a speechless petitioner. How did a man find words to ask for the hand of a female he had no desire to wed? Could any man not irretrievably lost to all sense of decency steel himself to proclaim an affection he did not feel? On the other hand, how could a man who claimed his honor demanded that he marry a particular female do less if he needed to secure a fond father's acceptance of his suit? She could perfectly appreciate the lacerated sensibilities of an honorable man in such a quandary, but perhaps Captain Wainright did not find that aspect of the situation at all troubling. Her Apollo had turned out to possess feet of clay beneath the surface charm.

Belinda was no less at a loss to predict her parent's reaction to having a complete stranger appear on his doorstep requesting permission to marry his daughter. For some reason or other she had never even mentioned Captain Wainright in her letters to her family from Somerset. She took comfort in the knowledge that, although not by nature a demonstrative man, her father held his only daughter in deep affection. He would not willingly enter into an arrangement that might jeopardize her future contentment. Naturally his response to Captain Wainright would depend in large part on his impressions of that gentleman at their meeting. It always came back to Anthony Wainright in the end. Once she had fancied that she knew him better than any man in the world, but that had been a child's air dreaming, based on wishful thinking, if not downright invention. Today she would not presume to claim the slightest understanding of the man he had become. No amount of speculation on the outcome of this journey produced a conclusion that had much appeal, but perhaps a temporary engagement would provide time in which to escape from Lady Ilchester's vaguely menacing presence. Deirdre would soon go off to London to join her husband, leaving Belinda free to return to Millgrove. She would be safe from Lady Ilchester's malicious

tongue there, and in due time the betrothal could be quietly
ended. After only a month in a more socially active environment, she longed for the uncomplicated life she had previously
led among people of solid worth and convictions.

It was on the afternoon that Deirdre first ventured out of her
suite that Captain Wainright reappeared at Archer Hall. The
women were in the small saloon when Drummond came in to
announce:

"Captain Wainright desires to speak with Miss Melville, my
lady. I have put him in his lordship's bookroom."

"Why did you not show him in here, Drummond?"

"Really, my dear Deirdre, would you deny the young people
a few moments of privacy at such a time?"

Lady Ilchester's tolerant little laugh seemed out of character
and grated on Belinda's abraded nerves as she folded her
sewing with unsteady fingers. She avoided the older woman's
eyes and tried to disguise her anxiety as she prepared to follow
Drummond out of the room.

"Bring him back here for tea, Bel," Deirdre called after her.

Belinda managed a little nod in acknowledgment but was
conscious of a painful dryness in her throat that was going to
make speech difficult. Her slow pace toward Lord Archer's
study reflected an instinctive reluctance to discover her fate.
Whatever the decision arrived at in Gloucestershire, her life
would never be quite the same simple affair again.

She entered the study and stopped one step from the door,
unsettled as always by the extraordinary appeal generated by
Anthony Wainright's sheer physical perfection. By virtue of
all that had passed between them, she ought to find the very
sight of this man distasteful, and she was chagrined that such
was not the case. She gripped her hands together against the
soft gray cotton folds of her simple gown and waited.

Captain Wainright, seated in an elaborately carved armchair
near a massive desk, closed the book he had been reading and
set it on the desk as he got to his feet. "Good afternoon, Miss
Melville."

Belinda inclined her head, swallowed with difficulty, and
continued to wait, her gaze never leaving his serious face.

Some fifteen feet still separated them, but now Captain
Wainright started to walk slowly forward, pausing as, without
moving her feet an inch, Belinda retreated, her eyes widening

still further and her shoulders pulling back. He resumed his progress and essayed a small smile. "Except that your eyes are gray, not brown, you look like a deer suddenly coming upon a hunter. I am not that, I promise you."

Or at least I am not your chosen prey, Belinda silently amended before asking, "Did you see my father?" There was a little creak in her soft voice but, thankfully, she had produced some intelligible sound at last.

He stopped a couple of paces away and some of the tension eased from her posture.

"Yes. I located Millgrove quite easily. Actually, I spent some time in that corner of Gloucestershire a few years ago and found the general area somewhat familiar once I arrived within a few miles of your home."

"Did . . . did you meet my stepmother and my little brothers?" Belinda asked quickly, her eyes sliding away at mention of a previous visit to her locality. She missed the flicker in his eyes as he replied:

"I fear I did not have the pleasure of meeting the rest of your family, but I found your father a most agreeable and well-spoken man."

Belinda sensed that Captain Wainright was exercising care in the selection of his words. "I . . . see," she said lamely into the silence that ensued.

"Sir Walter was very cordial, considering that my name meant nothing to him initially."

There seemed to be a question underlying this simple observation. When Belinda looked a query, he laughed, faint amusement in his countenance.

"Your father was quite understandably taken aback to have a total stranger ask for permission to pay his addresses to his daughter."

"I gave you a letter of introduction to him."

"So you did. Your father said it was this letter that persuaded him to give his consent to my request in the end."

"But I did not try to persuade him into anything!" For the first time there was some animation in Belinda's voice, animation bordering on indignation to be precise, and the amusement in Captain Wainright's expression took on a tinge of friendly mockery.

"So I discovered when Sir Walter handed me your letter to read. If memory serves, the pertinent part read 'the bearer of

this letter is Captain Anthony Wainright. I hope you will welcome him.' Your father, influenced no doubt by his understanding of your character, took that stark departure from what
he called your 'usual detailed and meticulous reports of all
small happenings' as an indication of your urgent desire that
he accede to my request."

"You must have misunderstood his meaning," Belinda said,
annoyed at his gentle teasing. "Did you tell him the truth—
about the situation with Deirdre, I mean?"

The friendliness died out of Captain Wainright's face. "I
told him nothing of that," he replied shortly.

"Then what did you say that made him give his consent so
readily?"

He shrugged. "I have already told you what *he* said. I
merely asked his consent to our marriage and assured him that
if he honored me with your hand, I would always make your
welfare my primary concern."

Belinda stared very hard at the man who would marry her to
save her cousin's—and her own—reputation, but that handsome face was a closed book to her probing intellect. If he
were to be believed, there had been no need to swear undying
affection; a mere promise to take care of her had been sufficient to gain her father's consent to give his daughter to a perfect stranger. For reasons as yet only dimly perceived, Belinda
experienced a rush of furious indignation to her brain strong
enough to make her light-headed. She did not trust herself to
speak but stood stock-still staring into space with her lips
pressed together while she endeavored to assimilate the fact
that she was of no real importance to anyone in the world, certainly not to this man who sought to marry her, and apparently
not even to her father if he could so lightly pass her into another's keeping.

Captain Wainright's voice brought her partway back to the
present. "If I have judged Lady Ilchester's nature correctly,
she will be timing this interlude. I am persuaded you will
agree that it will not do to let her accuse us of forgetting the
proprieties yet again in the grip of unrestrained passion, so
may I suggest that we proceed to wherever she is lying in wait
in order that we may make our happy announcement?"

Belinda turned blank eyes to his cold, perfect face and
barely repressed a shudder at the bitterness underlying his
grim humor. After a moment she laid her fingers on his ex-

tended arm and they proceeded in silence to the saloon where Deirdre and Lady Ilchester awaited them. Just before they entered the room he said in smooth tones, "Loath though I am to begin our betrothal on a carping note, I feel that this charade has no chance of succeeding if you will persist in presenting a face of tragedy to the world."

If Belinda's eyes had been daggers he'd have died on the spot, but the anger she needed to control gave her a pretty color as they joined the other women.

Apparently Captain Wainright's announcement passed muster because Deirdre and Lady Ilchester pressed felicitations upon the couple. As she struggled to produce acceptable phrases of appreciation, Belinda wondered if the hypocrisy of the whole affair was as nauseating to her temporary fiancé as it was to her. Any tendency to refine upon this thought was brought to a halt by Lady Ilchester's proposal to send off an immediate notice of the betrothal to the newspapers.

"Naturally my father will see to that when I return to Millgrove." Belinda turned to her cousin. "I shall go home as soon as you are well enough to travel to London, Dee."

"Well enough? Have you been ill, Lady Archer?" Captain Wainright turned a concerned gaze on Deirdre, who looked her usual beautiful self in a white muslin gown with a cherry red sash tied about her slender waist and grosgrain ribbon in the same color edging each of three flounces at the hemline.

"Did Sir John not inform you that my sister-in-law suffered a miscarriage a few days ago?"

"A miscarriage!" Shock rang out in the captain's voice as he looked from Lady Ilchester to Deirdre. "You never . . . I mean, I did not know—"

"No one outside the family knew I was increasing," Deirdre said hastily, cutting off any injudicious words her cicisbeo might utter in his present state of shocked disbelief, "but as you can see, I am recovering nicely and will soon be able to join my husband in town." She turned away from him then to address her cousin. "Will my uncle send his traveling carriage for you, Bel?"

"I shall write to him as soon as you make your own plans."

"I fear that it will not be possible for you to return to Gloucestershire in the immediate future," Captain Wainright said to his betrothed, wrenching his eyes away from Lady Archer, all expression wiped from his face as he explained, "I am sorry to have to tell you that your little brothers and two of the maids have contracted scarlet fever. Millgrove is quarantined at present. Your father and I had our meeting in the shrubbery. I never even entered the house."

"Why did you not tell me this earlier?" Belinda cried, jumping to her feet. "I must return home at once, on the stage if necessary. They will need me at Millgrove. Oh, those poor babies! I must pack—Dee, will you send Polly to—"

"No, Belinda," Captain Wainright said, stepping into her path and seizing both her hands as the agitated girl would have dashed from the room. "Your father does not wish to expose you to the disease." His face hardened as Belinda struggled to pull her hands free. "In fact, he has expressly forbidden you to return home at present."

"Don't be ridiculous," she said impatiently, giving another unavailing tug to gain her release from his grasp. "They will need me to help nurse the boys. My stepmother is of no practical use when the children are sick. She feels their suffering so dreadfully that she makes herself ill also. I can handle the boys better than Nurse, who is getting along in years now. Please, let me go!"

"No, Belinda. Your father told me how it would be when you learned about your brothers' illness. He assured me they are receiving the best of care, but he is concerned also for your health because you were so ill yourself last year and have recently undergone the great strain of nursing your grandmother through her final illness. I gave Sir Walter my solemn word that I would not permit you to go home until he feels all danger of contagion is past, and I intend to keep that promise."

The authority in Captain Wainright's tones had an effect on Belinda, who ceased her struggles as she looked up at him through a film of tears. "B . . . but what am I to do?" she whispered forlornly.

Lady Ilchester spoke up quickly. "It seems to me, Miss Melville, that the obvious course would be to go ahead with your marriage immediately, which would eliminate one of your father's burdens by solving the problem of where you are to go when Deirdre leaves for London. You will naturally go where your husband goes."

"Bel can come with me to London. I am persuaded that she will prefer this to a hasty, scrambling wedding with none of her family present," Deirdre said before either of the two whose future was being planned could comment.

Captain Wainright had released Belinda's hands when Lady Ilchester began speaking. Curiously enough, she had to exercise conscious control to keep from clutching his again as the import of the older woman's words sank in, pushing aside her concern for her little brothers for the moment. "Deirdre is right, of course. I could never consider marrying without my family to support me," she said firmly, emboldened by the need to make her position clear. "I know Ca—Anthony shares my feelings in this matter," she added as a clincher, fixing compelling eyes on her temporary betrothed.

"It pains me to have to disagree with you on any subject, my dear, but I fear I must in this instance. Under ordinary circumstances I do indeed believe that to marry without one's family present would be unthinkable, but changing situations alter cases." Captain Wainright looked away from his dumbstruck fiancée to point his next words at Lady Ilchester. "Belinda and I have had no opportunity to discuss my intention to rejoin my former regiment in Brussels, ma'am. I had expected to leave her safely with her family until my return, but with the uncertain climate at Millgrove I am now leaning toward an early marriage to ensure that she will have the protection of my name while I am away."

"No! I . . . I mean, there is no necessity for such drastic measures surely. A betrothal announcement should be sufficient to acquaint the world with our intention to wed. I . . . I am still in mourning for my grandmother."

"Given *all* the circumstances surrounding this betrothal," Lady Ilchester said with pointed emphasis, "I would not expect you to be so blind to the wisdom, indeed the necessity, of an early marriage."

Belinda's gentle gray eyes darkened with anger at the implied threat and her lips parted, but Captain Wainright spoke before she could utter any impulsive words that could not be retracted.

"I think you forget, ma'am, that Belinda has just this moment learned of a serious situation in her family that could conceivably end in tragedy. It is greatly to her credit that her concern is not for herself but all for them at this time."

Lady Ilchester gave a regal nod. "I do not question that Miss Melville seems to have a very proper regard for the welfare of her family and her duty toward them, but what you have said about Sir Walter Melville's wishes in the matter of her continued absence from her home makes it imperative to settle her future now before you must leave for Belgium."

"I quite concur, and since Lady Archer has been so generous as to offer her cousin a home with her in London for the present, the sensible thing would seem to be for us to marry in the next sennight or so. Obviously I shall have to go to London to procure a special license—"

"You intend to marry Belinda in my house?"

"I assumed that would be your preference," Captain Wainright said with a glinting smile for his perturbed hostess, "but I would not inconvenience you for the world, Lady Archer. If you plan to leave for London in the next few days, I will make arrangements to marry in London. Perhaps Belinda would prefer that?"

Panic rose in Belinda's throat and threatened to choke her at the realization that three persons who cared nothing at all for her preferences behind their civil masks were proposing to arrange her life for her. "No . . . I . . . it is too soon—"

"How thoughtless of me. Of course it is too soon after the distressing news of your brothers' illness to press you for decisions about our wedding. Please forgive me," Captain Wainright put in smoothly, with a convincing air of sympathy. "In fact, I am going to take myself off right now so you may be private and write to your family, for I am persuaded that must be your most pressing desire at this moment. You may wish to tell your father that I plan to obtain a special license to be held in readiness for when we make our decision. Whatever you decide about the location of the ceremony will suit me.

"And now, ladies," he added, turning to include their avidly listening audience in his remarks, "I'll bid you adieu again for a few days and thank you in advance for your assistance to my fiancée in planning our wedding. There is no need to ring for Drummond, Lady Archer; I'll show myself out."

With that, Captain Wainright swept all the women an inclusive bow and raised Belinda's limp hand to his mouth, ignoring the panicky protest rising to her lips as he walked rapidly out of the room.

Chapter Eleven

Rocked though she was by the double blows of bad news from home and the confident talk of an imminent wedding by people who took no notice of her reluctance, Belinda still had the presence of mind to avail herself of the temporary escape route Captain Wainright had provided with his hint that she must wish to write immediately to her family. That had been kind of him; indeed, he had been the source of any compassion existing in that room this afternoon, she acknowledged with some little surprise as she got out a sheet of pressed paper and seated herself at the desk in her room. Lady Ilchester had been bent on arranging the wedding of two near strangers, and Deirdre, now that her particular difficulties had been solved to her satisfaction, was too impatient to get on with her own life to spare much thought for someone else's troubles.

She closed her mind to her personal turmoil while she concentrated on sending a message of love and concern to her beleaguered family. Despite Captain Wainright's recapitulation of her father's feelings on the matter, she begged her parent to allow her to come home to help nurse her brothers, pleading that her own health was markedly improved by long walks in the good, clean air of Somerset. Having relieved her feelings and made her pleas, she brought the epistle to a close without mentioning that Captain Wainright intended to procure a special license in order to marry at once.

This defiance of her betrothed, not that she could think of him in those terms, of course, gave her a secret feeling of independence that did not survive her next meeting with Lady Ilchester at dinner. Her ladyship's calm assumption that a marriage would take place at Archer House within the next sennight, and her readiness to organize the details of the celebration sent Belinda early to her bed with a nervous headache.

The morning brought more of the same as Lady Ilchester sought to pin Belinda down to a time to drive into Taunton to order a gown in which to be married. Deirdre was no help at all, merely stating coldly that she saw no reason why her cousin should be rushed into marriage against her will, and repeating that Belinda was welcome to stay with her in London indefinitely.

"My dear Deirdre, have you given any thought to the awkwardness of your own position if you insist on sheltering someone whom nobody will receive?"

"If she is not received it will be due entirely to your loose tongue since no one else knows about the incident!"

"You are forgetting the servants. What servants know eventually becomes known to their betters. Also, there is my brother to consider. He has a right to be informed about the type of female residing under his roof and being presented to his acquaintances."

At this point Belinda fled to the garden, leaving the sisters-in-law to continue their quarrel alone.

In her haste to escape, she went out without hat or shawl, but the air was balmy and she held up her face to the sun, feeling her tensions draining away under its beneficent rays. A glimpse of golden daffodils at the edge of the home wood lured her in that direction. Thanks to dedicated gardeners of the past, she was transported over the green velvet lawn toward a sunny sea of daffodils, its breaking waves fringed in creamy narcissus. Feasting her eyes, Belinda strolled into the stand of trees surrounded by massive rhododendrons just coming into their glory. In the midst of so much beauty some of the stiffness in her shoulders eased and the pounding in her temples subsided as she wandered about the estate with no destination in mind, deliberately electing as far as possible to suppress all thought. Closing off her mind brought the other senses sharply into play and she was contentedly conscious of the woodland scents and the myriad sounds of insect and animal life, much of which was not even visible to the casual eye.

It had been nearly lunchtime when she had come outdoors, but no repast in company with Deirdre and Lady Ilchester held much appeal. Belinda had no clear idea how long she wandered about the grounds, but it was the rumblings of her empty stomach that finally drove her back to the house. She returned by a path that circled around the back of the stable block and joined one at the corner of the formal garden. Conscious of heated cheeks and an untidy head after repeated brushes with greenery, she had the intention of entering by the side door and getting to her room by a back stairway to freshen her appearance before going into the saloon. She was about to turn off toward this door when her name was called.

Sir John Hanks, coming from the direction of the stables, approached her with his long stride when she halted and turned.

"Good afternoon, Miss Melville. This is a piece of good fortune. I have dropped in at teatime in the hope of seeing and speaking with you."

"How do you do, sir. Is it really so late? I have been walking about the grounds admiring the spring plantings and have quite lost track of the time." Aware of a close scrutiny from Sir John's intelligent eyes, she raised a self-conscious hand to her temple and smoothed back an errant strand of hair. "I fear I am far too untidy to present myself in the saloon without first making repairs."

"Don't go in just yet, please, Miss Melville. You look charmingly ruffled but a bit fatigued perhaps. Shall we sit on that stone bench beyond the hedges while you gather your strength for climbing the stairs?" He guided her to the seat, saying with a self-mocking twist to his finely cut mouth, "In general, I am much quicker to take the hint when my company is not desired, but you have been much in my thoughts since Captain Wainright informed me this morning that he was off to London to purchase a special license so that you two might marry immediately."

He paused fractionally as she drew back and dropped her glance to her clasped hands in her lap, then went on when she kept silent, his marvelous voice very earnest. "I hope you know that I wish to be your friend. I have felt right from our first meeting that we could become good friends."

This time when he paused, Belinda raised her eyes and met his concerned look squarely. "Thank you," she said simply. "I have felt that way too."

"Then do you think you might confide in me—at least to the extent of calming my fears that there could be an element of . . . coercion involved in this sudden decision? I wish you to know that you may freely command my services—anything I can do to assist you, I shall do gladly."

"Thank you," she said again, her pewter eyes eloquent of gratitude. Her lip quivered and she looked away, obviously waging an internal battle. He did not press her and after a while she took a deep breath. "What explanation did Captain Wainright give for his actions?"

"A sketchy one at best. He said that after you decided to marry he went to Gloucestershire to obtain your father's consent. There he learned that your brothers had contracted scarlet fever. Rather than risk your health by allowing you to return to a house of contagion, he and your father determined that you should wed immediately by special license. You would then go to stay with your cousin in London and he would rejoin his regiment in Brussels."

"I . . . see."

"Is it true . . . substantially?"

"It is true . . . partially," Belinda said after a long pause.

"Ah."

The single syllable was pronounced with a questioning inflection, and after a moment Belinda stopped gnawing on her bottom lip and spoke quickly. "We had decided to marry, and my father gave his consent. He did say I wasn't to return home while the house was quarantined, but the special license was entirely—almost entirely—Captain Wainright's idea."

"*Almost* entirely," Sir John repeated. When this produced no amplification, he went on, "If you had the air of happy anticipation common to brides, I would wish you happy and retire, but I do not think this is the case. If I am wrong, you have only to tell me, and that will be the end of it."

"No . . . I . . . I did not agree to a quick marriage, but Captain Wainright and Lady Ilchester are determined . . ." Her voice trailed off and Sir John took her chin in his fingers and turned her gently to face him.

"How should they impose their will on you? What is this all about, Belinda?"

The deliberate use of her given name seemed to break down Belinda's resistance. "Lady Ilchester's maid saw Captain Wainright . . . and me in a . . . a compromising situation," she said in a lifeless voice. "According to Lady Ilchester, we must marry at once if I am not to lose my reputation."

Sir John's eyes narrowed as he contemplated her downcast face. "And Wainright agrees that this is necessary?"

"Yes."

"Ah . . . well, that would seem to limit your options." He released her chin and gently ran the back of his finger down her cheek, though he did not look at her directly, and he seemed lost in thought. "I believe I can comprehend your reluctance to marry so quickly," he said at last, "given that Wainright has been rather obviously taken with Lady Archer's charms of late." He pretended unawareness of her slight wince and continued, choosing his words with care. "You are young, not a child, but not, I believe, very experienced in dealing with men, apart from family members.

"I daresay relatively few marriages are based on so-called romantic love, although that would be most people's desire perhaps, at least, most young women's desire. These other unions, perhaps because they do not have unreasonable expectations, are often very successful in time, and contrarily, love matches quite often founder on the rocks of the unromantic day-to-day problems of living." He paused and said apologetically, "Forgive me if I sound as if I am preaching. Does what I have said make sense to you?"

"You are saying that I should not allow the fact that Captain Wainright is madly in love with my cousin to deter me from marrying him," Belinda replied, giving him a challenging look.

"Oh, no, my dear. I would not presume to tell you what to do," he said coolly, "but you are mistaken in thinking Wainright is in love with your cousin; he is infatuated with her, which is vastly different."

"Different . . . how?"

"Infatuation has nothing to do with the basic qualities of the adored object, who is perceived through a mind-dulling haze of desire as absolute perfection. When reason succeeds in intruding on such an unreasoning passion, it vanishes as swiftly as it arose."

"Suppose reason never does intrude?"

"It must eventually—we humans cannot long exist on that heightened emotional plane. It consumes one."

Belinda had listened attentively to Sir John's philosophy, her eyes grave. Now she rose and offered her hand and a small smile as he, perforce, got to his feet. "I must go in now. Thank you for your concern for my future, sir."

"May I say just one more thing, Belinda? One gets to know a man pretty thoroughly in wartime conditions. I lived and fought beside Anthony Wainright for four years and I tell you truthfully that it would be impossible to find a better fellow. He has a good heart, which can be said about few of us who dwell in this vale of tears, and he is a man of honor and principle." As Belinda preserved an unconvinced silence, he added, "This affaire with Lady Archer is an aberration. After years in the midst of cruel suffering and wretchedness that displayed all man's baser nature, the first sight of your beautiful cousin must have done something to him, affected him so powerfully that it blotted out the past. It sounds ridiculous to say he saw her as his salvation, but I cannot find another way to explain what has happened to him. One doesn't readily abandon such a dream, but reality will creep in eventually and push insubstantial dreams aside. One day he will see clearly again, I promise you."

Belinda summoned up Sir John's reassuring words frequently over the next difficult days as Lady Ilchester continued to act as though the marriage were a foregone conclusion.

"If Deirdre still feels unable to drive out as yet, I shall be pleased to take you to Taunton to commission a suitable gown for your wedding," she offered on the third day of Captain Wainright's absence.

"But I am still in mourning, ma'am," Belinda objected.

"I assure you, my dear Miss Melville, that your grandmother would wish you to look your best on your wedding day, and as your parents cannot be here, I should like to make you a gift of the gown in their stead."

"Th . . . that is most generous of you, ma'am, but I could not allow . . . I could not accept such a gift."

"Nonsense," Lady Ilchester said with one of those indulgent laughs that never rang true, "I am only too happy to play the role of your guardian in the unusual circumstances; in fact, I insist, so let us have no more discussion on that account."

After an imploring look to her cousin, who continued to sit silent and stony-faced, Belinda subsided and did her best to infuse some warmth into her expressions of gratitude of Lord Archer's formidible sister.

Deirdre had plenty to say that evening when she came into Belinda's room before going down to dinner, with a curt word, dismissing Polly, who was bustling about picking up discarded clothing. "So you have let that dreadful woman force you into marriage," she began the second the door closed behind the maid. "She has but to offer to buy your wedding dress and you capitulate."

Belinda gave her sneering cousin a level look but did not deign to rebut this accusation. "What would you have me do?" she asked quietly. "I cannot go home and I cannot go to London unless I wed Captain Wainright."

"Of course you may come to London. Archer won't listen to Lydia's tales. He'll scotch her gossiping tongue."

"Are you so certain he would even if it were possible?" Belinda asked, sensing the uncertainty beneath Deirdre's bravado. She shook her head. "I have no choice."

"That's not what you said a few days ago. You as much as said you'd rather lose your reputation than marry Anthony."

"A few days ago I had a home to run to where I could be safe from the gossip. That is all changed now."

"It's my belief that all that protesting you did was just a lot of fustian! I think you've really wanted to marry Anthony all along, but it won't do you any good. He's in love with me!"

"What a dog in the manger you are," Belinda said pleasantly, preserving her composure until Deirdre had stormed out of the room, whereupon she collapsed onto her bed, shaking like an aspen.

Belinda's set-to with her cousin did nothing to improve the atmosphere at Archer Hall, and she was more than willing to go off to Taunton the next day with Lady Ilchester in her carriage. It was second nature to her ladyship to maintain the decorous flow of impersonal inconsequentialities common between slight acquaintances, so there were no awkward silences to suffer through. Indeed, the older woman took pains to set Belinda at her ease, and the latter's thanks for an enjoyable day when they returned in late afternoon were quite sincere.

It was pleasant to drive about the pretty town, calling in at the best shops and partaking of an excellent luncheon at a delightful inn. Belinda made a few necessary purchases, among them three pairs of stockings manufactured in nearby Glastonbury. The gown that Lady Ilchester ordered for the wedding ceremony was to be made up in a supple silk of a creamy white that warmed Belinda's pale skin. The simple lines suited her admirably, but her ladyship ordered that the brief bodice and puffed sleeves be embellished by designs composed of pearls, which considerably increased the price. She brushed aside Belinda's protest with the laughing rejoinder that she had

never dressed a daughter and was hugely enjoying the rare opportunity and must not on any account be thwarted. The only
really embarrassing moment was when Lady Ilchester was
bent on presenting her charge with a night rail the like of
which Belinda had never dreamed, a diaphanous pale pink creation fashioned of a silk so delicate as to be nearly transparent.
Belinda blushed and protested that she could never wear such
a garment; her ladyship laughed and insisted on having her
way. After impressing the necessity for speed upon the dress-
maker, who promised to send out the completed gown in three
days, the ladies returned to the waiting carriage and headed
back to Archer Hall, more in charity with each other than at
any previous time in their acquaintance, at least on the surface.
Though she chided herself for her own ungenerous spirit, Belinda could not entirely allay the unchartable suspicion that
Lady Ilchester's present magnanimity sprang from some
source other than a generous heart. For some incalculable reason it suited her to play fairy godmother to a girl for whom she
had no real liking and whose character she demonstrably held
in contempt.

For Belinda, the next two days had a peculiar air of unreality about them. Perhaps she should not be surprised at this;
after all, she was about to act in a manner inconsistent with her
beliefs by marrying a man for the wrong reasons. Moreover,
she was going to marry a man who had taken her in dislike and
was yearning to possess another woman. Oddly, no one else
seemed to see anything abhorrent or even unusual in the situation. Everyone treated her as if they believed her to be the happiest of expectant brides, and behaved as though she and
Captain Wainright were the best-matched pair since Adam and
Eve. She found herself stealing looks at the servants when she
passed them in the halls, but no one appeared the least bit self-
conscious in her presence. Did they see nothing out of the ordinary or were they simply too well trained to betray unseemly
interest in the eccentric behavior of their masters? A pity she
was not so well schooled—she felt somehow divided in two
with the intelligent half of her unconcernedly observing that
foolish creature uselessly twisting and turning in the trap that
was inexorably tightening about her.

Belinda was dreading Sir John's dinner, where she could
expect to run the gauntlet of well-wishers concealing their curiosity behind polite smiles and felicitations. Lady Ilchester set

the ball rolling by asking Belinda that afternoon what she planned to wear to the party. On being told that she intended to wear the gray with the black bands, her ladyship protested, "My dear child, you ought to wear the sapphire gown for such an important occasion."

"I am still in deep mourning, ma'am."

"But this evening is unique, and since you have already worn the blue on one occasion at least, that consideration should not weigh too heavily with you." As startled comprehension sent rich color racing up under Belinda's fair skin, Lady Ilchester went on in coaxing tones, "Besides, I am persuaded that Captain Wainright deserves to have his betrothed looking her best when he presents her to his friends."

"Very well, ma'am, I'll wear the sapphire gown."

"I trust you did not plan to wear your blue dress, Deirdre," her ladyship said with a gay laugh, "for, I vow, people will be unable to tell you two apart."

"I am going to wear yellow," Deirdre replied through gritted teeth.

Put on her mettle by Lady Ilchester's veiled malice, Belinda gave Polly free rein with her hair that evening. The girl spent her spare time improving her favorite skill by dressing the heads of the other maids at the Hall, and she was in her element, brushing and rolling and pinning to her heart's content. The results merited the lavish praise her mistress bestowed on her as the maid moved the hand mirror carefully so that Belinda could see the cascade of curls at the back falling from an intricately swirled topknot. Since her mistress possessed no hair ornaments, Polly had to be content with weaving a matching satin ribbon into her creation for the final touch.

The effect, Lady Ilchester later assured Belinda, was delightful, and she ventured to predict that Captain Wainright would find his betrothed lovelier than he dreamed possible, Belinda could not deny the secret wish that this improbability should be true, and she despised herself for her weakness.

Deirdre was still sulking and Belinda was intent on achieving a serene appearance during the drive to Hilltop House. Even Lady Ilchester maintained a rare silence, seemingly absorbed in private ruminations.

Sir John's home turned out to be a beautifully proportioned building or rosy brick that looked to have been built in the middle of the last century. As its name promised, it was situated on an eminence that offered a distant view of the Bristol Channel on a clear day, Sir John told an admiring Belinda as he welcomed his guests at the entrance. Captain Wainright, standing slightly behind his friend, glanced quickly from one cousin to the other before coming forward to raise Belinda's hand to his lips.

"You look very charming tonight," he murmured before greeting Lady Ilchester and Deirdre with smiling courtesy.

"Do you know, I nearly had to browbeat this young woman into wearing what I am persuaded must be your favorite gown, Captain Wainright," Lady Ilchester said with an arch smile that made Belinda long to strangle her.

"Yes . . . it is indeed," the captain replied readily, just before Lady Barton, who was acting as Sir John's hostess, took the women off to remove their wraps.

The drawing room where Sir John's guests were gathered was a large rectangular apartment boasting a delicately patterned plaster ceiling in the style of Robert Adam. The same garlands decorated the graceful marble fireplace surround and were repeated in the good-sized carpet in the center of the room. The greens and golds against a creamy background had faded somewhat from their original splendor, as had the upholstery on sofas and chairs, but the furniture looked soft and inviting.

The evening was not nearly the ordeal Belinda had anticipated. All the guests were people she had met on similar occasions in the past weeks. Their felicitations seemed heartwarmingly genuine, though there were one or two good-natured accusations of slyness for concealing their courtship so thoroughly. When a dowager expressed surprise at the swiftness of the wedding, Captain Wainright, who had remained at Belinda's side like the adoring fiancé he was purported to be, made a touching story of Belinda's father's determination to keep her from being exposed to infection.

Unused to being the center of attention, Belinda was somewhat uncomfortable at first, but her shyness did her no disservice in the eyes of the respectable matrons who had occasionally raised disapproving eyebrows at young Lady Archer's free and easy manner with the gentlemen. Why, even tonight, less than a fortnight after losing her expected child, here she was shamelessly flirting with all the younger men in the room. Miss Melville might look enough like her cousin to be taken for her twin, but under the skin she was cut from a different bolt of goods. Some of the matrons recalled that Captain Wainright had seemed as bowled out by Lady Archer's extravagant charms as any of the other young fools, but obviously he'd been quick to spot the sweetness of expression that distinguished Miss Melville from her more vivacious cousin and betokened a sweeter nature. A sensible girl too by all evidence; they agreed that she would make him a good wife, and patted her hand maternally in their turn.

With so much goodwill directed at herself and Captain Wainright, Belinda would have had to be churlish indeed not to respond, despite her basic unhappiness. If she did not achieve the fabled radiance of a bride, there was yet a soft glow about her that was very appealing.

When the gentlemen rejoined the ladies in the drawing room after their port and cigars, Belinda was ensconced among the dowagers, who were plying her with good advice to take into her married life. Through the veil of her lashes she saw her cousin beckon to Captain Wainright. After a barely perceptible hesitation he walked over to the sofa she shared with Lady Barton just as that lady rose to seek out her husband. Deirdre patted the spot beside her but he did not avail himself of the invitation, standing in front of her during the conversation so that she got up after a moment with a smile and shook his arm playfully. He remained talking with her for better than five minutes, but Deirdre's smiles and flirtatious glances met with a grave courtesy on his part that Belinda had not before observed in his manner toward her cousin. She deliberately turned her shoulder on the tableau. His formality meant nothing. Naturally he would not wish to be seen flirting with Deirdre on the eve of his wedding. To his credit, Captain Wainright had given an impeccable performance as a happily betrothed man tonight—it was one more sacrifice he was prepared to make for the woman he adored.

Presently Captain Wainright sought out his fiancée and piloted her from group to group during the remainder of the evening, honoring her with a smiling attentiveness that must have seemed convincing to the other guests. Even if his actions were dictated mainly by his desire to shield Deirdre, he was demonstrating a concern for his intended bride's sensibilities that promised some of the kindness of heart for which Sir John had commended him.

Late in the evening while waiting for the Archer carriage to be called, Belinda and Captain Wainright found themselves inadvertently eavesdropping on Lady Ilchester in conversation with two of the older couples present.

"Yes, a beautifully matched couple." Lady Ilchester's well-modulated tones rose above her companions' less distinct voices. "Belinda is such a lovely girl—I declare I have grown prodigiously fond of her these past weeks. She will suit Captain Wainright perfectly. Such a pity her family was prevented from arranging her wedding, but I have tried to do what they would wish for their daughter."

Belinda's eyes flew to her fiancé's face as he pulled her a little beyond hearing range. "And they say eavesdroppers never hear good of themselves," Captain Wainright said with mocking humor.

"Lady Ilchester has been trying to give the impression that she is fond of me, but I know she thinks me lacking in principles and decorum," Belinda replied with a little shiver.

"She is leaving no stone unturned on her brother's behalf."

Belinda's eyes fell at the grimness in his expression but in a moment they rose again when he said hurriedly, "There isn't much time left, but I have wished to tell you—to assure you that I do understand how distasteful this whole situation is for you, and how difficult. I just wanted you to know that you have nothing to fear tomorrow. I would not dream of taking advantage of your loyalty to your cousin—in short, do not be afraid that I will expect to consummate this forced marriage."

Serious blue eyes looked deeply into shadowed gray ones for a long moment; then Belinda said softly, "Thank you."

Chapter Twelve

Belinda did not sleep well the night before her wedding. Depleted of all the nervous energy that had sustained her throughout the evening, she had felt exhausted in the carriage on the way home from Hilltop House, but her limbs would not relax when she got into bed and her eyes refused to stay closed. Also, her mind refused to empty itself of apprehensions about the future. It was no use telling herself that all girls must feel this way on the eve of their marriage, even those eagerly looking forward to beginning a new life with the man of their choice where mutual affection prevailed. The finality about her old life as of tonight was chillingly complete and she could see no source of happiness or reasonable satisfaction in the foreseeable future. Far from sharing a home with a loving husband, she was to reside under the roof of a cousin whose tastes and interests were incompatible with her own, and who had been constrained to make the offer. Deirdre had needed her at Archer Hall, but Belinda's usefulness had ended with the sham miscarriage. In London she would be an incubus to her pleasure-loving cousin, as well as an irritating reminder of Deirdre's near disaster.

Perhaps it would not be long before she would be able to return to Millgrove, and the capital itself would offer much to interest her. There would be some compensations for an enforced stay in Deirdre's house. She would not permit herself to fall into a fit of the dismals.

Belinda's thoughts roamed no further than a fairly brief sojourn in London. She did not allow herself to think about an eventual life as Anthony Wainright's wife. She had wasted quite enough time air dreaming about a splendid future with the fairy-tale prince who had kissed her on her fifteenth birthday, nearly five years of her life.

"Oh, my goodness!" she whispered, sitting bolt upright in bed as she began a mental scramble to recall the date. She had been so burdened by recent events that she had lost track of the time. After a moment of intense cogitation, Belinda was in possession of the final piece of irony:

She was going to marry her tarnished prince on her twentieth birthday.

Belinda's wedding day left nothing to be desired in the way of nature's favors. A cloudless blue sky and sweet, warm air greeted her on arising. As a bonus, when Polly came in with a cup of chocolate she brought her mistress a letter from home on the tray. Belinda fell on it with a little cry of pleasure. Perhaps her father had had a change of heart about permitting her to come home.

Belinda's eyes were misty when she refolded her letter a few moments later and took a sip of her chocolate. Her father had written in a loving manner, pleased and proud that she wished to curtail her wonderful visit but, though he thought the boys to be out of danger now, still adamant about keeping her away from Millgrove for the present. He had gone on to wish her a happy birthday and to inquire after her cousin's health, which reminded Belinda that she had neglected to inform her family about Deirdre's supposed loss. She would have to put that in her next letter home. There seemed to be no end to the deceit she was constrained to practice on those dearest to her these days.

It was the final part of her father's letter that had brought the tears crowding behind her eyelids. Sir Walter had expressed regret for the wretched circumstance under which he had been compelled to receive Captain Wainright and had gone on to assure her that he had been favorably impressed by the man's bearing and breeding. He was relieved that her intended husband was not a fumbling, tongue-tied youth, but a sensible and articulate person. He was sorry that she would have an anxious period while her betrothed returned to the army, but he quite appreciated the determination of the men who had fought Napoleon's forces for years to see the tyrant defeated once and for all. He and her stepmother looked forward to Captain Wainright's return to England when they would be pleased and happy to plan for her wedding.

Guilt and shame tormented Belinda, adding to her unhappiness as she forced herself to drink the chocolate and later went

through the process of getting ready for the late-morning ceremony. Gratefully she allowed Polly to manage the business,
following the young maid's quiet-voiced directions like an au-
tomaton. Somewhere in the deep recesses of her mind she realized that Polly had matured since coming to Archer Hall. She
had always been conscientious and quick to learn, but the experience of living in a large country house had increased her
confidence. Also, she possessed an intuitive awareness of Belinda's state of mind that regulated her flow of chatter and the
amount of assistance she offered in making selections and getting her mistress dressed. Belinda clung to her abigail's hand
for a second as she prepared to leave her room, thanking her in
halting words.

"That's all right, Miss Belinda. You keep your chin up
today; you look every inch a bride, just the way you should."

Belinda's rare smile appeared for an instant as she squared
her shoulders and headed for the saloon. Neither Deirdre nor
Lady Ilchester had come near her this morning, for which
blessing she was grateful, but both were in the saloon when
the footman sprang to open the door for her a few moments
later. Two pairs of critical feminine eyes assessed her appearance thoroughly.

"My dear Belinda, you look charming," Lady Ilchester said
approvingly, "sweet and solemn as befits a bride."

"That is a pretty dress, Bel, but it washes you out. Your
maid should have applied some rouge." Deirdre herself was
vividly beautiful in the red gown and matching bonnet and
spencer she planned to travel in.

"A painted bride is not to everyone's taste," Lady Ilchester
retorted, adding, "Your pearls and the wreath of silk roses that
we found in Taunton make the perfect finishing touches for
the costume, Belinda. Have you your gloves? Oh, yes, I see
you have. Good. Here is Drummond to tell us the carriage is
waiting, I make no doubt. Are you ready, girls?"

Another irony, Belinda reflected as they descended to the
carriage. Neither she nor Deirdre was "ready" for what this
day would bring. Stop whining, she admonished herself
sharply. There would be no last-minute rescue. She must simply keep her composure and carry on.

The drive to the church in the village was mercifully short
for the three women confined together in closer proximity than
any of them would choose freely. Belinda had visited it on one

of her walks that took her through the village so it did not seem strange to her, and she had met the vicar on two occasions also.

Captain Wainright and Sir John were waiting when the ladies entered the church, which had been decorated with several magnificent flower arrangements. Sir John presented the bride with a bouquet of pink-and-white hothouse roses from the groom before rejoining his friend at the altar. The heady perfume of the roses remained with her, but the vicar's sonorous voice reading the familiar service made little lasting impact. Belinda was overwhelmingly conscious of the utter strangeness of standing beside the strong, still figure of Anthony Wainright and trying to comprehend that the beautiful words applied to the two of them. After one swift look at his stern, carved features as she approached the altar, she had been unable to lift her leaden lashes again, not even when he took her icy hand in his and slipped a gold ring on her finger. Captain Wainright made his responses in clear uninflected tones; her own were nearly inaudible as her knees threatened to buckle. Why was everything taking so long? She identified slight jangling sounds as coming from Deirdre's bracelets but did not register the vicar's last words. Her lashes flew up when she found herself being drawn up against Captain Wainright's body by his hands gripping her upper arms, but she caught no more than a flash of the electric blue of his eyes before his mouth came down on hers, warm and firm.

Belinda was as bemused by this kiss as she'd been by the first one they'd shared five years ago. When she glanced up after he released her and stepped back, she saw that his eyes were not focused on her. She did not have to turn her head even one inch to know that Deirdre, standing at her side, was the recipient of that burning regard. Nothing could have been more efficacious in steadying her shaking limbs. Her chin came up and she met his eyes calmly when they came back to her. He offered his arm and she placed her hand on it, concealing her reluctance for the contact.

Belinda was surprised and touched when they exited the church to find a number of villagers gathered in front to offer felicitations to the bridal pair. Captain Wainright, helping her into Sir John's carriage for the return to the Hall, raised his brows as she waved to a woman standing with her arm around a young lad of about ten years.

"Do you know all these people?"

"Not well, of course; they are villagers whom I have met and talked with during my walks about the area."

"It was . . . rather pleasant to have people wishing us well."

"Yes." Belinda could think of nothing to add until she became aware again of the perfume of the roses in her bouquet. "Thank you for the lovely roses," she said with a tentative smile.

"Jack said you were particularly fond of flowers—most women are, I daresay."

Belinda's smile faded and she angled her head the tiniest bit to direct her gaze out the coach window. "I daresay."

That was the extent of the conversation between the newly wedded pair for the rest of the short drive. As they pulled to a stop in front of the double staircase at Archer Hall, Captain Wainright observed, "I believe we had a head start on Jack and the ladies."

The carriage door was opened by Drummond at that point, obviating the need for any reply. Captain Wainright exited first and helped Belinda to descend. Drummond permitted himself a small smile, an unheard of occurrence. "May I offer my felicitations on your marriage, Captain Wainright, Mrs. Wainright?"

"You may indeed, Drummond." Captain Wainright was smiling as he released Belinda's hand. The smile disappeared as his eyes fell on the heavily laden carriage and the armed groom on horseback just ahead in the drive. "That is Lady Archer's carriage?"

Drummond was saved from the necessity of replying by the arrival just then of Lady Ilchester's carriage, which he hurried to greet.

Belinda had spotted Meritt coming down the staircase carrying Deirdre's Moroccan leather jewel case. She arrived at the bottom just as her mistress was assisted out of Lady Ilchester's carriage by Sir John.

Deirdre sauntered over to the bridal couple and said with a glittering smile, "Well, I am off to London at last."

"B . . . but are you not coming inside for the wedding breakfast?" Belinda asked.

Deirdre's tinkling laugh rang out. "Do not be foolish, Bel, you know I can never eat before a long drive if I am not to be ill on the road. I'll see you in a few days, I expect." As she made a show of embracing her nonplussed cousin, Deirdre whispered in her ear, "You forgot to thank me for helping you to get what you never could have achieved on your own."

Stung, Belinda pulled back as Deirdre, still smiling brilliantly, turned to give her hand to Captain Wainright. Her cousin's farewells to the others did not penetrate her fierce concentration on reasserting control over her expression. She'd have remained rooted to the spot had not Captain Wainright pulled her forward as the party gathered around the viscount's crested traveling carriage to wave Lady Archer off.

As the matched team of grays set off at the crack of the coachman's whip, Sir John said cheerfully, "I don't know about the rest of you, but I am famished."

Lady Ilchester took her cue and herded the remaining three up the stairs, all the while exchanging bright comments on the recent wedding scene with Sir John in a praiseworthy attempt to create a festive mood after Deirdre's abrupt departure. Belinda tried to cooperate, responding to the best of her ability to all remarks made to her during the lengthy meal that followed, but she was never able to recall any of the details of the occasion afterward.

Lord Archer's chef had surpassed himself in the bridal couple's honor according to the others, but the few mouthfuls she managed to swallow sank like lead shot to the pit of her stomach. She smiled through Sir John's toast to the happy couple and kept it pasted on her lips during Captain Wainright's reply, though the words were just disconnected sounds that reached her ears but not her brain.

At last Sir John took his leave after again wishing the bridal pair happy, his thin attractive face expressing real affection for both. Captain Wainright excused himself to walk with his friend to the entrance, and Lady Ilchester, who had called her carriage for half after two, repaired to her quarters to check that her maid had followed all her instructions to the letter.

For the first time since Polly had awakened her that morning, Belinda was alone. She continued to sit unmoving at table, thankful for the solitude but too drained to take the slightest action. She looked up in surprise when Captain Wainright and Lady Ilchester returned within seconds of each other sometime later. Lady Ilchester was ready to depart, and the newly wedded pair escorted her down to her carriage where Captain Wainright bade her a formal adieu and stepped back to allow the women to say their good-byes unencumbered by a masculine audience. Drummond stood at the open carriage door a few feet away.

Lady Ilchester held out her hand. "Good-bye, Belinda and please accept my sincere wishes for success in your marriage."

"Thank you, ma'am, and once again I thank you for this beautiful gown; it is a magnificent gift."

Her ladyship waved away this earnest gratitude with one gloved hand, saying with unwonted bitterness, "Do not thank me for that; I'd have paid one hundred times that trumpery sum to protect my brother's honor had this been possible, but I did what I could to salvage the situation."

"Wh . . . what are you saying?" Belinda pulled back, but Lady Ilchester retained a grip on her hand.

"Do not imagine for one minute that I was taken in by your misguided loyalty to your trollop of a cousin. It was not you embracing that man in Deirdre's bedchamber. Once Captain Wainright supported the story, however, there was just enough of a possibility that my besotted brother would believe a tearful, injured wife that I dared not denounce her. All I could do was take advantage of the opportunity that ludicrous story offered to engineer a marriage that would remove Wainright as a threat to Lucius in the future. That is what you should thank me for, Belinda. I have seen the way you look at him when you believe yourself unobserved. Your cousin has noticed too, but she was powerless to stop what she had set in motion, and now she is hoist with her own petard. Do not look so sick, my girl; your husband is right behind us," her ladyship hissed. "I give you credit for possessing enough feminine guile to win your husband away from your cousin in time—he is not such a difficult proposition, and you have something Deirdre never will possess, a warm heart. I feel I have made an excellent match."

Lady Ilchester patted Belinda's limp hand in a manner that might have appeared maternal to masculine observers, and with a satisfied smile, allowed Drummond to assist her into the carriage.

Belinda remained stationary, her arms at her side, unaware that Captain Wainright had come up beside her. Glancing down at her white face, he said, "Good God, you look ready to swoon. You had best lie down for a while."

Avoiding his eyes, Belinda nodded. "Yes, I believe I should like to rest."

The sun was blindingly bright; it hurt her eyes as she stared at the mountainous flight of steps which wavered oddly in the light. An involuntary sigh escaped her lips.

Captain Wainright, quick to assess the situation, swept his bride into his arms before she could fall, and set off up the stairway at a steady pace. His breathing rate had barely accelerated when he followed Drummond into Belinda's bedchamber and laid her on the bed. "Send for her maid," he instructed.

The next time Belinda saw her husband was when she joined him in the saloon before dinner.

"How are you tonight? You look much better," he said, running an appraising eye over her serene countenance as he walked toward her. Her pale translucent skin was healthy in appearance, and in combination with darkly fringed light gray eyes, provided an intriguing contrast to the black gown she wore.

Belinda nodded as she allowed him to lead her to a chair. "I am perfectly fine, thank you. I have never fainted before in my life—the sun was so blinding—" She stopped, then hurried on, "Polly, my maid, says that you carried me upstairs, Captain Wainright. Thank you."

"Lord, girl, we're *married*! You cannot continue to call me Captain Wainright in that prim tone. My name is Anthony, or Tony, if you prefer."

Belinda blinked at the vehemence in his words, saying pacifically, "I beg your pardon. The trouble is that I don't think of you as Anthony." She stopped again, appalled to realize that the foolish epithet "Apollo" had popped into her head. "Which do you prefer, Anthony or Tony?" she asked quickly to erase the frown gathering on his brow.

"It doesn't signify," he said with a shrug. "They call me Tony at home."

"Where is home? I don't know anything about you, except that Deirdre said that you are a younger son." She regretted mentioning her cousin's name when she saw his mouth thin, but he answered readily.

"My family comes from Hampshire. My father has more or less turned the managing of the estate over to my elder brother, who married last year. Since then, he and my mother have done some traveling in Scotland, where Mama has relatives. They had planned a trip to the Continent this spring, but Bonaparte's escape has stopped that for now. I also have a younger sister, Martha, who is married and lives in Kent. She has two small daughters, babies really.

"How old are you?"

"Six-and-twenty. I know Deirdre is twenty, but I expect you are a bit younger."

Belinda responded to the inquiring tone. "No, that is, I am two months younger than my cousin but I am twenty also—today."

"I'm sorry—that I did not know, I mean. I'm sorry too that I cannot bring you to meet my family just yet—" He broke off with a mirthless laugh. "Let us just say that I'm sorry about a lot of things."

Drummond's entrance to announce dinner at this moment was regarded by the bridal pair with unadmitted relief. It had been heavy weather making conversation, each new topic serving only to illuminate the chasm of ignorance that lay between them.

Because both strove to overcome the awkwardness of their situation, the dinner hour was less unnerving than their earlier conversation. The presence of servants was also a spur to put forth their best efforts to keep the talk flowing. Belinda was genuinely interested in her husband's experiences in the Peninsula, and he obliged by relating several anecdotes reflecting the lighter side of campaigning. They also touched briefly on literature and music, revealing something of their personal tastes in these areas. Belinda relaxed enough to do justice to the chef's offerings, even forsaking her diet to consume a delectable orange cream.

The atmosphere between them had eased considerably by the time they returned to the saloon. When her bridegroom requested that she play for him, Belinda was only too happy to comply. She was never more content than when creating music, and there was also the secondary benefit of precluding conversation to be considered.

She played for over an hour, pleasing herself in the selection since Anthony had declined at the outset to request specific pieces. For a time all her problems were forgotten as she filled the room with beautiful sounds. She had even succeeded in smothering for once that unwanted extra sense that always told her when Anthony Wainright was physically near at hand. Therefore it was almost with a sense of shock that she looked directly into his brooding face as she raised her hands from the keys on finishing a series of Mozart compositions. Her eyes widened in dismay, the peaceful interlude shattered.

"That is one of Deirdre's favorite songs; she sings it magnificently," he said as though the words were forced out of him.

"Yes . . . I . . . I'm sorry." She looked away.

"Why should you be sorry—or even pretend to be? I am persuaded you agree that the sinner has gotten his just desserts."

Belinda clasped her hands together but did not rise to the bait. "I am sorry Deirdre hurt you so badly," she said softly.

"It was not your cousin's fault that I was such a fool. Her father forced her to marry Archer. I suppose I never really accepted that she was actually . . . committed to him. I believe— I hope—if I had known she was carrying his child, I'd have accepted defeat and gone away."

"Deirdre was not carrying a child."

He stared at her composed face. "Of course she was, she lost the child less than a fortnight ago."

Belinda shook her head. "She pretended the miscarriage just as she pretended the pregnancy. When she learned you were coming to Somerset she told her husband she was increasing and too unwell to travel because it was the only way she could remain behind. She sent for me because Lord Archer insisted she have someone to stay with her. He intended to ask Lady Ilchester to come."

"She *planned* our meeting? But she would not come away with me though I begged her often and often."

"She preferred the life Lord Archer offered her," Belinda said shortly.

A muscle twitched in Anthony's cheek, which was pale under its light coating of suntan, and his eyes darkened to steel blue. "You sound disapproving as always, but why should you save your cousin's reputation if you dislike her so much?"

For the first time in her unemotional disclosure, Belinda hesitated. "Deirdre and I have disliked each other all our lives," she said slowly, "but I could not stand idly by and see Lady Ilchester denounce her to Lord Archer."

"Especially if you stood to gain by your noble sacrifice?" he suggested with silky nastiness, his eyes boring into hers.

"Gain! Are you mad? I have been forced into a distasteful marriage!"

"Methinks the lady doth protest too much. It occurs to me that Deirdre may have been right last night when she hinted that you do not find this marriage so distasteful as you pretend. It also occurs to me that you and your cousin are sisters under the skin, both schemers. You don't possess her stunning beauty, but in any other company you would be judged a very pretty girl. I shall probably be the envy of the officer's mess."

The effect of this outrageous speech on his unwanted bride was not perhaps what Captain Wainright might have anticipated. Belinda was reduced neither to tears nor hysterics. She was deathly pale to be sure, but she displayed admirable control of her limbs and her temper as she rose from the piano bench under his sneering regard and headed for the door at a steady pace. As she passed his chair she gave him a direct look that equaled his in disdain and said dispassionately, "You are utterly despicable and I never want to see you again."

A harsh laugh followed her as she continued to the door. "If you say your prayers like a good little girl each night while I am in Belgium you just might get your wish. Meanwhile, I am going out early tomorrow morning. I shall spare you the sight of my despicable face until dinner, when I shall tell you the arrangements I've made for your allowance while I'm away."

The soft click of a closing door was his only answer. Captain Wainright stared balefully at its blank panels for a moment before thrusting himself out of his chair so violently that he dislodged a cushion in the process. He flung this item across the room and stalked over to the table against the wall where Drummond had thoughtfully left a bottle of Lord Archer's best brandy. He took the bottle and one of the glasses and headed for the stairs leading to the elegantly furnished guest suite that had been prepared for the bridal couple.

Belinda's poise did not desert her when she entered her old room and found Polly waiting to get her ready for bed. She submitted docilely to the abigail's ministrations, though she curtailed the nightly hair brushing and declined to don the gauzy night rail Lady Ilchester had bought her. She wished Polly good night in a calm voice and climbed into bed before the girl left. She did not, however, extinguish the light on the table by the bed.

Nor did Belinda remain in her bed, sliding out the moment the door closed behind the maid. She took the precaution of locking that door and the one leading to the dressing room before putting on her wrapper and heading for her desk, carrying the bedside candle. She unlocked a small drawer and removed the money therein, counting it carefully before depositing it in a reticule she took from a drawer in the dressing table. This done, she returned to the desk and wrote a short letter which she added to the money in the reticule. Only then did she climb back into bed, tucking the reticule under her pillow before extinguishing the candle. She did not require light to make her plans.

Polly looked startled the next morning to find her mistress up when she arrived in answer to a summons. Her surprise increased when she cast a surreptitious look at the bed and discovered the gray traveling dress and bonnet reposing thereon.

"Oh, good, Polly, you have brought hot water." As the maid filled the washbowl, Belinda said, "Will you send a message to the stables that I would like to have the gig brought around in an hour?" She began washing her face and arms then, and did not speak again until the abigail handed her a towel, when she said abruptly, "Polly, I am going to Northumberland to visit my old governess. Are you willing to come with me? I may be there some little time."

"Why . . . why yes, o'course, Miss Belinda—I mean, Mrs. Wainright—but I thought we was going to London to stay with Lady Archer."

"I changed my mind. Polly, do you think you could pack up my clothes and yours this morning without anyone finding out? Can you get the cases and keep the housemaids out of this room?"

"I know where the key to the box room is kept," Polly said, "but I reckon it would be best to ask the maid to come early and then pack up after she finishes in here."

"That makes good sense. Now for the hardest part. I have racked my brains but I cannot think of a way to get the baggage away from here without it being seen by Drummond or the footmen. I must tell you that I am hoping Sir John Hanks will drive us to wherever the mail coach departs from, or perhaps the stagecoach."

The maid looked into her mistress's anxious face and thought a moment before saying slowly, "I can bring the bags down one at a time to that back gate you pass on the way to the stables. I could hide them in the shrubbery there and wait for Sir John's man to come, unless you are coming back here in the gig, Miss Belinda?"

"I don't know." Belinda frowned and pulled in the corner of her mouth. "Let us say that if I do not return within two hours, you will bring the baggage to that gate and wait there for a carriage from Hilltop House. Bless you, Polly."

Belinda spent the drive to Hilltop House trying to maintain a casual mien while fretting that Sir John might be away from home.

She was in luck. Sir John's butler showed her into a small study, where she was joined within a couple of minutes by her host, on the point of going out.

"Belinda, this is a pleasant surprise," he said, tossing his gloves onto a side table as he came into the room. "Shall I send for coffee?"

His smile gave her dwindling resolution the necessary boost to begin as she returned it with a rueful one of her own. "Sir John, forgive me for bursting in upon you like this, but you did say if ever I needed help you would be glad to assist me."

"And I meant it," he replied promptly. "What may I do for you?"

"I don't wish to stay with my cousin in London. My old governess has invited me to visit her in Northumberland, and this is what I would like to do. I have nearly ninety pounds left of the money my father gave me, certainly enough for stage fares for my maid and me—I don't know about mail coach—but the problem is in getting to a town where we can meet the stage."

"Why are you running away, Belinda?" he asked bluntly. "Tony would arrange your transport if this were something you two had agreed on. I have every intention of helping you, but you must be completely candid with me."

Judging from the varying emotions crossing Sir John's countenance as she began with the reason for Deirdre's invitation to visit with her, the truth was more than he had bargained for, but he interrupted the tale only once, saying, when she related the incident in her cousin's bedchamber, "I had a strong suspicion it was not you who was caught in a compromising position with Tony. No, don't stop—go on with your story."

His mouth tightened on hearing Deirdre's taunt to her cousin before she left for London and again when Belinda repeated Lady Ilchester's final comments, but he did not speak until she finished detailing the quarrel with her husband.

"You have had a lot to bear," he said. "None of the three has been at any pains to spare your feelings, though I believe Tony hit out at you out of his own pain. Not that that excuses him, of course, but I am persuaded you will find that already he deeply regrets his part in your quarrel."

Belinda's smile was real if not wholehearted as she interrupted Sir John's attempt to heal the breach. "I do understand, really, but you see, I have been thinking over what you told me about infatuation, and suddenly last night 'reason intruded' and I could see clearly that *I* have been infatuated with Anthony Wainright for five years. Last night for the first time I saw him as a very ordinary individual beneath that handsome face, and not one whom I can admire. It felt wonderful to be free of that unreasonable attachment; it took the sting out of Deirdre's and Lady Ilchester's attacks which had made me so miserable just a few hours earlier."

"I am glad; I hated to see you so unhappy, but do you not feel that you and Tony can discuss the whole situation now and perhaps come to a better understanding?"

Belinda shook her head. "No. I meant it when I said I never wished to see Anthony Wainright again. I cannot hold myself completely blameless in this affair—not that I am the schemer he called me—but if I had not clung so obstinately to the hope that he might come to love me instead of Deirdre, perhaps I might have found a way to avoid the marriage. It was only yesterday when I was determined not to stay under Deirdre's roof again that I remembered Miss Fenton's invitation," she added with painful honesty. "Why did I not recall this possibility earlier?

"It is better for Anthony too that we part immediately. I credit him with a sense of responsibility toward me, even though it was his feeling for Deirdre that forced him to assume the role. If I remove myself without his knowing my destination, he will be able to go off to Belgium with a clear conscience about me. Hopefully the separation might make it possible to obtain an annulment at some future time. I have already written to Miss Fenton, and my maid has agreed to accompany me to Northumberland, so if one of your men would drive us to the nearest town where we may make travel arrangements I would be exceedingly grateful."

Sir John's eyes had not budged from Belinda's face during the whole of this speech. If the logic of her argument left him unconvinced, the steady conviction and self-possession with which it was put forth must have persuaded him, for he said, "I am prepared to help you, but only if you accept the stipulation that I shall assume complete responsibility for your journey. You will travel in my coach with my people driving and accompanying you—"

"But I could never impose such an obligation on you!" Belinda cried, aghast at the mere idea of such a degree of indebtedness.

"You must if you wish me to assist you. If you attempted to arrange this lengthy flight on your own, I would feel compelled in your own best interest to inform Tony of your intentions." As Belinda sat seething, he added, "I don't doubt he would intercept you before you had gone half that distance."

Belinda didn't doubt it either. Though she did not scruple to express her indignation at this blatant example of moral blackmail—which condemnation Sir John accepted with a rueful stretch of his mouth—her determination to get away from Archer Hall and Anthony Wainright was too all-consuming to permit the luxury of sweet independence. After a swift discouraging review of her alternatives, she swallowed her pride and accepted her friend's conditions with as good grace as she could manage.

Sir John's quick smile mirrored his understanding of her predicament as he plunged into a discussion of practicalities. He listened unwinkingly to a description of the precautions she had planned to take to cover her tracks, then suggested with convincing diffidence that it might be just as well to simply inform Drummond by message that she was leaving Archer Hall and request his assistance in getting Polly and the baggage to the entrance in good time to be collected.

"Do you think so?" Belinda said doubtfully. "It is just that Anthony might be a trifle . . . put out at first to find me gone so unceremoniously. I do not wish to compromise the servants or you if he should think it not quite the thing to have aided my efforts."

Sir John nobly concealed the certain knowledge of just how "put out" his old comrade would be at the man who enabled his wife to run away as he soothed her anxiety on this point with smooth phrases. He went off to the stables to make his arrangements, leaving Belinda to write two short messages for the gig driver to deliver at Archer Hall, one informing her husband of her decision to leave in polite but distant terms, and the other, couched in rather warmer language, instructing Drummond in the distribution of vails among the servants of the money she was enclosing.

Chapter Thirteen

The solitary horseman crested the rise in the road and pulled his mount to a walk before leaving the road surface to pick his way over springy turf and stop near a large tree. A comprehensive glance around the rural scene revealed that, with the exception of a lumbering farm cart several hundred yards farther along the road, his was the sole human presence at the moment, though there were long-faced sheep grazing in a pasture in the middle distance. He relaxed more deeply into the saddle, relishing the peaceful atmosphere he had once despaired of experiencing again. There was no other place where the air was so sweetly refreshing—he'd dreamed of scenes like this, especially during that endless night before Waterloo which they'd spent shivering in the rain-soaked fields of rye and corn where it was impossible to stay dry.

The rider removed a gray beaver from his head and ran a gloved hand through golden waves, soliciting the currents of air stirring the hair to caress his scalp. He lifted a deeply tanned face to the sun, appreciating as always the difference between the burning blast of the Spanish sun that he'd suffered for several years and England's benevolent rays, which invited communion.

After a few mindless moments of soaking up the sunshine, the horseman sighed and replaced his hat, turning the handsome bay stallion back to the road. His physical well-being had certainly improved tenfold since his return from the Continent last week, he reflected. A pity the English air and climate could not work similar wonders on his moral and personal well-being, currently in a deplorable state of decline. At this point he jolted himself upright mentally. It was more than time to cease wallowing in self-pity and regret and to take stock of his blessings. First and foremost, he had come through one of the bloodiest battles in history without a scratch—an undeserved blessing, considering that the recently acquired habit of morbid musings on his failings had put him in an uncaring frame of mind that disregarded danger. It had not been courage but a darker trait that dared, perhaps even invited, destruction. He should be—and was—humbly thankful that his personal recklessness had not cost the lives of any of his comrades or his men. It had served a purpose at the time, but military commendations could not invest it with value. No point in dwelling on this subject; that part of his life was finished forever. He'd witnessed and participated in enough senseless butchery to last several lifetimes. By rights he should be dead, but since he'd been spared despite himself, it was time to put the gift to some better purpose.

He'd made a right royal mess of his life up to and including the present. From the first instant he'd clapped eyes on Deirdre St. John nearly a year ago, he'd somehow surrendered personal control of his fate without at first being aware of this horrifying condition. He'd been unable to see past Deirdre's beautiful face to care about anything except his consuming desire to possess her. Her marriage to another man had done nothing to bring him to his senses. He'd convinced himself that she had been coerced, that she loved him, not her husband, and most incredible of all, that this last delusion removed any moral impediment from the path of his continued pursuit. Looking back, he still found it nearly impossible to accept that he could have been so willingly self-deceived, so enslaved by a lustful desire that he would toss away his honor with scarcely a twinge of conscience, but so it had been until the advent of Belinda Melville. Those rainwater clear eyes of hers had held up a mirror to his conscience, but gratitude had been the emotion furthest from his heart. He'd resented her knowledge of his adulterous intentions and heartily disliked her for the unspoken but implacable disapproval he always sensed in her.

It was galling to acknowledge his colossal stupidity, but at the time he had believed his Deirdre to embody every feminine grace and virtue; he was blind to any slightest defect in his goddess. Even when the scales had been forcibly torn from his eyes by Deirdre herself with her demand that he shield her reputation at the cost of a loveless marriage to her cousin, he'd convinced himself that his love for her was great enough to encompass the sacrifice. Oddly enough, it was learning of the trick she'd played on her husband to enable her dalliance with him that had finally opened his eyes. He'd been sickened by the callousness that could prompt such a deception, but, typically, had taken out his fury and disgust on Belinda, who had had the temerity to shine the light on Deirdre's shortcomings. Small wonder she had run away from him.

His initial anger upon discovering Belinda's absence had been somewhat forced, though he'd gone through the motions of dressing down Jack for abetting her flight. Although genuinely angry that no argument or threat would persuade Jack to divulge his bride's whereabouts, he'd known its source was a sense of responsibility for Belinda's welfare rather than any desire to see her and try to achieve some sort of peace between them. With the wisdom of hindsight he could now accept that Jack had been correct in insisting that a period of separation was necessary to permit him to come to grips with the realities of his life. At first he'd balked at introspection and avoided any close examination of the affair, but no amount of busyness, military or social, in Brussels had enabled him to banish the subject from his mind for long.

It had been a painful process—perhaps self-revelation always was since it was generally achieved at the cost of the comfortable opinion of one's character that sustained the unthinking majority, to which he belonged. Surprisingly, letting go of his dream of Deirdre had not been difficult in the end. Once he'd acknowledged his own culpability in the affair, her face had faded rapidly from his memory, shaming evidence that what he'd felt for her was infatuation instead of the deathless love he'd believed it to be.

Forgiving himself was another matter, especially since his was not the only life he'd ruined. Belinda had done nothing to deserve her fate. She despised him with good cause, but he was her husband. He'd not managed to get himself killed, which, he recalled with a grimace for the immaturity that had produced the taunt, he'd almost literally promised to do for her. Her face had haunted him for months. It was a lovely face, something he had never wished to concede in his childish resentment of the role she had played in his life. She did not smile very often and had not Deirdre's sparkle and vivaciousness, but there was nothing amiss with her understanding and

there was a sweetness in her manner (except to him) that had
won her many friends in Somerset. He had no doubt that she
would make some man a charming wife if she respected his
character. Unfortunately, he could see no reason why five
months' absence should have produced a change for the better
in her estimation of his own character, but he was resolved to
try to come to a better understanding with her. Her busi-
nesslike farewell note had urged an annulment, but annulments
were not easy to come by, and in any case, he'd just as soon be
married to Belinda as any other female of his acquaintance. He
wasn't in love with her, of course, but that was all to the good.
He never wished to experience that sort of enslavement again.
He would do his best to make Belinda a good husband if she
was willing to give him a chance, and that would content him
quite well.

Anthony had been so intent upon his own thoughts he'd
paid little attention to his surroundings for the last quarter
hour, and now he paused to get his bearings. He was on a
country lane that seemed familiar, which was nonsense; there
must be hundreds of nearly identical lanes all over England.
Trying to recall Belinda's directions when he had gone from
Somerset to Millgrove, he was fairly certain there had been no
longish stretch of similar narrow lane included. Her home was
within a half mile of the road he had taken last time. Leaving
the inn where he'd spent the night, he'd followed the landlord's directions today, cutting across country since he'd been
in no particular hurry and had little taste for wheeled traffic.

He came to a place where the lane met three roads. The
landlord had told him to go toward the village of Denton,
where anyone would be able to direct him to Millgrove. As he
headed in that direction he noted with surprise that the road to
his right was posted for Lynton Abbas. He'd spent a happy
sennight near Lynton Abbas years ago before he'd begun his
military career. He hadn't thought of that in ages. No wonder
the area looked familiar. He must try to contact his friend Ned
Breen while he was in Gloucestershire, but for now he was approaching a village and had best look out for someone to direct
him to Millgrove.

It was midmorning when Anthony rang the bell of Belinda's
home and saw the door immediately opened, not by a butler or
housemaid but Sir Walter Melville himself, dressed in
breeches and topboots. His eyes dilated in surprise but he

stuck his hand out promptly. "How do you do, Captain Wainright. I am happy to see you've come through that dreadful carnage unscathed. Come in, come in."

As Sir Walter moved back, Anthony stepped into a high-ceilinged hall, but by now he had taken in the low-crowned hat and gloves that made up part of his host's costume. "I fear I have caught you on the point of going out, sir."

"No, no, pay that no heed. Take off your hat," the older man urged, removing his own as he spoke. "Beddoes!" he bellowed, causing Anthony to start slightly. A palpitating quiet lasted for a second or two until advancing footsteps announced the appearance of a soberly clad man enveloped in the dignity of his station. "Bring a bottle of the best Madeira to the library," Sir Walter said to his butler, and, "Come this way, lad," to his visitor.

Sir Walter waved his unexpected guest into a well-worn brown velvet chair and seated himself behind his desk. That he had been taking stock of his son-in-law was evident when he said abruptly, "I take back that remark about emerging unscathed from the war. You look older than when we last met, also thinner and somewhat drawn. Have you been ill?"

"No, I am fine, but I have not asked about your sons yet, sir. I trust—I hope they have made a complete recovery?"

"Oh, yes, the boys are perfect, unless you include their behavior in that description—they're a pair of scamps, those two. Did Belinda not tell you they had recovered?"

"I have not heard from Belinda since I left England," Anthony admitted, meeting his father-in-law's noncommittal gaze. Belinda had her father's clear, watchful eyes, he realized suddenly, eyes that sought the person behind the public facade.

"I see. I knew that you had survived because I sent your letters, three of them, on to Belinda, but she has not mentioned your name in her recent letters."

"Are you saying that Belinda is not here?" Anthony stared at Sir Walter in consternation, but before he could question his wife's whereabouts, Beddoes entered the room bearing a tray. He sat in simmering impatience while the butler deposited his burden on the huge scarred desk and poured out two glasses, which he handed to the silent men. "Where is Belinda?" he asked the moment the door closed behind the servant.

"All in good time," said his host, raising his glass. "To your safe deliverance from war."

Anthony contained his impatience under his father-in-law's grave regard. "Thank you," he murmured, sipping the wine in turn. Sir Walter was playing the perfect host but the friendliness that had marked their first meeting, even while distraught over his children's illness, was missing today.

"I gather that Belinda has told you the story behind our marriage," he began, in the interest of having matters clear between them.

"Since she is female, I strongly doubt she has divulged the whole," Sir Walter said, "but she has written an account of the events leading up to the marriage that, needless to say, disturbed us greatly. Is it correct to state that it was not Belinda but Deirdre with whom you were in love, and you and Belinda married to shield her cousin from the consequences of her adulterous behavior?"

A muscle jumped in Anthony's cheek and his teeth were clenched shut as the words struck him like blows. His glance did not waver, however, as he said quietly, "That is nearly correct, though it is the worst possible connotation to put on what happened."

"I am eager to hear your version of how the marriage came about."

Anthony did not spare himself in telling of his pursuit of Deirdre and his intention of running away with her. "I'd have taken her away that night if she'd have agreed to it, but in the end she would not. I must tell you, in Deirdre's defense, that no actual adultery occurred, though I confess I let Belinda believe it had when she railed at me for trying to seduce her cousin. She had seen us together that evening also, as well as Lady Ilchester's maid."

"Not the most discreet pair of illicit lovers," Sir Walter put in dryly. "Still, I have never understood precisely why the affair culminated in such a hasty marriage."

"That was all Lady Ilchester's doing. You did not want Belinda coming back home while her brothers were ill, and Lady Ilchester threatened to blacken her character to Lord Archer so that he would not wish her to stay with them in London. In those circumstances I felt it was incumbent upon me to give Belinda the protection of my name as soon as possible. Lady Ilchester told Belinda after our wedding that she never doubted it had been Deirdre with me that night. She engineered the marriage simply to remove me as a threat to her brother's honor. Belinda did not tell me this; I had it from my friend Sir John Hanks, who acted as her friend throughout."

"What a vicious woman!" Sir Walter declared. "And stupid too if she really believes she can shield her brother from the natural consequences of marrying Deirdre St. John. You may have been the first, but you will not be her last liaison. She may acquire discretion in time; she most certainly will not learn loyalty. My poor Belinda."

Anthony flushed darkly at this bald summation. It was with difficulty that he admitted, "It took an inordinately long time for me to recognize what an egregious fool I had been about Deirdre, but I always knew that I treated Belinda very badly." He met his father-in-law's implacable gaze squarely. "It is no excuse to say that I treated her badly because her opinion of me was so patently low, but her every look was a reproach, the justice of which I would not acknowledge at the time. I have given it a lot of thought lately, and I believe this to be true. It is small wonder that she ran away from me."

"Ran away did she? She didn't tell me that. She wrote that you two had agreed to live apart and would seek an annulment eventually. I did wonder why your letters continued to come here." Sir Walter's tones contained a trace of satisfaction for a mystery solved, but his shrewd eyes never left his son-in-law's rigid countenance. "Do you hold this view about getting the marriage annulled?"

"No!"

Sir Walter's brows climbed toward his hairline as he said mildly, "Why would this not be the best course since you've all but admitted that you dislike her?"

"I *don't* dislike her. Even when I thought I did, it was mostly because she so obviously disapproved of *me*. I think Belinda is a naturally sweet person, kind and gentle and very loyal."

"Aye, the opposite of her cousin. She is all that—and a stubborn little mule at times too."

"Where is she, Sir Walter?" Anthony asked softly when his father-in-law had apparently fallen into a private reverie, staring into his glass.

There was nothing absentminded about the sharp glance Sir Walter flashed him. "My daughter also has a loving heart. It is a rare gift that I do not desire to see bestowed on an undeserving man. No, don't make me any promises on that head," he said as Anthony's lips parted. "There is only one promise I would like from you. I'll tell you where Belinda is, but I want your word as a gentleman that you will not put any pressure on her to resume the marriage if she is reluctant. If after seeing you again and talking the matter over, she still feels the marriage was a mistake, then I expect you to abide by her wish to seek an annulment."

"You have my word on it."

"Belinda is in Northumberland visiting her former governess, who inherited a small villa just outside of Alnwick."

Anthony's jaw slackened visibly. "That's nearly in Scotland," he said faintly.

Sir Walter's grin was tinged with malice. "When Belinda does a thing, she does it thoroughly. There will be ample time on the journey to marshal your arguments." He rose from his chair and came out from behind the desk to lay a hand on his son-in-law's shoulder. "But first, I hope you will give us the pleasure of your company for a few days while you prepare for the odyssey. I believe my wife is in the music room at this hour. Come and meet her."

Anthony nodded weakly, still working out the distances in his head as he allowed his host to lead him up a beautiful old oak staircase lined with family portraits.

On seeing that her husband was accompanied by a stranger, Lady Melville rose from the piano bench, a too-slender woman of middle height with fair curls clustered beneath a pretty lace-edged cap, and large, slightly unfocused blue eyes beneath pale brows in a thin face. Her lashes were pale too and contributed to the overall impression of a gentle but not very positive personality. Her timid smile and soft voice when she responded to the introduction confirmed Anthony's assessment, but she seconded her husband's invitation with apparent pleasure at the prospect of entertaining her stepdaughter's unwanted husband.

Still reeling from the news that his recalcitrant bride had even fled her own family in her desire to place herself outside his reach, Anthony gratefully accepted his in-laws' hospitality, both as a practical matter and because he felt he had much to learn about Belinda. There was no better place to begin the process than in the bosom of her family. He spent three days with the Melvilles, riding over the estate with his father-in-law during the day and dining quietly *en famille*, having been told apologetically by his hostess that none of the neighbors knew of Belinda's marriage since she had not been home since the event had taken place.

Anthony met his wife's brothers before dinner the first evening when their nurse brought them into the drawing room. "They are fine boys," he said to their proud parents after the lively pair had departed, "but I had no idea Belinda's brothers were quite so young."

"Louisa and I have only been married five years," Sir Walter said. "Belinda's mother had died the previous year after a lingering illness."

"We were married in my home in Bath," Lady Melville said, taking up the tale, "in the early spring, and Sir Walter brought me to Millgrove a few weeks later, without, I must tell you, having advised Belinda and her grandmother of our marriage. We arrived unheralded on Belinda's birthday. I shall never forget that poor child's stunned face when she tried to make me welcome." She cast a look of loving exasperation at her husband, who smiled ruefully.

"What a peal she rang over me when she later discovered I had forgotten my daughter's birthday. The two have been in league against me ever sine. Eh, lad, is something wrong? You look as though the pianoforte had just fallen on you."

"I . . . I just recalled something I had not thought of in years." Anthony summoned up a smile and said to Lady Melville, "Did you know that Belinda and I were married on her birthday?"

"Why no, she did not mention it in her letter telling us the news. I do hope you and Belinda will be able to solve your difficulties," Lady Melville said earnestly. "She is such a dear girl."

"I agree with you, ma'am."

Sir Walter drew his son-in-law's attention to a picture on the wall behind his chair. "That was painted at her mother's request when Belinda was about thirteen. Go ahead," he added with a nod toward the portrait when the younger man made an involuntary movement as if to rise.

Anthony stood motionless in front of a half-length portrait of a young girl with long black hair tied with a ribbon at the nape and falling over one shoulder. He gazed intently into a vivid, smiling countenance and seemed to see there instead a ferocious scowl and soft pouting lips begging to be kissed.

"Flower face," he murmured on a mere breath of sound.

* * *

The day Anthony was scheduled to leave for Alnwick on
the mail coach there was a letter for him among the batch
brought into the library by Beddoes. "It's from my parents,"
he said, turning it over to scan the envelope. "I spent a few
days with them last week on my return from the Continent. I
had not previously told them of my marriage, having tried and
given up the attempt to explain it in a letter. They knew I was
heading here with the intention of bringing Belinda back to
Hampshire with me eventually. I hope there is nothing
wrong."

"Go ahead, open it," Sir Walter urged.

Anthony did so. He sat quite still for a moment after master-
ing its contents, his expression somewhat dazed. Catching his
father-in-law's concerned gaze, he extended the single sheet
across the desk. "I would like you to read this, sir, in the event
it becomes necessary to corroborate my word that I had
formed the firm intention of persuading Belinda to honor our
vows before I ever heard about the bequest mentioned in this
letter."

"Very well." Sir Walter rapidly perused the epistle, saying
as he returned it to his son-in-law, "Congratulations, my boy.
This is good news indeed."

"I would rather it had been delayed by a year or so," Anthony replied, a worried crease in his brow, "and I can only
hope your felicitations are not premature. Belinda has a very
poor opinion of my character."

"But a loyal and forgiving nature," Sir Walter reminded
him. This produced a faint twist to the young man's lips
though his eyes remained shadowed.

Although doubly anxious to reach Belinda following his extraordinary recovery of the lost memory of their first encounter, Anthony had enjoyed his peaceful stay at Millgrove.
His wife's parents were good, kind people and he found Sir
Walter in particular to be a compatible spirit whose questing
mind challenged his own. After months of self-castigation and
confronting his deficiencies, it was good to feel that his father-
in-law liked him despite his past sins and wished him well.
Though Sir Walter would permit no undue pressure on Belinda
to resume a marriage that was distasteful to her, it was cheer-
ing to know he would be welcomed into the family, given the
chance.

Anthony found himself constantly reliving his long-ago meeting with Belinda on the journey north, marveling that he could now recall in exact detail an event that had lain long buried in his memory. Or perhaps the real mystery lay in how he could ever have forgotten in the first place. His heart had gone out to the valiant, unhappy girl that Belinda had been five years ago, and his senses had responded to her too, the silky length of inky hair that his fingers had brushed behind her shoulder, the delicate bone structure and straight little nose, the creamy skin of rose petal perfection that he'd longed to touch. But she had been little more than a child, and he had been filled with vainglorious notions of military heroics to come. He'd had the good sense—and yes, the consideration—to keep the tone light and casual, not even permitting an exchange of identities. And then in the end those beautiful melancholy eyes had been his downfall; he'd cast caution, sense, and consideration to the winds and given in to self-indulgence by stealing a kiss. Her dazed expression had quickly brought him to his senses, and he'd loped off before he could give in to a strong temptation to repeat the offense. He'd taken a delightful memory with him to Portugal, where it had gradually dimmed and dissolved under the weight of brutal, ugly scenes of war, more nightmares than memories in some cases.

There was no denying he *had* forgotten the charming incident, which he could never sufficiently regret, for it was patently clear that Belinda had remembered. Here then was the explanation for that short-lived radiance that had bloomed over her face when they met again in Deirdre's saloon. It had embarrassed him at first, piqued his curiosity briefly, then stuck like a nettle in a dark corner of his mind to sting on the rare occasions when his obsession with Deirdre's charms had allowed any sustained thought of another female. It had never even risen close enough to the surface to become an elusive memory to be tracked down, but the irritation remained. Belinda had irritated him too. He had been aware that his reaction was irrational though he had tried to rationalize it, blaming his reaction on the disapproval of himself he sensed in her.

Deliberately recalling the fleeting expression on Belinda's face that day in Somerset, Anthony experienced a quickening in his pulses as he pursued the cause. She must have remembered him with joy. He shifted uneasily in the swaying mail

coach and his pulses steadied again as a bleakness settled over
his features. He had summarily destroyed any joy associated
with her memory of him, unwittingly at first by his total lack
of recognition, but later quite savagely as he alternately ignored and belittled her. And then on their wedding night he'd
crowned his oafish efforts by taunting her with having
schemed to marry him. He groaned inwardly and his jaw went
rigid. Lord, she must hate the very mention of his name!

On the heels of this thought a picture of Belinda as she
made the announcement that she wished never to see him
again flashed into his head. It had not been anger, which was a
volatile emotion that could vanish as swiftly as it arose. Her
whole bearing had expressed calm disdain, which was infi-
nitely more lethal to his hopes of establishing a friendly footing upon which to begin their marriage. The fact that she had
replied to none of his letters was discouraging, to say the least,
but dogged persistence would seem to be his only course. Her
father extolled her sense of loyalty, Deirdre had flagrantly ex-
ploited it, and he, it would appear, was about to try to do the
same. He was not proud of himself, he deeply regretted the necessity, but the alternative was to stand by and accept the final
loss of all their youthful dreams.

Everything in his being rose up against that conclusion.

Chapter Fourteen

Alnwick, Northumberland

The notes of a finger exercise sounded, hesitantly at first and then more fluidly as the player gained confidence. When triumphant fingers were raised at the conclusion, the second person on the piano bench said, "Once again." This time the exercise was played with definite verve and earned unstinted praise. "Excellently done, Betsy."

The small musician, no more than eight years old, beamed a gap-toothed smile upon her teacher and begged, "May I play my new piece now, Miss Melville?" Belinda glanced at the clock on the mantel and hesitated, prompting renewed pleading, "Please, Miss Melville, just once?"

Belinda laughed and gave the child's shoulders a quick hug before rising from the bench. "Very well, Betsy, but just once, mind. Your mother will worry if you are late home." She left the little girl to get on with her practicing and moved over to take a chair in front of the window.

One of the many charms of Anthea Fenton's small villa was its situation on the outskirts of Alnwick on the road approaching the town from the southwest. Set well back behind a lawn and flower gardens that were the joy and the achievement of Miss Fenton's life, Hollyhock House escaped the dust and most of the noise of the road while providing its inhabitants with an ever-changing view of local traffic when their activities within doors ceased to hold their interest. Never having lived near a town before, Belinda found the parade of humanity available to her eyes and imagination a source of endless diversion. She glanced out the window now from force of habit, noting a couple of farm workers trudging homeward after working in the nearby fields, their scythes over their shoulders. They would be in the center of Alnwick in less than ten minutes. This proximity to town was a decided advantage of living at Hollyhock House since Miss Fenton's income, while adequate to running the property, was insufficient for the maintenance of a stable. Except in the most inclement weather it was a pleasure rather than a hardship to walk into town.

Belinda was only marginally aware of the painstaking performance of the young musician behind her as she studied the sky over the fields across the road. There was a sharp little wind with a foretaste of winter's icy breath that was whipping clouds across a pale blue sky faded from its summer depth of color. She had only seen the best Northumberland had to offer, starting with the first joys of spring—her second this year—on her arrival late in April. Anthea assured her the winters were long and cold here.

Where would she be when winter came, she wondered abruptly, a shade of apprehension darkening her mood. It was nearly inconceivable that she could have been in Northumberland for close on five months; the time had sped by on wings. When her visit had reached the six-week point her conscience had demanded that she fix a definite date for its end, but Anthea had flatly refused to listen to any argument arising from considerations of conscience or social delicacy. She had declared with convincing sincerity that her former pupil's companionship gave her inestimable pleasure and she must not dream of curtailing her visit unless prompted by stronger claims or her own inclination. Belinda had been only too pleased to comply, consulting for the first time in her life nothing save her own inclination.

She had been made to feel more welcome and privileged in Anthea Fenton's modest home than her close ties of kinship might be thought to have entitled her to feel in her cousin's mansion. With her acute perception and genuine concern for the sensibilities of others, Anthea had refrained from questioning her guest about the sudden change of heart that had brought her up north on the heels of a short letter that shed no light on the subject, and in a private carriage belonging to someone of whom Belinda had never given the least intelligence before. Miss Fenton had merely embraced her former charge with smiling affection and proceeded to cosset her beyond her desserts.

After less than a fortnight of simple living, a pleasant routine, and the valued companionship of a truly refined mind and liberal spirit, Belinda's own bruised and battered spirit had recovered to the point where she was able to give her friend a detailed account of everything that had taken place in Somerset. Until then she had let Anthea assume that her little brothers' illness and her father's proscription on her return home had inspired the visit to Northumberland. Her friend had listened to the sorry saga with a grave attentiveness that could not quite conceal an inner perturbation on Belinda's account that more than did justice to the feelings expected of a close family member, and she had expressed her sentiments on the subject with uncharacteristic heat.

"That something of this kind should happen, not from the evils or foolishness of your own nature but that of another, and one moreover who has done nothing to merit such loyalty, is a misfortune almost past bearing. That wretched girl! It challenges the very foundations of one's Christian beliefs to refrain from deploring that she should go merrily on her selfish way, unchastened and presumably unrepentant. One's heart goes out to Lord Archer in the contemplation of what the future must hold for his domestic happiness if your cousin does not learn to care more for her duty to the husband she freely chose."

Anthea's warm championship could not be other than soothing balm to Belinda's heartache, but Miss Fenton's partisanship did not preclude sympathy for Captain Wainright also. In her own eyes Belinda had been scrupulously fair to her husband in the recounting of their clashes, but she was still a little surprised and, though she could not be brought to own the debased feeling even to herself, piqued at the degree to which her friend thought him deserving of pity. Anthea had commiserated with Belinda on the heartburnings that had accrued from having to watch Anthony's blind devotion to Deirdre, but in the emotional, as distinguished from the unfortunate practical consequences which the two shared equally, she held that Captain Wainright was more to be pitied than her friend. "For," she had said to an astonished Belinda, "if your heart and feminine pride were grievously wounded, it was not permanently, since you have concluded that your feelings for him were not love but infatuation. *He*, on the other hand, has all the sharp-edged and lasting pain of knowing that his infatuation has led him to act in a manner incompatible with his personal honor. *That* knowledge, you know, my dear, must be a source of permanent regret and shame to any man who was used to thinking well of his own character."

This aspect of the situation was new to Belinda and unwelcome; she had no desire to pity Anthony Wainright, especially when she was so thoroughly occupied in pitying herself. Life at Hollyhock House proved to be too full of interest and variety to spare much time for the most dedicated self-pitier, however, which Belinda was not. She was absorbed into Miss Fenton's circle of friends, which included such diverse elements as political pamphleteers, persons with literary pretensions, and a number of people, largely female, of valetudinarian habits, whose acquaintance she had inherited along with Hollyhock House from the great-aunt with whom she had been used to spend summers when a child. The spring days sped by with the two women happily occupied with domestic concerns, gardening, music, and the society of friends.

The only qualification to her contentment was the fact that she was not being completely honest with those people whose lives touched hers in Alnwick. It had begun by accident at the moment of her arrival when she discovered that Anthea, not knowing precisely when to expect her guest, was entertaining several ladies of her acquaintance. After the initial flurry of greetings, Belinda had realized too late that she was being presented as Miss Melville to her hostess's friends. The enormity of trying to explain away the mistake in front of a roomful of strangers had kept her silent. She had felt a great guilty relief at the reprieve because the idea of divulging the sordid tale to the governess she had not seen in nearly five years had been so tormenting and humiliating as to make her ill on the long journey north. She had been in such a shattered state that all she wished to do was escape from the reality of her unhappily changed circumstances. She was fleeing to Anthea Fenton but was so dreading the necessary revelations that she had sworn the faithful Polly to secrecy about the marriage. It had taken time to restore the balance of her mind, something that Anthea had freely understood when Belinda had finally overcome her reserve and unburdened herself about a fortnight into her visit. Upon serious reflection Anthea had decided that remaining silent on the matter was the lesser of two evils, and so Miss Melville she remained in Alnwick.

The first letter from Captain Wainright had arrived early in July after the Battle of Waterloo. It had obviously been sent to Millgrove and had been included with a letter from her father. Belinda had been so successful in banishing the whole episode from her thoughts that the inscription in a strange hand to Mrs. Anthony Wainright had meant nothing to her at first glance. When comprehension dawned she had dropped it as if it were a hot coal, and it had been many minutes before she'd overcome her reluctance and opened the missive. It had been short; beyond stating what she'd known by inference— that he'd survived the military engagement—it contained only a brief statement of his intention to remain with the army until all threat of a French resurgence was safely past, and a personal apology for his part in their final quarrel. There was nothing to be read between the lines; it was what it was—a necessary communication perhaps, but not one that required or invited any response from her. He did not mention an annulment, but that could wait upon his return to England. She had put the letter away and, after a day or two of feeling slightly on edge, had found it easy to resume her present life.

The second, equally brief communication from her husband, received in August, had been little more than a description of his travels and duties, plus a request for news of herself that she ignored. The third had arrived a few days previously and was the cause of the amorphous apprehension that had crept into her most satisfactory existence like a fog bank on the horizon. Anthony had announced his intention of returning soon to England and expressed the desire to meet and discuss their future. This time there had been something to read between the lines. Unless she was vastly mistaken, there had been a confident assumption that their future lay together. He had also expressed disappointment at not having heard from her.

As Betsy continued to pound away on the pianoforte, Belinda stared out the front window, unseeingly now as she attempted to bolster her uneven spirits and chided herself for her cowardice. She had always known that the meeting An-

thony spoke of was inevitable, had she not? Surely she was
not a simpleton expecting to drift on this gentle wave of contentment in Northumberland forever. Thanks to Anthea's
comforting support and the healing passage of time she had
recovered completely from the fancied wounds to her heart
and the real ones to her amour propre. She had even come to
accept her wise friend's assessment of Anthony's sufferings
as much greater than her own, and she could feel sorry for his
pain.

None of this made the least difference to her desire to
wipe out the forced marriage. She felt she deserved something better, and so, for that matter, did Anthony. Whatever
quixotic sacrifice he was prepared to make for the sake of
his honor, she wanted no part of it. She would find the
strength to hold her ground if he tried to convince her otherwise.

The sudden silence in the room brought Belinda's wandering thoughts to a halt. "That was nicely done, Betsy," she said,
hoping her words were true. "Miss Fenton should be coming
up the road any moment. Shall we go along together to meet
her on your way home?"

A swift glance around the room revealed that the shawl she
had worn while gardening before Betsy arrived for her lesson
was on top of the piano. She and the little girl headed down
the walk a few minutes later, just in time to open the front gate
for Anthea. Her friend had recently started a school to teach
the children of millworkers to read, and she was finding it exhausting work in the early days.

"You look fagged to death," Belinda said when they had
waved Betsy off and started to stroll slowly toward the front
door, stopping to admire a group of dark orange dahlias. "Did
something happen today?"

"Josh Duggan happened!"

"Ah, the limb of Satan himself," Belinda said with a smile.
"What did he do?"

"He keeps the class in a constant uproar and disrupts the
lessons."

"Is he capable of learning? Perhaps he is disruptive because
he doesn't understand and is afraid the others will laugh at
him."

"He is always ready with a quip and seems to have a
quick mind, but he doesn't concede the value of being able

to read and write." Anthea was taking off her pelisse as she spoke.

"Well, I am persuaded *you* know the value of a cup of tea, and I am going to make you one right this instant. Sit down over here and relax."

"Mrs. Higgins will be in the midst of dinner preparations; she won't want you in her kitchen."

"Mrs. Higgins and I have reached an accommodation," Belinda said gaily, waving away her friend's feeble objection. "As long as I don't make a mess for her to clean up she tolerates my presence in her bailiwick. Do not fear that my bumbling will cost you your treasure," she added as she headed for the kitchen.

She had merely been teasing but Belinda recognized the truth in her last remark as she bustled about the well-scrubbed kitchen where Mrs. Higgins was rolling out pastry while her two young daughters were engaged in cleaning vegetables, and Polly was ironing. It had certainly been a stroke of uncommon good fortune that Anthea had taken possession of her inheritance shortly after Samuel Higgins, a lawyer's clerk in Alnwick, had died of pneumonia, leaving his family virtually penniless. A position where she and her orphaned children might live in had seemed the answer to the widow's prayers, and Anthea was frequently heard to say that Mrs. Higgins had been the answer to hers, since her great-aunt's servants had grown old with her and had been pensioned at her death. The arrangement had worked most satisfactorily for nearly five years. Fortunately, the willing Polly had been accepted early on by Mrs. Higgins as good company for her daughters, and the three girls happily shared a large room in the attic.

Anthea's eyes were closed when Belinda reentered the front sitting room. The younger woman was conscious of both affection and gratitude as she looked at her dozing friend in the high-backed chair. At first glance people might tend to underrate her personal attractions, but the pleasant plainness of her features was improved by a tall elegantly proportioned figure, beautiful long-fingered hands, and aristocratically narrow feet. Her abundant hair was a rich reddish brown, her carriage was erect and graceful, and she had an innate sense of style that lent her an air of distinction whatever her company. Belinda considered that her former teacher's looks had improved in her thirties over what they had been in her twenties, never thinking that the perceived improvement might be accounted for by a greater maturity in her own power of discernment. She only knew that she greatly admired Anthea's presence and humbly hoped one day to acquire some degree of her self-assurance. She was possessed of a fine mind and a lively intellect allied with an equable temper and a deep tolerance for the foibles of mankind despite her own strong principles. Anthea Fenton created an atmosphere of rationality and unsentimental kindness wherever she was that drew people to her. One of her strongest attractions was the gift of intelligent listening unaccompanied by any urge to impart unsolicited advice. Belinda had liked and respected her enormously when her pupil, and she was excessively grateful for the opportunity to continue their friendship on a more equal footing.

Anthea's eyes opened as Belinda set down the tray, and she smiled, displaying slightly irregular but beautifully white teeth. "That looks wonderful—strong, just the way I like it," she said as Belinda poured out a cup and handed it across to her friend. "I shudder to contemplate a world without tea," she added after her first sip. "Thank you, I feel refreshed already. What did you do today? Did anyone call?"

"No one called, but while I was tying up the tall dahlias that were in wild disarray after last night's storm, Mr. Stoddard walked by on bank business. He was going to see old Mr. Amberwyth, who has been feeling too poorly to go into town lately."

"I must ask Mrs. Higgins to prepare some of her calf's-foot jelly for Mr. Amberwyth. He swears by it when he is feeling out of frame."

"I'll take it to him tomorrow afternoon if you like," Belinda offered, adding, "Oh, Mr. Stoddard plans to come by this evening to escort us to the meeting of the literary circle. I told him we would be glad of his escort on the way home but did not wish to trouble him on the way into town when it will be full daylight. He bore down all my arguments, however, and insists on calling for us after dinner."

Anthea took another sip of her tea before saying, "Actually, I am feeling a bit tired and would prefer a quiet evening at home, so it is fortunate that Mr. Stoddard will be coming for you."

"Oh no, if you do not wish to go, I shall remain home too. I'll send Polly into town with a note for Mr. Stoddard."

As Belinda got up with the obvious intention of carrying out this action, Anthea said hastily, "No, no, of course you must go. I would not for the world curtail your enjoyment, and Mr. Stoddard will be so disappointed."

"Mr. Stoddard's transitory disappointment is of no great moment in the broad scheme of things," Belinda said with cheerful brutality. "I would much rather stay at home with you. If you're not too tired we can have a game of chess before retiring." And she took herself off to write her note before Anthea could press her further.

Mr. Stoddard called on Sunday afternoon to see how the ladies did, timing his visit close to their dinner hour so that hospitality demanded that he be invited to partake of this meal with them. After polite protestations and apologies on his part and equally civil refutations and insistence on the ladies' part, he was persuaded to sink his scruples and accept what they were genuinely pleased to offer.

Belinda liked Mr. Stoddard unreservedly. She had met him at a meeting of the literary society shortly into her visit and soon realized that he was one of Anthea's small circle of intimate friends. In his late thirties, he had been widowed for nearly ten years following a happy but tragically brief marriage. Anthea confided that when she arrived in Northumberland Mr. Stoddard had been the subject of much matchmaking activity among mothers with daughters to establish and widows looking to improve their state, but continued lack of success had gradually thinned the ranks of hopeful contenders. It was now pretty well conceded that Mr. Stoddard was a lost cause, although he enjoyed the company of women and was much sought after as an extra man at dinner parties. His manners were excellent, his character unimpeachable, his mind well informed and liberal, and he possessed a natural chivalry that made him a great favorite with the fair sex. The only defect Belinda could see in him, and that not a fault at all, was a disposition to be universally serious. It was not that he failed to appreciate a witicism or see the humor in a joke, but there was an intrinsic gravity in his manner that left her with the lowering suspicion that her own nature might be rather frivolous.

Mr. Stoddard had been very kind and welcoming toward the newcomer, as indeed had all of Anthea's friends. In recent weeks, however, the suspicion had darted into Belinda's mind that this gentleman's interest in her was becoming more personal than an avuncular kindness for his good friend's young visitor. The first time she had noted a warm light in his eyes she had dismissed the startled notion as wildly improbable; after all, the difference in their ages must be close to twenty years. The suspicion returned on subsequent occasions, however, when he sought her out in company, and refused to be as easily dislodged. There was nothing smacking of courtship in his manner—he was not a man to pay fulsome compliments—but she was nearly persuaded that he cherished a decided preference for her society, and the idea caused her increasing concern on her friend's account. Anthea had not uttered one syllable on the subject, yet Belinda had the idea that she was cognizant of Mr. Stoddard's preference and was wounded by it.

Much as she admired Anthea, and dear as her friendship was to Belinda, the relationship had only recently been elevated to a more or less equal footing, and here too there was a considerable gap in their years and experience of the world. In short, they did not stand upon such terms as would encourage Belinda to challenge the older woman's deep personal reserve.

On the day after Mr. Stoddard dined with them, Belinda's mind was occupied with speculation about the emotional leanings of her two friends while her hands were busy among the flowers in the front garden. It was as plain as a pikestaff to her eyes that they would make a most attractive couple, both tall and well made, with an air of breeding and distinction about their persons. Their minds too were compatible, both so rational and well regulated, and their tastes were largely similar. Even the differences in their temperaments would seem to promote domestic felicity, for Anthea's optimistic and contented disposition would balance Mr. Stoddard's less sanguine outlook and lighten the weightiness of his general spirits. Hearts were such awkward things, she reflected gloomily, attacking the dead heads on the asters with sharp clicks of her shears, often blind to the existence of qualities in other hearts that would best suit them, and attaching themselves stubbornly to those that were bound to cause them grief in the fullness of time, the possibility of this latter mistake increasing proportionately with the degree of physical beauty possessed by the owner of the undesirable qualities.

Coming to the end of a row of asters, Belinda paused to dissect her last thought and burst out laughing. She had just made the profound observation that the Deirdres of the world ensnared unwary hearts.

"I wish you would tell me what is so amusing in a clump of flowers."

Belinda, on her knees among the rows and absorbed in her reflections, had not heard the gate latch open. She started, and glanced over her shoulder. "Anthony! Good heavens, what are *you* doing here?"

There was an odd expression in cornflower blue eyes that stared down at her. "My word, you look exactly like—"

"My cousin," she finished when he broke off the eager words. "I am aware, only without her stunning beauty." She got to her feet in a smooth motion, ignoring his outstretched hand, and proceeded to dust off the knees of her faded gray cotton gown.

"I was going to say that you look like a twelve-year-old in that straw hat, with your hair tied back," he corrected gently. "As for your question, I am persuaded you have already guessed why I am here."

She passed over his infelicitous comparison, saying coolly, "I must suppose you wish to discuss the steps to be taken to end our . . . this so-called marriage, but I do not at all comprehend why you should have put yourself to the trouble and expense of traveling all this way when a letter would have done quite as well." Belinda was removing her gardening gloves as she spoke. When her eyes returned to his face after tossing them into the trug, she saw that he had been studying her appearance keenly. By the exercise of strict self-discipline, she resisted the urge to straighten her hat or smooth her hair, keeping her hands still at her sides and a noncommittal expression on her face.

A shade of—what?—disappointment?—crossed his brow before he said with a whimsical plaintiveness, "True, I might have written a letter, my dear Belinda, except that I have discovered at first hand that you do not reply to written communication."

His quizzical look drew a reluctant little smile from her. "There was nothing I wished to say to you," she replied, neither apology nor aggressiveness in her voice.

This time his disappointment was unmistakable. "I had hoped, not from any increase in merit but just because one *does* allow oneself to hope, that the memory of our last acrimonious conversation might have grown less bitter with the passing of time; in short, that you might have accepted my apology and might not find me quite so despicable at this distance."

"It isn't that," she said hurriedly. "Pray believe that I did realize even by the next morning that you had been goaded into unjust retaliation by the pain that Deirdre's actions caused you, or"—when he would have spoken—"perhaps even more by the understandable irritation of having those shocking disclosures made by someone you disliked."

"But you still ran away."

"Oh yes, I had borne enough. I wished nothing more to do with you."

"And you never acknowledged my apology."

She stared him straight in the eye and said firmly, "There was no hint in your apology that my reaction was of any importance to you. You felt, quite rightly, that your conduct had been unworthy of a gentleman and you apologized. *I* did not come into it."

"And my other letters?"

"I can only repeat that I had nothing to say to you."

"Vastly uncivil, but it does have the virtue of clarity. There is no longer any excuse for my misunderstanding your feelings, but you still have a few misconceptions about mine. We have much to talk about, Belinda, but this little breeze is turning chill," he said as the brim of Belinda's straw hat flattened against her cheek, then blew straight up, so that she was forced to remove the hat for safekeeping. He scanned the rapidly gathering clouds. "I should not be surprised if it were to rain shortly. May we continue our conversation inside?"

"I'm afraid Anthea is not home at present," she replied with a negative motion of her head.

"All the better; we shall be assured the necessary privacy to talk about ourselves."

"But I cannot invite a man into Anthea's house!"

"I am not 'a man,'" he reminded her with a friendly smile. "I am your husband, therefore perfectly unexceptionable company."

"You don't understand," Belinda said, moistening her top lip with a nervous movement of her tongue. "No one in Alnwick knows I am married, except Anthea." At his quick frown, she added defensively, "It took some time before I was able to tell Anthea about my—our marriage. The whole episode in Somerset had been so upsetting that I could not bear to think about it at first. In any case, there were people with her when I arrived so that I was naturally introduced as Miss Melville, and . . . and it seemed advisable to remain Miss Melville afterward."

"I see." He made a little grimace. "Then may I call on you this evening? Presumably there is somewhere we may speak in private without inconvenience to Miss Fenton."

"N . . . not tonight, I fear. Some elderly friends of Anthea's are to dine with us."

"Very well, I'll hire a gig from the White Swan Inn where I am staying and we'll go for a drive tomorrow."

"Yes, all right," Belinda assented with a patent lack of enthusiasm that thinned his mouth. She looked hastily toward the front gate. "Where is Titan?"

"At Millgrove. I came up by the mail. It will rain soon. I'd best leave now if I am to escape a wetting. Till tomorrow, Belinda. I'll call for you around ten."

Before Belinda could respond he was off down the path, a tall, straight figure exuding sheer masculine vitality as he walked swiftly along the road toward the town.

When Anthony called for his bride the next morning there was no danger of repeating his error of saying Belinda looked like a twelve-year-old—something he'd instantly regretted when he had substituted it for the impulse to remark that she looked like she had at their first meeting on her fifteenth birthday. The only similarity between the vision who met him at the door and yesterday's working gardener was that both wore hats made of straw. Today's version was a leghorn bonnet with a high crown, a large brim, pale pink ribbons, and nestled against the crown, a darker pink rose that matched her elegant carriage gown of polished cotton. She was pulling on white gloves as she stepped outside, and a frilly white parasol was tucked under her arm as protection against the warm sun. Except for the blue gown she had worn at Sir John's party the night before their wedding, Anthony had never seen Belinda wearing anything but mourning. Today with color in her cheeks and a sparkle in her eyes she was a picture to gladden the heart of any escort, and a far cry indeed from the mournful waif who had kicked pebbles on a dusty lane because her father had surprised her with a step-mother on her birthday.

He offered his arm. "A mere gig seems woefully inadequate to carry a young lady of such decided fashion," he declared with a twinkle in his eyes.

"It would amaze me to discover that I was not the *least* fashionable lady of your acquaintance," she returned coolly, allowing him to assist her up into the vehicle before he untied the horse from the gatepost and climbed up beside her.

"Then you must prepare to be amazed," he replied, giving the horse a flick of the whip. "Do not forget that for most of the past five years I have been off in the mountains of the Iberian Peninsula, where ladies of fashion are not to be found."

"I have read about all the fashionable goings-on in Brussels this past spring right up to the moment of the battle," his reluctant bride retorted.

"I fear I was in no great humor for society last spring," he said, "especially feminine society."

"Was . . . was the battle very terrible?" she asked, refusing to be drawn down that path.

"It went on for three days that should have satisfied any man's craving to shed another's blood for a lifetime," he said dampingly before changing the subject. "The innkeeper told me there is a pretty valley north of the town. I thought we would head in that direction unless there is somewhere else you would prefer to go?"

"Oh no, that is the best drive. Keep following this road into Fenkle Street and head for Alnwick Castle, which is the seat of the Duke of Northumberland. It is atop a steep hill, at the bottom of which there is a bridge across the river with a statue of the Percy lion on it. On the far side is a lovely grassy valley with stands of trees dotting it."

Neither spoke much while Anthony was negotiating the gig through unfamiliar streets, except when Belinda pointed out a building of some distinction. He chuckled at the long-tailed lion guardian of the bridge and pronounced himself delighted with the peaceful valley that lay before them when they had crossed the Alne River. A little farther along they entered a belt of beech trees on the right to see the cross that marked the spot where the Scottish king, Malcolm, had been killed in 1093 after his army had burned most of Northumberland in retaliation for the lack of respect in which he had been held by William Rufus.

Anthony listened politely to Belinda's recounting of the affair and even asked one or two questions before saying, "Judging by your enthusiasm for Northumberland history, as well as your blooming looks, you have enjoyed your stay in the area."

"Oh, I have indeed. Just being with Anthea again would have been sufficient—we seem to share so many interests, which is not surprising since she was my governess for over three years—but this is the first time I have ever lived in— almost in—a town, which is also a most enjoyable experience."

"I can see that your stay has been beneficial," Anthony said, eyeing his bright-eyed companion approvingly. "You've lost that . . . haunted look you wore in Somerset toward the end, your skin glows with lovely color and you have learned how to smile."

"I've been very happy here," she said simply.

"Yes. I just wish you would not look at me as if fearing that I meant to change all this. There is nothing I desire more than a chance to make you happy, Belinda—" he began, to stop as she shook her head.

"Please, Anthony, I don't wish to be married to you. I believe in your heart you know we should not suit, and that it would be wise to dissolve this marriage."

"Well, that's plain enough," he said with a chagrined little laugh, "but your judgment is based on misunderstandings. You believe I dislike you, which is very far from the truth, though I admit a disinterested observer could have arrived at the same conclusion based on my behavior which, I am well aware, was indefensible. You have your father's eyes that look below the surface, did you know that? I was often aware of them disapproving of my pursuit of your cousin. They supplied pricks to my conscience, and I did not want my con-

science aroused. I slapped it down whenever it reared its
head, and I slapped you down too, figuratively speaking, with
my abominable rudeness. Those honest eyes were a constant
reproach to me."

They were driving north again along the road to Berwick.
Except when the horse required his attention, Anthony angled
his head to gauge Belinda's reaction to his words, but there
was little to be read on her composed countenance. It might
have been more hopeful had she argued or denounced him as a
liar—at least then he could be assured that what he had to say
was of vital interest to her. He had no choice but to press on;
he had to make her respond.

"Perhaps it is not my feelings toward you but yours toward
me that are the real crux of the matter?" he ventured after a
moment when she did not speak. Her eyes flew to his with a
startled question in their depths. "I have no earthly right to
complain if you despise me based on a belief that I am a man
without honor or moral principles, but that is not true—at
least it never was before I met Deirdre, and it isn't now. What
I did—tried to do—cannot be justified or perhaps even understood rationally. God knows I have had oceans of time these
past months to review the whole episode and question my actions, and I could arrive at no more satisfactory explanation
than to describe myself as incapable of moral judgment at that
period. I was like one bewitched. Please do not imagine I say
this to lay any of the responsibility at Deirdre's door. *I* was
the one who was determined to leave no commandment un-
broken in order to achieve my heart's desire. You cannot
think more poorly of my lack of moral fiber than I do myself," he said as Belinda's lips parted, "but this I believe I can
say with conviction: the madness that afflicted me, that fever
in the blood, for want of a better description, is like smallpox
in that it carries its own immunity. If one survives the disease,
one is safe from it thereafter. I do believe in the sacredness of
marriage vows, Belinda. I am not the libertine you must have
thought me."

The clopping of the horse's hooves was suddenly loud in
the silence which seemed to echo between them. Was she
going to refuse him any glimpse into her heart and mind?

"Belinda?"

"Anthony, I would like to ask you one question, if I may?"

She wishes to know if I am still in love with Deirdre, he thought, but that was not the question Belinda asked when he said, "Of course, anything."

"Do you believe Deirdre would have refused to go off to America with you had you been as rich as Lord Archer?"

"No," he said readily. "Do not fear that I still have any illusions about the beauty of Deirdre's character. She all but admitted that night in her room that she did not wish to give up her luxurious life, but even that did not cure me of my infatuation. I thought she was reluctant to hurt her husband, and I was fiercely resistant to admitting that I had been an utter fool over a heartless woman."

"She said you would not fail her when Lady Ilchester asked which of us you had been seen embracing, and she was right."

"Yes, I was still enslaved by her, but from that point on, Belinda, you must know that it was *your* reputation I acted to protect."

"And your own," she riposted.

"If Lady Ilchester had not been so bent on avenging her brother, a betrothal announcement would most likely have settled the matter, and it might have been forgotten in time. It did not satisfy her, however, and I could not let you pay for what Deirdre and I had done. I was going away; it was you who would be exposed to the cruel tongues of society."

"Anthony, I have no desire to be introduced into society in London. I don't believe an annulment of this marriage will ruin either of our lives forever. Do you—honestly?"

"I don't know; all I know is that I do not wish to have it annulled."

"Why? You cannot wish to be married to me. Despite the physical resemblance, I promise you I am not at all like my cousin."

"If you were, I would not be so reluctant to dissolve our union. I wish I could give you a reasoned argument but I cannot. I simply feel that, with goodwill on both sides, we could have a successful marriage. I promised your father I would not put any pressure on you to continue with it, Belinda, but the last day I was at Millgrove—"

"The *last* day?" She was clearly startled. "How long were you there?"

"Three days. Your family made me very welcome and I liked them all very much. This letter arrived just before I left," he said, removing a folded sheet of paper from inside his coat. "Before you read it I must impress upon you that your father will corroborate that I was determined to continue the marriage before I received this. I feel I must show it to you, not to put any additional pressure on you to accommodate me, but because it might make a difference to your own interest. I know I was no great catch as a husband. Like your cousin, you might well have looked higher for a match."

A puzzled Belinda read what was obviously a letter to his son from Anthony's father saying that the news of his marriage had decided Mr. Wainright's uncle, Thaddeus Wainright, to make Anthony his heir following the death in Belgium of the great nephew who had been his designated heir previously. It concluded with a pressing invitation that Mr. Wainright had been asked to relay from his Uncle Thaddeus to Anthony, to bring his bride to Meadowbrook at the earliest moment since his health was in a precarious state and he wished to settle his affairs. She read it through a second time before gazing at Anthony uncertainly. "Does this imply that your great-uncle would change his mind about making you his heir if you were not married, or were no longer married?"

"That is my understanding of the matter. There are two other cousins, besides my brother, who bear the same relationship to him that I do."

"But it is monstrous to be put in the position of depriving you of an inheritance!" Belinda cried. "I do not know what I should do."

"I was persuaded you would feel this way and I hated to introduce the matter and put you in such an unenviable position if you still detest me. On the other hand, you had to know all the circumstances, and I *would* not have you find out in the future and suspect me of wanting the marriage for this reason. As for your decision, do what your heart tells you. If the idea of being married to me is abhorrent to you, I would prefer that you let that be the end of the matter. I will try to obtain an annulment, though I must warn you they are not readily granted, and the process can take a long time. Do not give me an answer now. Take time to think on the matter; discuss it with your friend, who has your best interests at heart."

"Very well."

"One more thing must be said before we leave the subject and try to enjoy this lovely day." His eyes were darkly grave as they met hers. "Please do not fear that an agreement to continue the marriage would mean that I would expect conjugal intimacy in the beginning. You have my word of honor that that decision will rest entirely in your hands."

Chapter Fifteen

The entrance to Meadowbrook is just ahead."

Excitement deepened the timbre of Anthony's voice as the yellow post chaise swept around a bend in the road. Belinda smiled at him, catching something of his anticipation. A few moments later she grabbed the strap above the window and clutched it tightly as the chaise lurched from one pothole to another along the rutted drive.

"Are you all right?" Anthony was frowning now as he turned back to the window when she gave him a reassuring nod. "This was used to be a beautiful approach to the house, the avenue lined with mature copper beeches."

"They are still here for the most part and they are quite magnificent," Belinda pointed out, but her husband refused to be cheered.

"The undergrowth is rampant. I'd say there has been no maintenance for years. My God—that unkempt hayfield on the left was the south lawn when I was last here!"

Belinda only vaguely heard her husband's mutterings. She was gazing with fascination at the complicated structure coming into view ahead of them. "Goodness—I had not expected it to be so . . . so extensive!"

"It's certainly a rambling old pile," he agreed, "all angles and ells, and a regular rabbit warren of corridors and passages inside. That wing totally smothered in ivy dates from the Tudor period and probably should have been pulled down long since. The roof leaks, the chimneys smoke, and there is rising damp everywhere."

"It sounds uncomfortable, but that wing lends a romantic visual appeal to the entire house that would be sorely missed."

Anthony grinned at her. "You may change your tune if my great-uncle has stashed us away in there."

The team pulled to a stop at that point and the postilion opened the door to assist the much-jolted passengers to alight. Anthony put a steadying arm around his wife's shoulders for a moment and then looked toward the entrance, a smile breaking over his face as a roly-poly individual with a round cherubic face and a sparse ring of white hair beneath a bald dome made his careful way down the steps.

"Crimmons!" he cried, going forward to wring the butler's hand. "It's good to see you again. I vow you don't look a day older than when I was last at Meadowbrook. And how is Mrs. Crimmons these days?"

Belinda saw that the butler did his best to conceal a wince after this enthusiastic handshake as he smiled and murmured that his wife was as usual. "And you, sir, if I may be so bold, have changed almost out of recognition from the scrawny lad who plagued the life out of us all with his tricks twelve years ago."

"Has it really been as long as that, Crimmons?"

"Aye, sir; it was the summer before the mistress died when you and your brother spent a month with us. And now you are both married, I understand?"

"Yes. I beg your pardon for leaving you standing alone, darling," Anthony said, recalled to the present by the gentle hint. "Crimmons and I are old friends. He and Mrs. Crimmons have taken care of Uncle Thaddeus for over thirty years. This is my wife."

When Belinda and the butler had exchanged smiling greetings, Anthony asked, "How is my uncle, Crimmons?"

The butler's face took on a lugubrious cast. "I fear you will not find him in plump currant, Master Anthony, sir, but he has been eagerly awaiting your arrival since your letter reached us two days ago. If you will follow me now, Mr. Wainright has moved into quarters on the ground floor these past two years; the doctor felt the stairs were putting too great a strain on his heart."

Belinda brought up the rear as her husband questioned the butler more closely about the exact state of his great-uncle's health. She could not fail to note the dingy condition of the floors and walls along their route even in the dim light. The glimpses she had into rooms they passed en route were no more reassuring. It was a relief, therefore, to emerge from a dreary corridor into a sunlit area at the back of the house overlooking a colorful though overgrown garden that could be reached through a glassed door at the end of the hall. There were rooms on either side of this hall.

Crimmons led them into the one on the left, announcing, "Mr. and Mrs. Anthony Wainright."

It was the first time Belinda had ever heard herself so titled and it took a moment to recover her mental equilibrium to focus her attention on the figure in the Bath chair whom her husband had hurried across the room to greet. Whatever picture of his great-uncle Anthony might have retained in his memory, it could not have coincided with the frail appearance of the man whose skeletal hand he was grasping with the care one would extend to a rare piece of Venetian glass, Belinda thought, pitying both men.

Mr. Thaddeus Wainright must have been a tall man in his prime, judging by the position of his knees under a woolen lap rug, but his bony frame was sadly underfleshed beneath a velvet coat that hung loosely from his shoulders. He had a noble head, covered with thickly waving white hair, the mournful brown eyes of a Byzantine saint, and the gentlest smile Belinda had ever seen.

The smile was directed at her as Mr. Wainright said softly, "Please forgive me for keeping you standing, my dear child."

"This is my wife, Belinda, Uncle Thad," Anthony said, drawing her up to the man in the wheeled chair.

Belinda returned her host's smile as she took his cool, dry hand into hers. "I am very happy to meet you, sir."

"And I you, my dear. You are quite the loveliest creature to enter this house since my wife died over a decade ago. You have something of the look of my Hannah about you with your dark hair and fair skin."

"What a lovely thing to say. Thank you, sir."

"Forgive me for not rising to greet you," he continued, retaining her hand for another second. "I am confined to this confounded chair these days. Please sit here on this settee beside me while we get acquainted."

As Belinda obeyed with a smile, Mr. Wainright addressed himself to his great-nephew again. "You may remember that this was used to be your aunt's morning room."

"I do indeed, sir. She always kept a jar of sweetmeats on that table for us children. It seems strange to think she is no longer here to judge whose fish is larger or settle arguments between my brother Hugh and me."

"She is here with me always in spirit," Mr. Wainright said, "and I had that portrait brought here from the red saloon when Dr. Abernathy insisted I moved my quarters to this level to avoid having to climb stairs."

Following the direction of his glance, Belinda gazed over her shoulder into the smiling painted face of a dark-haired woman who appeared to be in her early forties. "She was beautiful," she said softly, smiling at the old gentleman.

"Except that her hair was gray when I was a child, that is exactly how I remember Aunt Hannah," Anthony said, his eyes on the portrait.

"She liked this room best because she could always look out at her special garden," Mr. Wainright said. "I had that glassed-in cabinet brought in to hold my favorite books; otherwise, the room is exactly as Hannah left it. We've converted the music room across the hall into a bedchamber, and this is where I shall spend my final days."

"Do you ever go out for a drive in fine weather, Uncle?"

"No, never. Sometimes I sit in the garden for an hour, and Mr. Jones, the rector of St. Swithin's, calls occasionally to give me a game of chess, but anything more active and I'll find myself sadly out of breath in five minutes. I make no complaint; I have had a good life, but the years since Hannah died have seemed very long. I shall be glad when I am done with it."

Belinda's eyes met Anthony's and saw that he shared her desire to say something of comfort and the unhappy conviction that there was nothing anyone could say that would accomplish this purpose.

After an awkward silence Mr. Wainright seemed to recollect himself from his reverie and he dragged his gaze away from the portrait of his dead wife. "I beg your pardon. One falls into bad habits when there is too much solitude. I desire you and Belinda to regard Meadowbrook as your home, my boy, from this moment. Why should you have to wait until I am in the ground to have a home of your own? There is much to be done about the property, I fear. My bailiff will be overjoyed to have someone who will listen to his pleas to take this or that action. Of late I have found it too exhausting to bear with him. I have asked Mrs. Crimmons to prepare the suite that Hannah and I used for you and Belinda, but if, after you go over the place, you feel you would prefer to be situated elsewhere, the choice is yours."

"You are very generous, Uncle."

"Not at all, my boy. This place will be yours soon, and it will give me great pleasure to have you here with me."

"I thought we would stay for a fortnight, and then I have promised to bring Belinda to High Chimneys to meet my family."

Mr. Wainright nodded. "Very well. I hope you will then return to Meadowbrook permanently." He put a hand up to his throat as his voice weakened.

"Would you like a glass of water, sir?" Belinda asked, spotting a pitcher on a nearby table. "I fear we have tired you."

"No, thank you, my dear. Crimmons will be bringing my cordial presently, and Mrs. Crimmons will show you to your rooms. I have grown so lazy of late that I have my breakfast in bed and I take my other meals in here, but tonight I shall do myself the honor of dining with you and Anthony."

Several hours later Belinda dawdled about the business of preparing for bed in the large apartment that had belonged to Mr. Wainright's late wife. She had sent Polly home to Gloucestershire from Alnwick, and she preferred to do without the services of a maid rather than deal with a stranger tonight.

She felt oddly unlike herself, full of emotions she could not quite pin down as she wandered about the unfamiliar room that was to be hers in future. The delapidation common to much of Meadowbrook was not evident in here where the graceful furnishings, fashioned mostly of mahogany and dating from the middle of the last century, had been painstakingly maintained in a high state of preservation. It was added proof, had any been needed, of the great love Mr. Wainright had borne for his Hannah. It made her feel fluttery inside to contemplate being so cherished even beyond the grave. Hannah Wainright had been a fortunate woman indeed, and from things Anthony had said during the journey and incidents related by Uncle Thaddeus tonight, thoroughly deserving of her blessings by virtue of a loving and sympathetic nature that drew people to her all her life.

She was about to embark on the same journey Hannah had made when she came to Meadowbrook as a bride fifty-five years ago. As she studied her serious reflection in the dressing-table mirror, a small prayer rose to Belinda's lips that she would prove a worthy successor to the last mistress of Meadowbrook.

The start of her marriage had been marked by such hostility that she had desired only to expunge all memory of it during her stay in Northumberland. She had succeeded so well that Anthony's arrival and his pleas to continue with the marriage had cast her into a state of acute anxiety. She recalled with shame that she had cravenly begged Anthea to tell her what was the right thing to do, a questionable service her sagacious friend flatly declined to perform. What Anthea had done was to listen patiently while Belinda carried on a frenzied debate with herself, occasionally interjecting a comment or posing a question that reduced the complexities of the situation for the younger woman. The maze of conflicting desires, ingrained conceptions of duty, imponderable qualms, and a paralyzing reluctance to act had eventually boiled down to two opposing points: She felt she could not bear to have Anthony lose his inheritance through her fault, but she was fearful that she would be miserably unhappy as his wife. Anthea had gently pointed out that even brides who were madly in love had some of those qualms—or should have—because no one's happiness was assured in life, least of all in marriage.

She had clung desperately to her friend before climbing into the post chaise Anthony had hired for the trip to Meadowbrook. Among the recurrent themes in her apprehensions before making her decision had been the daunting fact that she was married to a stranger. Until that fateful day in Alnwick they had spent fewer than four or five hours in each other's exclusive company, most of those on their wedding day. To make matters worse, an undeniable thread of animosity had run through most of their previous encounters.

Anthony had not tried to charm her on the journey south. She'd been on guard against that, aware from observing his manners toward the matrons of Somerset that he possessed effortless charm. No, that was unfair. It would be more accurate to say that, at a time when he was obsessed with his feelings for Deirdre, he had made the considerable effort to be civil and attentive to the other ladies who desired some of his society.

Conscious perhaps of all that had gone before, the couple had conversed haltingly, tentatively at first, but the confined space inside a moving and swaying carriage imposed an intimacy that soon did away with awkwardness. Anthony told her about his boyhood in a closely attached family, and she responded with stories illustrating the unique relationship between her mother and Deirdre's, and the twins' unavailing efforts to recreate their closeness in their daughters. He had asked about the time following her mother's death, and she'd told him about the loneliness that even her grandmother and Miss Fenton had not been able to assuage, described her great relief that her father's second wife had proved such a sweet person, and recounted some of the delights of watching two lively little brothers grow. Anthony had not been able to satisfy her curiosity about Meadowbrook, having visited there only twice during his childhood. He did recall that he and his brother had found the overgrown grounds greatly to their liking and had enjoyed fishing in the brook that gave the property its name.

By the second day they were exploring each other's tastes in everything from food to poetry, sparking some spirited discussions, with each party vigorously defending his own position and giving no quarter. A reminiscent smile flitted over Belinda's lips as a picture flashed into her memory of Anthony's exasperated expression at one point when he'd declared that her father had not exaggerated when he'd warned him that his daughter could be as stubborn as a mule. She had not denied the charge as she gave him a cheeky look that earned her the delighted smile that had formerly been reserved for Deirdre's antics.

At this point it was fair to say that she and Anthony were friends, Belinda decided as she blew out the candle and settled among the pillows—friends and partners too in the great enterprise that lay ahead. Something that Anthony had said in Northumberland suddenly flashed into her mind. He'd insisted that, despite their past history, he was persuaded they could have a successful marriage with good will on both sides. At the time it had sounded pat and simplistic, but today, after observing her husband's affection for his aged relative and even for Crimmons, she had seen clearly that he *was* a man of good heart, as Sir John had promised. She would do her part to match his goodwill, she vowed before sliding into slumber.

* * *

"Good morning, sleepyhead."

Belinda's black lashes flew open and she stared into her husband's teasing face just inches above hers for a dazed moment. Confusion and alarm must have been written clearly on her countenance because Anthony pulled back quickly, even his ears going red.

"I beg your pardon; I didn't mean to frighten you," he said. "I just wished to let you know that I shall be riding over the estate all day with my uncle's bailiff. I hope you will not find it too boring here on your own."

"Oh no, I am never bored," she replied cheerfully, responding to the uncertainty in his manner. "If your great-uncle does not object, I will explore the house and gardens a bit."

"Uncle Thad will no doubt have Mrs. Crimmons standing by to conduct you around the house at your pleasure, and I know he will enjoy your company too. I'll see you at dinner." Anthony had been heading for the door between their rooms as he spoke. With one hand on the handle he added softly, "May I say that you look very sweet when you are sleeping?"

He left the room on the words, so he did not see the tiny smile that played about his wife's lips for a moment before she threw back the covers and bounded out of bed to greet the day.

That was the way she greeted every day as time sped by at Meadowbrook. While Anthony rode over the estate with the revitalized bailiff, Belinda spent many hours reading to Uncle Thaddeus or playing cribbage when he felt strong enough to challenge her. She listened willingly to reminiscences of earlier days at Meadowbrook when he and his adored wife had frequently entertained family and friends for weeks at a stretch. His servants, though devoted, lacked direction, and the standards that had prevailed in the kitchens and housekeeping when Mrs. Wainright was alive had slackened deplorably. Taking care not to alienate anyone, Belinda found ways to make the invalid more comfortable. As had been the case with her grandmother, Uncle Thaddeus had little interest in food, but by tactful intervention in the kitchens she had succeeded in getting the staff to prepare some nourishing broths and custards that she cajoled him into eating when she kept him company during his light repasts.

Uncle Thaddeus treated Belinda with the gentle courtliness of a bygone era, charming her thoroughly. She was unaware that she blossomed like a rose under the spell of his affection, but she derived a great deal of satisfaction from the fact that he had ceased entirely to speak of death as imminent and desirable and was speaking instead of inviting some of his neighbors to meet his heir and his bride when they returned from their visit to Anthony's family.

"I shall miss you sadly while you are away, my dear child," the old gentleman said the evening before their scheduled departure. "You have brought warmth and sunshine back into this house." The three were in Mr. Wainright's room after dinner, and he turned to his nephew. "I felicitate you with all my heart, my boy, for being as fortunate as I was in the choice of your life's companion."

"Thank you, Uncle. I realize the truth of this increasingly with each day that passes."

Both men smiled at Belinda, who blushed delightfully but protested that they praised her far beyond her merit.

"That would be quite impossible of achievement," Mr. Wainright said gallantly. "And now, kiss me good night, my dear, for I find I am a bit fatigued with all this planning. I shall leave everything until tomorrow and retire, if you will ring for my valet, Anthony."

The young people complied with their relative's requests and said their good nights.

Belinda was awakened by a hand on her shoulder and a voice repeating her name. She opened her eyes, aware at once that it was barely dawn. One look at her husband's face in the dim light brought her sitting upright. "What is wrong? Is it Uncle Thad?"

Anthony swallowed with difficulty. "Yes, he is dead. His valet just told me. Evidently he felt ill and rang for Morton, but he was already gone when Morton entered his bedchamber."

Seeing the moisture in her husband's eyes, Belinda threw her arms about his shoulders and held him tightly. "Oh, my dear, I am so sorry. I . . . I was persuaded his health had improved since we came to Meadowbrook."

"His spirits and his outlook were much improved, thanks largely to your affection and companionship," Anthony said, cradling her in his arms, "But when I mentioned this to the doctor the other day, he speedily undeceived me about his health. I did not tell you because there was no call to sadden you before time. He might have gone on for some little while yet, but the doctor felt the final attack could come at any time. I am glad for the servants' sake that it did not happen while we were away."

A shaky little murmur against his chest signified Belinda's agreement with this sentiment.

"There will be much to do presently," he warned her, "so dry your eyes, and pray do not grieve for Uncle Thad. He is with Aunt Hannah at last."

Chapter Sixteen

December, 1815 Hampshire

Belinda Wainright sat at the rosewood table desk in her sitting room and prepared to compose a letter to her family. In front of her on the desk was a letter from her father expressing the hopes of everyone at Millgrove that she and Anthony would be able to come to them for a visit at Christmas. Glancing at the date, she found it hard to comprehend that Christmas was nearly upon them and that less than three weeks remained in what had proved to be the most eventful year of her life. Little had she dreamed when she headed for Somerset in early March that she would not return home for over nine months.

Uncle Thaddeus's sudden death in October had meant the instant assumption by Anthony and Belinda of full responsibility for the running of Meadowbrook. The burden of preparing to receive the relatives who would shortly arrive for the funeral fell upon young and inexperienced shoulders, but the couple had instantly, albeit unconsciously, forged a working partnership that cooperated to achieve the well-nigh impossible. That description had been bestowed upon their efforts by Anthony's mother, who had been a tower of strength to the young bride during the hectic period following the master of Meadowbrook's death. Belinda had met a large number of family members and had had the felicity of knowing that her liking for them was well returned.

Nibbling on the tip of her quill, she reflected that the unusual circumstances of her introduction to Anthony's relatives might have been designed to conceal the true relationship between bride and groom. They had each been so busy in their separate spheres while seeing to the comfort of their guests that interaction between them was necessarily much less than would have been the case had *they* been guests at his father's or sister's home. Belinda could say with complete honesty that there had been no embarrassing moments or incidents during their relatives' visit. They had behaved quite naturally, like the friends they were; anything else would have been inappropriate, given the sad circumstances that had brought about the convocation of family members.

Their friendship had strengthened and deepened in the weeks that had elapsed since the departure of the guests had left them to the enormous challenge of bringing the estate into better condition. She might have known her husband from the cradle, so confident was she of anticipating his reaction to a wide spectrum of events. Anthony was the soul of generosity, she had discovered, without a mean or petty bone in his body. She admired his kindness to his tenants and dependents, and respected his determination and willingness to labor long and hard to restore the property. She also delighted in a dormant sense of fun that was being liberated in him as they settled into a routine at Meadowbrook. She had never shared so much laughter with anyone before and felt her own spirit could be aptly described as greatly liberated of late.

Which left the question of why she was dithering over a reply to her father's invitation to spend Christmas at Millgrove. When in the grip of the initial joyful reaction to her letter this morning she had relayed the invitation to Anthony, he had cheerfully agreed to the request, foreseeing a pleasant interlude away from daily labors. Belinda glanced around the faded elegance of their private sitting room, her eye lingering at a door in the fireplace wall leading to her bedchamber, and beyond that, Anthony's. There would be no suite of rooms put at their disposal at Millgrove. Her father and Louisa had both written to express their pleasure and best wishes in response to the letter she'd sent upon their arrival at Meadowbrook, a communication that had merely announced that she and Anthony had decided not to seek an annulment of their marriage. She might request separate bedchambers, of course, but Anthony's family had no reason to suspect theirs was not a normal marriage, and she was reluctant to expose their arrangement at Millgrove, even though her family, unlike Anthony's, was cognizant of the circumstances that had produced the marriage.

Belinda pushed back her chair abruptly and walked over to a window, staring out at nothing while her brain churned away furiously. Her father's invitation had jolted her into a delayed realization that she had been coasting along, reveling in the challenges and delights of her daily existence with Anthony but refusing to look beyond the immediate present or to examine her feelings for her husband.

She set her mind to these tasks now, an exercise that was completed in seconds and resulted in sweaty palms and a racing pulse, but also in honest perplexity. During her stay in Northumberland she had firmly believed that her romantic attachment to Anthony Wainright was over, an aberration of the past. Even when Anthony had appeared without warning on the walk outside Hollyhock House, her heart had jogged along at its accustomed rate and her senses had registered nothing beyond an aesthetic appreciation of his extraordinary good looks. This present agitation must be panic at the idea of being ever again at the mercy of such an irrational passion. She took a deep, calming breath and relaxed the fingers that had curled into fists, bringing them up against her hot cheeks while the panic subsided and her heartbeat steadied again. This was *not* a recurrence of that fever in the blood of which Anthony had spoken. Apart from fluttery physical sensations, everything was changed now—*she* had changed. She had witnessed and to some degree experienced the destructive power of such obsessive attachments, and the experience had matured her. She no longer expected some nameless benevolent force to gift her with a fairy-tale romance.

Having said all that, Belinda admitted with a self-mocking smile that the road to maturity had led right back to the beginning. She loved Anthony now as she had five years ago. This time, however, her love was grounded in friendship, admiration, and respect for the person he was. Considering the unpromising conditions that had prevailed at the inception of this marriage, she was fortunate indeed, and this would still be true if Anthony never came to love her in the manner of a fairy-tale prince—but oh, it would be wonderful if he did! She was confident that he liked her very much and enjoyed her company. Sometimes his face would break into delighted laughter at some nonsense of hers, and occasionally a tender light would appear in his eyes, but beyond that she dared not speculate, especially since he seemed quite content with the status quo. Surely if he were in love with her this would not be so; he would be trying to make her fall in love with him. Now that she really thought about this, it struck her that Anthony rarely touched her these days. When his family had been in residence, he had often pulled her along by the hand or draped an arm about her shoulders when they were standing together in conversation with one or another of their guests, but it had been quite some time since he'd done anything that intimate.

Belinda was gnawing at her bottom lip and frowning at the gray sky as she recalled how relieved and grateful she'd been when Anthony had told her the decision to consummate the marriage would rest in her hands. She was still grateful—at least, she should be—but it would help to know if he had kept his word so scrupulously for *her* sake or because it suited his own feelings in the matter.

"What are you doing in here without any light to speak of?"

Belinda jumped at the sound of her husband's voice behind her. "I . . . I came in to reply to my father's letter."

"You didn't get very far," Anthony said with a laugh, glancing over his shoulder at her blank paper as he lighted another candle from the holder on the side table. "Does your pen want mending?" he asked as he placed the candlestick on the desk. "I am a champion pen mender at your service."

"Thank you, but it is fine. I was just looking out the window."

"I imagine you are all excited at the prospect of returning home after such a long time away."

"Oh yes," she agreed, returning his smile warmly.

"I too am looking forward to spending Christmas with your family, but right now I must get rid of all this dirt before changing for dinner. We've been digging postholes and mending fences today," he said, heading for the door again.

Belinda's expression was wistful as she watched her husband go out of the room whistling a military air. Had there been anything significant in his avowal of pleasure in their plans to spend Christmas at Millgrove? Or in the smile he had given her when offering to mend her pen? For once she wished she had her cousin's knowledge of men's behavior, as well as Deirdre's confidence in her power to enchant. How would Deirdre go about discovering Anthony's true feeling were she in Belinda's place right now?

Two days later Belinda was no closer to an answer to her dilemma as she bade her maid good night and climbed into her bed, tying her long hair at the nape for sleeping. Other than questioning Anthony directly, something she could not summon up the courage to do, she had been unable to think of a way to discover what was in his heart. As for telling him she wished to put their marriage on a regular basis, she might as well attempt to fly—a burning desire would not produce an efficacious action. She lay stiffly in her bed for hours, her overactive brain preventing her body from relaxing into sleep. She heard the muted noises behind the wall that meant Anthony was preparing to retire, and the eventual silence indicating that he slept. She was drifting into welcome unconsciousness when indistinct sounds behind her brought her to full alertness once more. Anthony must be dreaming again. She'd discovered soon after their arrival at Meadowbrook that he was subject to a recurring nightmare that bedeviled his repose. She'd questioned him one morning after he'd cried out in his sleep, and he'd admitted that he was troubled occasionally by a dream of the last battle of his military career. He'd dismissed it, and her concern, brusquely, but though she had not mentioned it again, she'd always known when the dream recurred. Happily, the frequency had dropped off steeply in the past few weeks. She'd even dared to hope it was behind him for good.

It was worse than usual tonight, Belinda realized when the thrashing around next door became grunts, and the grunts cries. She groped for the tinderbox on the table and succeeded in lighting her candle. She didn't take the time to don robe or slippers, her only thought being to put an end to the incoherent agony in the next room. She padded barefoot into her husband's room, the wooden floor striking cold where the carpet ended.

Anthony was flailing about on the bed, having thrown off all covers. He was muttering something about keeping the squares intact, and he did not respond to Belinda's soft enunciation of is name. She deposited the candle on his bedside table and put her hand firmly on his shoulder. "It's all right, Anthony, you were dreaming. It's only a dream," she repeated in a slightly louder voice as he twitched away from her hand.

Suddenly he flung his head around, staring at her with wild eyes that held no recognition. "It's all right, Anthony, the dream is over now," she reiterated, and after a second he drew a long, shuddering breath and threw his arm across his forehead, wiping the sweat from his brow and sweeping the damp gold curls off it. Belinda poured water into a tumbler and handed it to him when he removed his shielding arm.

He accepted it with a murmur of thanks. "What are you doing in here?" he asked, his eyes still containing remnants of remembered horror as he pushed up on his elbows and gulped down half the water.

"I heard you moving about and calling out. You haven't had one of these nightmares in some time."

"No, I had hoped I was done with them. Thank you for coming to the rescue, flower face."

Belinda, oddly disturbed by a new intensity in his glance, was reaching for the candle she'd put on his night table when the appellation reached her ears. Her head spun back toward him. "Wh . . . what did you call me?" she whispered.

"What I called you the first time we met—flower face."

"But you gave no sign—I was convinced you had forgotten." Her eyes were wide with shock, and the hand he seized trembled in his.

He leaned over and replaced the tumbler on the table, retaining her hand to pull her closer as he gazed up into a young and delicate face in the shadows. "I am ashamed to confess I *had* forgotten until I was at Millgrove in September. Something about the lane teased at my memory, and then your stepmother spoke of arriving at Millgrove on your birthday. It was the portrait of you that clinched the matter though; as I looked at it, every delightful detail of the meeting came back to me."

"Why did you say nothing until now?"

"I meant to tell you. I thought about little else all the way to Northumberland, but you were less than welcoming when I arrived, you may recall, my darling girl, so determined to send me to the rightabout that I lost my nerve."

"And you a big, brave soldier," she scoffed.

"It was pusillanimous of me indeed," he agreed solemnly, gently brushing the long tail of silky hair that had fallen forward back behind her shoulder.

"Why did you not mention it some time before this," she persisted, her voice unsteady, either from lingering shock or some new sensations caused by his hand stroking her ear and the side of her neck above the modest collar of her cotton night rail.

"I needed to prove to you that my word meant something, and it was vital that you learn to trust me. Until then it seemed wiser, indeed crucial, to avoid such a personal topic. You are very lovely indeed, and I am not made of stone, but I had promised that the decision to consummate our union would be yours. Do you not think, my darling, that tonight would be an excellent time to begin our real marriage?"

Anthony was sitting on the edge of the bed now, his hands holding Belinda's arms lightly. The real pressure was being exerted by his eyes which she would swear were drawing her heart right out of her body. "Yes please," she whispered.

Those were the last coherent words she would produce for a long time as his mouth came down on hers, warm and persuasive, producing a jolt of pure pleasure deep inside her being. She was barely aware that her husband had expeditiously removed her tentlike bedgown until he said in a hoarse whisper, "My word, but you are even more beautiful than I dreamed. Did you not know that I have been starving for you, you stubborn little mule?" The epithet was uttered in caressing tones and punctuated by delicate forays of his fingers tracing her form as if he intended to reproduce the curves in marble or bronze.

Of their own accord Belinda's arms went around his neck, removing any obstacles to his exquisite explorations. Her lips began their own exploration of his jawline until he shuddered and pulled her tightly up against him, flesh against burning flesh, as they fell back onto the bed. All rational thought dissolved, along with bones and muscles, as Anthony's delicious depredations reduced Belinda to a state of quivering response. The rapid changes in his breathing indicated that he was in a similar state. She followed where he led without hesitation or fears, only gasping a little at the inevitable pain, but soothed too by the words of love and comfort he repeated until her body accommodated itself to his. She was transported by the subsequent ripples of delight that rose to a crescendo of sensation, and afterward could only cling weakly to the man who wielded such sweet power over her being.

"My beautiful Belinda, I think you must be a miracle," her husband said, smoothing back the silken tangle of hair that covered both their shoulders, "because I've done nothing to deserve you." He was tracing the curves of her mouth as she smiled sleepily at him, then his lips replaced his finger and traveled the same route.

Belinda awoke in her own bed with only the haziest memory of being carried there by her husband. The morning was well advanced and she was alone. Her disappointment was eased when she spotted a note on the pillow, the contents of which considerably increased her temperature and the sense of well-being that flooded through her.

Happiness bubbled like a fountain inside Belinda now that Anthony was her lover as well as her friend. She looked forward eagerly to their visit to Millgrove, knowing she would be able to set her father's mind at rest about her future. Her days were filled with preparations and planning, her nights with the joy of discovering the secret world that belongs only to those in love.

Three days before Belinda and Anthony were due to leave for Gloucestershire, she found two letters at her place when she joined her husband for luncheon in the small bright room on the ground floor that she had converted for use as an informal dining room when they were alone. A pleased smile lighted her face as she pounced on the top envelope. "This is from Anthea—finally. I had begun to wonder at her continued silence. You do not mind if I read it now, do you, Anthony?"

"Of course not, my love. I had already begun to glance through my own correspondence while I waited for you."

She wrinkled her nose at him. "I am late so that your lunch would not be. Mrs. Greavy was in a tizzy because the kitchen boy was idling about and let the chicken burn on the spit. I whipped up a sauce while she salvaged the best bits of it."

"I keep discovering new and delightful talents in you," he said gravely, but with an exaggerated leer that brought the color flaring up in Belinda's cheeks as she glanced quickly at the butler to assure herself that he had not witnessed the look.

She maintained a dignified silence until the server left them alone, then protested, "*Really,* Anthony!"

"No, no, do not scold. I freely admit it was deplorable of me to put you to the blush—literally—in front of a servant, but you look so enchanting when you color up that I cannot always resist the temptation. I beg your pardon. Ummmn, this sauce is delicious. Am I forgiven?"

"You didn't promise to mend your ways," she pointed out, pursing her lips.

"I didn't, did I?" he returned affably. "And I should perhaps warn you that provocative pouts could get their perpetrator kissed, servant or no."

She looked at the door through which the butler had vanished and hastily picked up her fork as her husband laughed softly.

A few minutes later Belinda exclaimed, "Oh, how marvelous! Anthony, Mr. Stoddard has asked Anthea to marry him. Isn't that delightful news?"

Anthony smiled into his wife's glowing eyes. "Delightful indeed—surprising too. From his attitude toward me when we met, I got the distinct impression that the banker had been having thoughts in quite another direction."

"Oh no," she said quickly. "I always felt he and Anthea would be ideally suited, but Mr. Stoddard had been widowed so long it was thought that he had quite decided against remarrying."

"Something must have given his thoughts a new direction."

"Anthea says they will marry in the spring," Belinda went on, deciding to ignore her husband's odd humor. "I should love to invite them to spend some time here with us next summer if you have no objection."

"I have no objection to anything that would give you pleasure, my love. You have another letter also." His eyes were watchful as Belinda slipped Anthea's letter into its envelope and picked up the other, so he did not miss her slight recoil when she read the inscription.

"It . . . it's from Deirdre," she announced.

"I rather thought so when I saw it was franked by Archer."

Belinda was turning the envelope around in her hands. "I have had no communication with her since our wedding. I wonder how she knew my direction?"

"My uncle's death was reported in the London papers."

"Oh, of course, that must be the answer. I cannot imagine what she should wish to communicate to me."

"Well, there is one certain way to find out," Anthony said cheerfully.

Belinda looked at him blankly for a second. "Oh, yes, of course." She opened the letter and began to read, her frown of concentration suggesting that the handwriting was more than usually difficult. A moment later the silence in the room was broken by her gasp. "Good heavens, they wish to come here!"

"Who wants to come here?" Anthony looked up from his own post.

"Deirdre and Lord Archer. She says they are planning to spend Christmas with friends in East Sussex and they would like to stop here one night on the way."

"When?"

"On the eighteenth. When is that?"

"Tomorrow."

"Tomorrow!" Belinda looked aghast. "But that is impossible. There is no time to prepare—I shall write and tell her we are unable to receive—"

"It's too late. They will have left Somerset before your letter arrives. You cousin has put you on your mettle, my love." He rose from his chair and smiled at her. "You coped magnificently when close to a score of my relatives were here in October. Two guests and a couple of servants should not be a problem. If you will excuse me now, I was supposed to meet my bailiff five minutes ago. We'll talk more at dinner."

Belinda's thoughts defied description as she watched her husband amble out of the room. Gone in the stroke of a pen was the euphoric cloud in which she had dwelled these past few days. Her appetite gone also, she pushed away her half-filled plate and got up slowly. As she passed through the door she caught sight of the listless droop of her shoulders in a pier glass in the hall and her mood changed again, this time to anger—not at Deirdre for merely following her usual selfish course, but directed where it rightly belonged—at herself for lack of gumption. Had she learned so little this past year that the prospect of seeing her cousin again could bring on the anxious competitiveness she should have left behind with adolescence? She shook her head at her own folly and went in search of the housekeeper. She and Deirdre were grown women, their separate natures and talents fully formed by now. Deirdre was definitely favored in the category of physical endowments, she acknowledged without rancor, but she did not consider herself to be her cousin's inferior in any mental quality or feminine accomplishment or virtue.

A few hours later, Belinda entered the set of rooms that she'd had prepared for Deirdre and her husband in the best-preserved wing of the house, casting a housewifely eye around for anything left undone. At the time of Uncle Thaddeus's death, she and Anthony's mother had canvassed the whole house and brought the best pieces to these rooms, most of them dating from the early part of the last century. The furnishings would not be to Deirdre's taste, of course, but nothing at Meadowbrook was modern enough or opulent enough to please her cousin. At least the housekeeper's cabinets had produced some very fine linen for the beds; she took an appreciative sniff of the lavender-scented air as she checked the mahogany washstand for soft towels and the fragrant soap Deirdre liked.

Lord Archer's bedchamber was next to his wife's, not separated by a sitting room as at Archer Hall, something that gave Belinda a mean little satisfaction she had the grace to be ashamed of when she walked into the handsome apartment and smoothed out a wrinkle in the French toile covering the bed. There was not the slightest doubt in her mind that Deirdre meant to exercise her charms to the fullest on Anthony during the brief visit. Her devious mentality was an open book to one who had known her from birth. Deirdre's relief in escaping the scandal her sister-in-law had tried to initiate had been fleeting, swamped in a jealous resentment that the cousin she despised should get the man she wanted to keep on a string. Anthony had played the part of willing bridegroom a little too well for her liking. She could not be quite sure that he was still her devoted slave. Belinda would wager her grandmother's pearls that Deirdre would use the stay at Meadowbrook to try to reexert her power over him. The challenge of doing so under her husband's nose would increase her pleasure in the accomplishment. Belinda was quite cool in making this analysis because she had finally realized that Deirdre had no power to hurt her; only Anthony could do that.

When Lord Archer's traveling carriages pulled up at the entrance to Meadowbrook late the next afternoon, Belinda and Anthony were enjoying a cup of tea together in the best saloon, a rare occasion with Anthony's heavy work schedule. Belinda had spent hours in the kitchen earlier, striving to foresee and guard against the multiplicity of disasters to which the erratic staff was susceptible. No one meeting her at present would be able to guess from her smiling and relaxed demeanor that she had lifted a finger to anything more strenuous than pinning on the cameo brooch she wore at her collar.

When the butler announced the viscount and his lady, Belinda looked up, her face sparkling with laughter at something her husband had just said. She got to her feet swiftly and crossed the room with the gliding grace her grandmother had bequeathed to all her descendants. "Forgive me, Dee, for not coming out to meet you but we did not hear the carriage pull up, way back in this room. How do you do, Lord Archer. Welcome to Meadowbrook."

Deirdre's tinkling laugh rang out as she embraced her cousin. "It's lovely to see you, Bel, but I cannot believe you are still wearing mourning!"

Belinda blinked. "Anthony's great uncle has been gone barely two months," she explained, but she could have spared her breath, for the viscountess had turned immediately to the man who had just reached the group in the doorway.

She held out both hands and tilted her head as she said gaily, "You do not have the appearance of an old married man, Anthony."

Anthony obliged his guest by raising one of her gloved hands to his lips, saying with a smile, "If you are hinting that I should perhaps look hag-ridden, you do not know your cousin. You look ravishing as always, Deirdre." Anthony turned to Lord Archer, whose expression of calm civility never wavered. "I believe we were introduced at Tattersall's last autumn by Colonel Hugh Trevor, Lord Archer. May I add my welcome to that of my wife?"

As the men shook hands, the viscount said, "Thank you, I recall the meeting. I was grieved to learn that Trevor fell at Quatre Bras. I was at Harrow with him, you know. He was the best of good fellows."

"And a very fine officer." Anthony gestured toward a grouping of sofas and chairs behind them. "Please come in and sit—"

"Is that a teapot I see?" Deirdre interrupted in tones of exaggerated delight. "Just what I have been craving to wash the travel dust out of my throat. Lead on, Macduff." She seized Anthony's arm and pulled him toward one of the sofas. He went with her good-naturedly but resisted being pulled down beside her, promising with a laugh to bring her the tea she craved.

Belinda had seated herself behind the tea table and was already preparing a cup for her cousin while Anthony inquired

about the viscount's preference in beverages. He handed
Deirdre her tea, then poured out two glasses of Madeira, giving one to Lord Archer, seated in a chair at right angles to the
two sofas.

As Anthony joined his wife on one, Lord Archer raised his
glass to the couple with a smile. "May I propose a toast to
your happiness and offer my belated felicitations on your marriage?"

"Thank you, sir."

As Anthony raised his own glass, the viscount said, "Please
make that Archer, Wainright. With Deirdre and Belinda being
so closely related we are bound to see a lot of each other from
time to time."

"Archer it is then. How did you find the roads after all the
rain we have been having?"

With the men embarked on a discussion of road conditions,
Belinda inquired if her cousin would like to be shown to her
room and Deirdre accepted, declaring herself in desperate need
of a bath and a rest. She had almost nothing to say beyond a
few commonplace comments on the age of the house until
they reached the rooms that had been prepared for their use.
Belinda made no apologies for the old-fashioned furnishings;
she pointed out the door to Lord Archer's room, promised to
have hot water sent up for bathing whenever Deirdre was
ready, and announced the time they would gather in the saloon
before dinner. "I see your baggage is already here. Shall I send
Meritt to you immediately?"

When Deirdre signified assent, Belinda expressed the hope
that she would have a good rest, and headed for the door, turning back when her cousin said abruptly, "Bel, is your marriage
everything you expected?"

Belinda looked into Deirdre's curious face and shook her
head. "No," she said softly, "it is everything I hoped." She
closed the door gently, aware that Deirdre was staring after her
with narrowed eyes.

The evening proceeded exactly along the lines Belinda had
envisioned. Deirdre, perhaps in honor of the season, chose to
wear a gown of crimson velvet trimmed with white fur, and
around her lovely neck hung rubies and diamonds that would
not have disgraced a coronation. She was in rare form at dinner, keeping the gentlemen in a constant state of amusement
with her sparkling wit, demonstrating that she was au courant

with all the *on dits* involving the elite of English society. Belinda, keeping an unobtrusive eye on the servants to ensure that the dinner service went smoothly, could not be said to have contributed much to the success of the conversation, never having met any of the people featured in her cousin's stories. At one point when Deirdre was entertaining Anthony with news about acquaintances of his, Lord Archer sounded Belinda out on her opinions of Lord Byron's poetry and the two entered into a lively discussion that became a friendly argument that eventually involved the other two when Anthony jumped in on his wife's side.

Deirdre's scintillating performance ended when she and Belinda returned to the saloon. After sitting on a sofa for a moment or two she jumped up and began wandering about the room, examining various objects on tables and mantel. Belinda, poised with her embroidery, wondered at her cousin's restlessness and was thankful to be in her own house where Deirdre's moods need not concern her.

Deirdre launched into an enthusiastic description of the large house party they were to join in Sussex while Belinda continued to set stitches serenely, making encouraging noises whenever there was a pause in the narrative. Both were relieved when the men rejoined them in short order. They were discussing Anthony's plans to rehabilitate the older wings of the house when they entered, but Deirdre demanded music or cards.

"Not that I would not adore to be conducted all over this fascinating old place tomorrow, Anthony, but bricks and mortar and wood worm are not my idea of evening entertainment," she declared.

Lord Archer said, "I'm afraid a tour must wait for another occasion, my love, since we need to make an early start tomorrow, but I would be greatly entertained to hear Belinda play and then to hear you sing this evening."

"I'll play for Deirdre," Belinda offered, knowing her cousin would not be pleased to sit through a long instrumental selection.

After one song, Deirdre demanded that Anthony join her in a duet. He obliged willingly and they sang a couple of the songs they had sung together in Somerset. Deirdre was about to suggest another when Anthony turned to the viscount, watching the performance with his usual pleasant civility, and invited him to take a turn.

Deirdre laughed gaily. "Archer doesn't sing a note."

"But you must concede that I am a splendid audience, most content to listen to such talented performances."

Anthony smiled at his wife. "What was that lilting air I heard you singing the other day, sweetheart, when I came back to the house to get another pair of gloves?"

"An Irish melody. Do you know it, Dee?" Belinda played a few bars and Deirdre shook her head. At Lord Archer's request, she sang the song. Her voice, though not as strong as her cousin's, was sweet and true.

"That was lovely, Belinda, thank you. You might like to learn this song, my dear," the viscount said to his wife. "It would suit your style."

"I made a copy for my stepmother, Dee. It is in my morning room. I'll give it to you and copy it out again for Louisa while we are at Millgrove for Christmas."

"Oh, you are planning to travel yourselves soon?"

"The day after tomorrow." Belinda's eyes were shining.

Lord Archer apologized for having put them to the trouble of receiving guests at a time when they were busy with their own travel plans, and was reassured of their pleasure in so doing by both Wainrights. He took over the direction of the conversation at that point so skillfully that Belinda didn't realize until it was time to retire that he had put an end to the duets between his wife and Anthony as well as guiding the talk into impersonal channels, heading off every attempt on Deirdre's part to claim Anthony's undivided attention.

The same held true the next morning at breakfast where, ably abetted by Anthony, the viscount continued to keep up a light discussion around a sulky and silent Deirdre.

A message from the kitchens caused Belinda to excuse herself near the close of the meal. When she returned a few moments later the viscount was finishing his coffee in solitude.

"Where are Deirdre and Anthony?"

"Deirdre remembered the music you promised her and they went off to fetch it a moment ago," Lord Archer replied.

"I doubt Anthony will find it easily as it is tucked away among some other things I am taking to Millgrove. I'd best go get it for her."

The viscount set down his cup and rose. "I'll come too if I may. Deirdre will need hurrying if we are to get away when I planned." As they walked he thanked Belinda for her hospitality, his eyes examining her face. "Happiness becomes you, my dear. There is a bloom about you these days that should make your husband feel ten feet tall."

They had come up to the morning room as Lord Archer spoke, stopping in front of the door, and Belinda looked into hazel eyes that were kind but remote. As her lips parted to reply, Deirdre's voice drifted out through the partially open door.

"I have missed you quite dreadfully, Tony."

"Don't, Deirdre. You made your decision, not once but twice. There won't be a third opportunity."

Though low, Anthony's firm tones carried well enough to reach the paralyzed pair outside the door. Deirdre's mocking laugh was sharp. "This from the man who swore eternal devotion and begged me to run away with him!"

"Once I was besotted enough to cast all honor to the winds. I shall be eternally grateful that your mind remained clear enough to choose the honorable path. Never was a sinner so undeservedly rewarded as I have been, and I shall be happy to spend my life trying to merit my good fortune."

"You can't mean *Belinda*?" Incredulity rang in the fluting voice.

"Most certainly I do, but I have no intention of discussing my feelings for my wife. Ah, here is the music on the desk."

In the corridor, Lord Archer turned to Belinda, his customary control in place, though his eyes were hard. "It seems we have both had our suspicions confirmed," he said evenly.

She was staring at him in troubled sympathy when the door was pulled back and Deirdre walked out, an angry glitter in her eyes. Consternation was succeeded by assumed gaiety as she held up the music. "It took simply ages to locate this. Is it time to go, Lucius?"

"Yes, my dear, the pleasant interlude has come to an end, I fear." The viscount looked over his wife's head into the guarded face of his host. "I have been trying to express my gratitude to Belinda for all your hospitality," he said. "I would not for the world have missed the opportunity to wish you happiness in your future life together."

Twenty minutes later Anthony turned to his silent wife as the Archer carriages pulled away from the entrance. "You heard, both of you?"

She nodded. "Oh, Anthony, I feel so desperately sorry for him!"

"I feel like a worm myself. I never thought of him as a real person who could bleed when I was pursuing Deirdre. This must have been a terrible shock, but he carried on as cool as you please."

"I do not believe it was a shock," Belinda said slowly, "at least not entirely. He said something about having our suspicions confirmed just before Deirdre came bursting out of the room."

"It would have been no more than I deserved if he'd called me out instead of thanking me for my hospitality," Anthony said morosely. "I cannot undo a thing, and I can't make it up to him."

"Deirdre is the only one who could do that, and it is clear from what she said to you in that room that she has chosen instead to continue to betray her husband. Don't you *dare* to take all the blame on your shoulders! Deirdre could have stopped your pursuit with a single word at any time, and she did not do so until you forced a final choice on her. Remember that always, Anthony."

Anthony stared down into the militant countenance of his gentle bride for a long moment. Light came back into his eyes as he wrapped his arms strongly about her. "My loyal little love," he murmured. "I meant everything I said to your cousin. I am the most fortunate man alive, and I'd like to shout it to the whole world."

"That sounds very nice," Belinda said with demure mischief. "You may begin by shouting it to everyone at Millgrove."